Black Lightning

Zook's Place

Jo Hammers

Paranormal Crossroads & Publishing

Zook's Place

ISBN 978-0-9849879-1-7

www.paranormalcrossroads.com

Cover Art by Jo Hammers, 2012.

Table of Contents

Black Lightning

Zook's Place

Jo Hammers

Paranormal Crossroads & Publishing

CHAPTER ONE

The Death of Amish Twins

It was late December and the wind was fiercely blowing causing the house's windows to rattle in their frames. Christmas was over and New Years was only three days away. Hannah Zook, seventeen, had completed her regular chores around the house and had settled down to tend to her two little brothers who were mentally challenged, or God's Will children. Hannah was Amish and unmarried. At seventeen she was considered an old maid. All her friends married right after the eighth grade when their schooling was finished. Hannah wanted more than what her Amish world had to offer. However, it didn't look like she was going to get it.

In two weeks, when she turned eighteen, she would have to join the church and marry. Her father had chosen two new suitors to call on her. They were deemed suitable by her father, but not by her. One was a second cousin named Uziah Zook, a tall, lanky, blonde, second cousin who had spent most of the last two summers and falls working for a teacher who had a neighboring farm. Her father assumed he was earning and saving money to take a wife. That was a good and responsible endeavor in her father's thinking. The other suitor was a second cousin from the other side of the family who would work and take over his father's two hundred acres. He was short, round, and had a bad habit of picking his nose. Hannah found him very unpleasant and just didn't see what her father saw in him other than he was an only child and would inherit well. Hannah wanted to run as far as she could thru the snowy fields and not return. She did not want either suitor calling on her.

The care of her two little brothers was time consuming and never ending. She hated that her parents didn't make her siblings help with their care. She just sort of inherited them as her charge when she graduated eighth grade. Being an old maid, nose wiper to two God's will children was not how she wanted her life to be. She wanted more and was burnt out with the care for her two brothers. She had definitely made up her mind that she would never have children.

There were ten Amish families who owned farms near each other and they made up her world. Over the last fifty or so years, there had been extensive marriage between the ten families. As a result, shared genes from having the same grandfathers and great grandfathers, was producing mentally challenged, or God's Will children. She had learned about Gene pools when she was caring for the Widow Belier whose children were deceased from having been afflicted with Maple Syrup Disease. The visiting nurse from the city explained to Hannah about the silent incest, the combining of family genes that pop up when all of a social group originates from the same gene pools. She explained to Hannah that was the reason the widows children had all died young and that it was the reason for so many mentally challenged children amongst the Amish families.

Hannah knew that if she married either of her second cousins, her father had chosen as suitors, she would stand a great chance of having multiple mentally challenged children because the population shared the same three or four grandfathers. Hannah, taking to heart what the nurse had taught her, decided she was not willing to chance having children born with challenges. She was a smart young woman and wanted to make good decisions for herself. Knowing she carried genes for deformed or mentally challenged children, she wasn't willing to produce them. She had made a conscious decision to not reproduce.

So, here she was looking out the window wishing she could escape and choose a life. She just didn't know how. She knew no one in the English world and had no money to start a new life on her own.

She could not discuss wanting to leave with her mother or sisters. They would see her as selfish and not wanting to do the Godly thing and care for her two little challenged brothers who were five and seven years old. They had the minds of two year olds. To her, her brothers were not God's Will children. They were the products of two willfully ignorant people who had chosen to marry their cousin when they should have known better. Hannah was appalled at the backwoods thinking of her family and those of her community. They claimed to be holy in God's sight and would never commit a sin. However, they would share genes, a silent form of incest. She wanted a different life, a responsible, educated one.

A knock sounded at the door. Hannah left her two little brothers to roll a ball of yarn back and forth and went to answer it. She had cabin fever bad and welcomed company, any company to relieve her boredom.

Opening the door, she saw that it was her second cousin Uziah standing there. He took off his stocking hat to speak with her. She wasn't happy to see him. She thought that perhaps he had came to call on her and that aggravated her. It was the middle of the day and she had food down the front of her dress where her two little brothers had grabbed her before she could wipe their hands.

"Uziah, would you like to come in?" She asked politely. It was cold outside. She would have to let him in. If it were summer she would make him stand on the porch and tell him to get lost when her parents weren't listening.

"Just to warm myself while your mother grabs her things. My mother's baby is coming. I need your mother to come now." He said stepping inside the door but no further.

"I will get her," Hannah stated and hurried upstairs to fetch her mother who was the community's midwife.

Bursting into her mother's upstairs bedroom which had its door open she stated excitedly, "Your cousin Martha's baby is coming. She has sent Uziah for you."

"Get your things, Hannah. You will be going with me. It is time you started to learn to deliver babies. I am getting older and I will always have the boys to care for. I need the help. You may end up being an old maid at the rate you are running off suitors. Being a midwife could be a good occupation for you. You could trade your services for whatever you would have need of in your older days. You could barter your skills."

"I don't want to be a midwife. I get sick at the sight of other people's blood. Please don't make me go with you. Take one of the other girls." Hannah begged. She also didn't want to walk with Uziah and give him the idea she might be interested.

"It has been decided by your father and I. You are the only one in our family that isn't likely to marry and you must have a skill to survive without a husband or children in your old age. After these two suitors, your father has decided not to further match you up with anyone. We both agree that we don't know where we went wrong with you. You have had plenty of chances to marry boys of our faith with means. You almost shame us, Hannah. Now get your long cloak and heavy hat. It will be a long walk across the snowy fields. Martha needs us. She is an older mother and knows how to time the arrival of her babies. We won't be there long. Young mothers know nothing and they may send for you a day and a half too soon. We will be at my cousins for two hours at the most."

Hannah did as she was told with tears in her eyes. It was the first time that her mother had ever spoken of being ashamed of her. The words cut her heart to the core. She fought back her tears, bit her lip, and avoided her mother's eyes. She didn't want her to see that she had hurt her.

At the door they joined Uziah who took her mother's medical supplies and carried them for her. They walked across the field, thru a grove of trees, and then he helped her mother climb under the barb wire fence between the farms. However, he didn't help Hannah. He left her to climb under by herself. She was instantly peeved about it and decided he definitely would not be accepted as a suitor. A boy who wanted to court you, would definitely help you under a fence. He was a definite no, a rude piece of Amish trash.

It took about thirty minutes and they arrived at the farm house where Martha was in labor. Hannah's mother told the children to stay in the kitchen till the baby was born, and to watch out for the little ones making sure they were fed and diapered. Uziah had four sisters and three brothers. One of the sisters and one of the brothers were God's will children. His mother had also lost three besides them to Maple Syrup disease. Hannah knew that his gene pool was as bad as hers. Both were doomed when it came to having a family.

Hannah accompanied her mother to the bedroom and helped

with what she could. Uziah was told to go to the kitchen and run the house till they called for him. Martha's husband was away for two days attending a funeral out of state. He had gone by bus and wouldn't return till the next morning. Uziah was the man of the house till he returned.

It didn't take long for the baby to make its appearance. Hannah's mother quickly wrapped it in a towel and handed it to her cousin and then did the strangest thing. She told Hannah to go to the kitchen and stay there till she called for her. That was fine with Hannah. She wasn't enjoying the experience to begin with and left immediately.

In the kitchen she ate a cookie that the older girl offered her. Uziah, however, didn't say a word to her. He just ignored her and bounced his challenged little sister on his knee amusing her playing ride the horse. That was alright with Hannah. She didn't want his attention anyway. She was not accepting any suitor rude suitor. She would run away first, if she could figure out how to accomplish that feat.

About half an hour later, Hannah's mother made an appearance in the kitchen door way and asked Uziah and Hannah to come with her. They followed thinking they were going to get a peek at a squealing new baby. However, when they entered the bedroom, they found Uziah's mother in tears holding two bundles wrapped in towels not one. She had twin boys.

Uziah hurried to his mother's side and asked her what was wrong and why she was crying.

Hannah's mother said to him, "They are with Jesus, Uziah. They lived five minutes. Both are God's will children."

Uziah picked up one of the little bundles and looked at it. His eyes filled with tears and he quickly gave it back to his mother and left the room.

"Go after him, Hannah. Tell him the babies are better off with God. Both are deformed and have the mentally challenged look. They would not be an asset to life if they had lived. Life would have been unkind to them. Tell him his mother can try again for twins."

Hannah was appalled. Why would any woman with bad genes want to keep trying to have more children? Was her mother nuts? She left the room and went after Uziah who had put on his coat and hat and was heading outside. She called after him. "Wait for me! I will walk with you till mother is finished."

He waited on her, but she could see in his face that he wasn't happy about it. She grabbed her cloak and hat. When she got to the door, he walked out ahead of her in a rude fashion. She could feel her blood rising, but she held her peace. This wasn't the time to set an Amish man straight concerning his rude manners. It was a time of grieving.

Outside, they stood on the long, rambling, snow covered front porch to talk.

"I am sorry, Uziah. The babies are with God. They were God's Will children. God in his mercy has taken them. They would not have grown up to have good, productive lives."

"Don't be an idiot, Hannah. Our parents have God's Will children because they are cousins. If anything, God will send both of our sets of parents to Hell for their ignorance. The babies are not God's Will children. They are the products of a silent incest in the genes."

"I thought I was the only one who understood gene pools." She replied. "I share your sentiment. The genes of shared grandfathers in us are like little bombs ready to explode and give birth to incestuous children."

"Why do you wish me to call on you, knowing the great, silent sin of our people?" He smirked.

"My father arranged for you to call on me, not I." She replied equally as rude.

"I am going to be blunt with you Hannah. I have no intentions of courting you. My father is insisting I marry and join the church. I have no intention of doing either. I plan to leave after the babies are buried." He replied harshly. "I have been purposely rude with you so that you will turn me down and give me a little more time to plan my departure. However, you are hounding me this morning. Back off!"

"My plan has been to tell you to take a hike when my parents weren't aware of it. I have no intentions of marrying you. I want an education and a life amongst the English where women aren't required to marry, if they don't choose."

"My father said that you were a spit fire. He thought you could break me like a wild horse. That is the reason he agreed with your father concerning our courting." He stated.

"I am a spitfire? You can tell your father he is a jackass and that I wouldn't accept you as a suitor even if I was looking for a husband. I know what I want out of life and it isn't a marriage to a rude mannered, second cousin. I dislike tall, long legged, farm boys. It will be an educated man if I should ever decide to choose a husband."

"Well, I am glad we have the courting issue settled. I am just putting in time till my father returns and the babies are buried!" He replied. "Before I have to explain to him that I have been turned down by you, I will walk away into the night and a new life."

"You are lucky that I don't turn your tall, lanky frame over my knees and teach you some manners for being rude to me and calling me names!"

"My father was right. You would tackle a grown man, if the need arose." He laughed. "You need a wimp for a husband, a simple little man that you can control. I can picture in my mind your telling him to hop, jump, and roll over at your every word. That is not me. In my thinking it would be I that would turn you over my knee." He replied defiantly folding his arms across his chest.

"I guess we have been up front with each other right down to our gene pools?" She replied in a huff folding her arms also in a defiant stance.

"I would say that we understand each other. I find you full of yourself and you find me rude. What more is there to say, except that I will not miss you when I go off to the city?"

"And you think I will waste my time thinking of the caller that I intended to turn down?" She stated with fire in her eyes.

"Now that we know that we definitely do not want to court each other, we can go back to being family and second cousins."

Hannah grinned when he returned the conversation to them being family. "I respect your wish to further your education. I dream of going to high school and then college. I do not want to be an old maid, Amish midwife."

"I do not wish to be a farmer. I want to be a doctor and that is why I am running away to the land of the English." He replied.

"I have enrolled in the university for the coming January semester."

She replied. "How did you manage to complete high school? I have heard nothing of it from our relatives."

"I have been working for a Biology professor a couple farms away in the summers and in the evenings. He has home schooled me two hours a day when my parents thought I was working. He said it was his way of giving back. He was an orphan that a kind old gentleman took in and saw to it that he had an education. I must pass it on someday. That was the deal with him. I must see that one more person gets an education that doesn't have a chance to have one. I graduated high school the end of summer. My family doesn't know. They would see it as my taking charity. The professor has helped me enroll in classes at the university in town and has paid for my first semester of tuition and books. After this semester, I must have a part time job to continue. He has explained to me how to recycle and survive in the world of the English. I will leave as soon as the babies are buried. Classes start after New Years and I must find a room or an apartment and settle in."

"Had you thought of taking a relative along and letting them have the benefit of an education. I would love to go to high school. I could be that one that you pay back and see to it has an education." She stated. Hannah was not shy when it came to her opinions and what she wanted out of life.

"Take you with me? Are you crazy? Our parents would catch up with us and kill us both."

Hannah suddenly grinned, "I will leave my mother a note saying that I have run away on my own and will return after I am educated and that I do not intend to marry."

Uziah looked at her with a serious face. "If we share an apartment in the city as cousins only, would you be willing to work hard and do your part to keep the two of us afloat? There is every possibility that the community here, as well as our families, will shun us? The price of an education could be a sad one. Once we leave here, it will be either sink or swim for us. There can be no turning back."

"I am willing to do anything short of sin to escape being an old maid midwife. I want to finish high school and then go to college." She replied enthusiastically.

"You are willing to live as cousins and do as I say? I will make the final decision on all issues in our shared home like your father does. It is God's will for the man to head the house." He stated eyeing her to see if he thought she was reliable with her words.

"You may head the house as long as your decisions are not sinful. Perhaps it is God's will for us to start a new Amish community of two amongst the English."

"You must agree not to write your parents till you are out of high school and start college. My father is intent that I take over the family farm. I would not put it past him coming after both of us with a bull whip. I am afraid of my father. My mother is afraid of my father. When I am a wealthy doctor, I will go back and rescue those of my family that are willing to flee him. I have younger challenged brothers and sisters who will need me when they grow older. I plan to take them to live with me in the land of the English. I must make enough money as a doctor. Unlike your father, who I assume is a Godly man, my father has bad genes and is crazy and mean at times. I cannot let him find me. You must agree to no communication with your family and the Amish community. Is that a term that you can live with?"

"I am willing." She replied excited. "My mother won't be lonely without me. I am not her only child. She has a house full of children to keep her busy. I will leave her a note and tell her that I will get in touch with her four years from now so she will have that to look forward to. You will be a grown man and out of college."

"That is agreeable." Uziah stated. Then he added, "I will take you with me under one other condition. The English world is not a safe place for women like the Amish community is. English men openly rape and use women when they can. The English seem to lack a sense of morality. I think it would be safest, in order to protect you, that we tell everyone that we are a married couple. The English men would not see you as someone they could easily seduce or use. I feel I owe this to your father, to be your protector in his stead. Neither of us have plans to marry. So, we have no need of projecting ourselves as single and available. As cousins, we share the last name of Zook. No one will question our one little white lie. It is a necessary one for your protection. The men of the English world are predators from what I am told. They look for innocent girls like you to prey on. They pay little attention to married ones."

"I don't want suitors, so that is fine with me as long as you know that I don't intend to do anything with you that a married couple would do. You are my cousin and nothing more or ever will be."

"The same goes here. I actually find you to be a little homely, mouthy, and full of yourself. However I won't be married to you so it doesn't matter. Your flaws will be between you and God, not you and I. I actually don't like you very much as a girl. As a cousin you are alright."

"Well, we are in agreement then. We will tell everyone we are married. We will share an apartment, finances, and chores.

Other than shared responsibilities, we are both free to do as we will within the pretend boundaries of marriage." Hannah stated firmly.

"Can you cook? I am a lousy cook and I was dreading eating my biscuits." He inquired.

"Yes, I cook and do all the things an Amish woman is taught to do."

"Whatever day the babies are laid to rest, we will leave that evening at sundown. The babies cannot be laid to rest till my Father returns which possibly could be tomorrow. Meet me at your outhouse at sunset. It will be easier for us to run away if we have night to travel in. Stuff your cloak pockets with your personal things and carry only what is comfortable to carry in a pillowcase. I will do the same. Consider very carefully what you put in that case. It may be your only possessions for quite a while till we get settled. I have enough money saved to rent us a cheap apartment for two months. We must find work to pay for our shelter after that."

"I have fifty seven dollars that I earned caring for the widow Belier when she was ill. You may have it to add to our shared finances. I promise you, I will do my part and find work." She stated.

Hannah's mother suddenly called for her from the doorway and their conversation ended abruptly.

"Be at the outhouse at sundown after the babies are buried". He whispered as she turned to walk away.

"I will be there!" She whispered back and went to see what her mother was wanting.

Running Away

As the sun was starting to set, Hannah slipped out the back door to head for the outhouse. Supper was over and it was her sister's turn to do the dishes, so no one would miss her. She had filled her pillowcase earlier in the day and had stuffed her cloak pockets with her necessary underwear items. In her pillowcase was her Sunday dress, Bible, sewing supplies, socks, and dress patterns. Also, tucked safely in her Bible was a handkerchief her mother had given her for eighth grade graduation. It was the most important of all next to her Bible. Everyone had attended the funeral for the God's Will twins who lived five minutes. Hannah's family was so caught up in the event that they paid no attention to her or her sly stuffing of her cloak pockets and the pillow case on her bed. She had removed the pillow and hid it under her bed before leaving for the funeral. All day she added things to the case as she thought of them.

When everyone was busy at sunset, Hannah slipped out the door and hurried to the outhouse with her pillowcase of things hidden beneath her cloak in case any of her family was watching from the many farmhouse windows. Reaching the privy, Uziah stepped out carrying a feed sack with what he could carry in it. Immediately, he took her hand and they started across the field in a run. It wasn't a fast run with the snow being five inches on the ground. It was a laborious run. Once they reached the woods of the fence line, he released her hand and they rested panting. Running in the snow was not easy. Then they started walking across the neighbor's fields heading for the main highway into town. As the sun sank lower in the sky, they relaxed knowing that night was hiding their journey. They stopped a couple of times to rest, However, they kept moving in case their parents had discovered them missing.

"I am really cold, Uziah," Stated Hannah as they walked in

the dark. The temperature was dropping and there were giant snowflakes in the air suggesting that the sky was going to dump a new batch of snow on their heads.

"Another ten minutes, Hannah and we will be at the highway. I am sure that someone will stop and give us a ride in to town from there. No one would leave a couple stranded in the dark, out in a blizzard, to freeze on a highway shoulder."

"Let us hurry then. I welcome a ride in a warm stranger's car right now."

"We are paying the price of being cold tonight to buy a good tomorrow and an education. We will survive! Just keep thinking about the wonderful life that is ahead of us in the land of the English. The cold and darkness may have us in its grips tonight, but the sunshine of education will have us tomorrow."

"You have a gift of saying things beautifully."

"I must study and work hard to get where I am going. I do not regret being Amish and having a gift of beautiful words. However, it is the healing words of a doctor that I wish to be known for. Our people feel that an eighth grade education is enough. I say it is just enough to keep you ignorant. All the important subjects and beautiful words are taught after the eighth grade. I am very thankful for the Biology professor farmer that I have worked for. He has taught me to seek out the beautiful words of books. I have always wondered what was beyond our farms and life. Our people are willingly ignorant and pass it on in limited education to their children. I wish to be an educated man and know the mysteries of life. I am a thinker and have thought my way out of the ignorance of my roots that I am abandoning as we walk away tonight!"

"What about God?"Hannah asked tying to keep her mind off

of the biting cold.

"God I will keep. He is the mystery that lives in everything and everyone. I will seek him in new ways and cherish his presence in all knowledge. Satan is ignorance. I will seek God as intelligence."

"That is okay with me, as long as you do not abandon God. I want an educated life, but abandoning my belief in God is not an option." She replied. "I must pray and keep Satan at bay for both of us. If God is knowledge, Uziah, is Satan the lack of it? I have always thought he had horns and a pitchfork tail."

"You will be a thinker to. I hear your thinking in your words." He stated and then suddenly pointed ahead of them to car lights. "There is the highway, see it?" Stated Uziah pointing.

Hannah looked where he was pointing and saw a couple cars in the distance creeping down the snow covered highway.

"Yes, thank God. I cannot feel my toes."

"I will thumb a ride as soon as we reach the highway, we are almost there."

Within another five minutes they were standing on the shoulder of the highway. They set their sacks of possessions down in the snow so they could rest and catch their breath. After a moment or so, headlights appeared in the distance heading their direction. Uziah turned and put his thumb up to hitch a ride. His Biology professor had explained a lot of things to him and this was one of them, how to hitchhike to save traveling expenses.

The vehicle slowed and came to a halt beside them. It was a jeep with a younger man in his twenties who swung open the passenger door speaking, "Would you like a lift? This is a bad night to have a girl out hitchhiking wearing a dress. Are you nuts or something?"

"We are newlywed." Uziah replied. "Hannah and I were married a few minutes ago by a minister living in that house in the distance. We are running away to live in the land of the English."

Hannah blushed and didn't say a word.

"Get in. I am headed for the university. You have sure picked one heck of a night to elope! Wouldn't summer have been a better choice?"

"That is a good point," Uziah stated helping Hannah in to sit in the middle and on the edge of the passenger seat. They would have to share the seat for one. "When one's heart races, the weather doesn't always cooperate."

"Where are you headed?" The driver asked.

"Hannah and I are students. I will start my first semester at the university and Hannah will be finishing high school near the campus." Uziah replied climbing in and slamming the passenger door closed.

"I am pleased to meet you, Uziah. My name is David and I am also a student at the university. I am a sophomore."

Hannah thought to herself that the man was rude acknowledging Uziah by name but not her. Did she not exist? Why hadn't he said I am glad to meet you Hannah?

"We are pleased to meet you David. We are the Zooks, Hannah and Uziah." Uziah once more stated.

"My last name is Goldstein. I wish I had a pretty girl out with me tonight to keep me warm. My feet are cold."

Uziah laughed. "Hannah is indeed pretty and I am one lucky man. Don't you have a lady friend? Most male college students have a girlfriend, or so I am told?"

"The one I was living with last year, transferred to another college out of state. I am once more single and looking for a new girlfriend to move in with me."

"You lived with a woman and now look for another to do the same?" Asked Hannah before she thought. The words just popped out of her mouth in shock. Uziah was right. English men used women.

"Lots of college students live together. Does that shock you?" He asked turning and eyeing the bundled up dimple faced Amish girl and suddenly realized how pretty she was. His heart skipped a beat. That surprised him. He didn't as a rule go for young, plain types.

"It is a sin to live with a woman that you are not married to. Have you never heard of the sin of fornication?" Hannah asked unsmiling.

"Er . . . Uh . . . of course. My father is a Rabbi," replied the driver who was caught a little off guard by her gouging words.

"Hannah, I think it best that we not pry into our generous driver's private life. He is not Amish. He is English and one of those I have told you about."

"I apologize, Mr. Goldstein. It is not up to me to judge you for your sin of fornication. However, please speak with your Rabbi father concerning it. I would hate to reach Heaven one day and find that you, our generous driver, is not there because no one was willing to point out your sin." She replied.

Uziah cringed. He was going to have to talk to her about what was appropriate to say to the English. He could tell she was offending their driver named David.

David Goldstein, removing his eyes from the snow packed road for a brief moment, took a quick serious glance at the girl. She had a mouth on her and the prettiest face he had seen in a long time. He didn't know how to reply.

"Please excuse my Hannah, David. My wife is opinionated and holds very tightly to our Amish values. I am sure they are not yours and I apologize. What are you studying at the university?" Uziah asked changing the subject.

"I am just taking the basics for now, the prerequisites. I am considering a degree in Religious studies. My father wishes me to be a Rabbi like him. My grandfathers are diamond merchants. To be honest, I don't know what I want to be. For now, I am just enjoying the freedom of college life. It is great being away from mom and dad and staying out as late as I want with a pretty woman. Don't get me wrong. I study and make good grades. What is your major?" David asked turning on the windshield wipers. The snow was starting to fall hard and fast.

"I will one day be a doctor. Like you, I will be getting the beginning required classes out of the way. I plan to go to college year round and graduate in three years. Then I will tackle my master's degree and move on the medical school, possibly in Chicago."

"What about you, Mrs. Zook? Aren't you a little old to be in high school?" He asked not thinking about what he was saying.

"It is rude of you to refer to my age. It would be like me making references to your nose as overly large and ugly. Yes, I will be an older student as well as your nose being what it is."

Once again the driver glanced at Hannah with a serious look on his face. "You are right; I apologize about the age comment."

"I do not apologize about your nose. The truth is the truth. Does your family all have large noses? I bet your mother and your sisters stick them in everyone's business. Am I right?" She asked being insulted over the age comment. She didn't let her suitors get by with rude comments. Why should she let him get by?

"Actually, you are right. I live in a family of busy bodies. That is why I have chosen to attend college five hundred miles away from home. However, my large Jewish nose had to come with me."

"What a shame." Hannah stated. She hated rude men. She would not let him win their war of words. "I bet you don't find many English girls who wish you to call on them, with that nose."

David took an exit ramp from the highway shooting them off into the city and the university area.

"Where would you like me to let you and your aging, opinionated wife off? Will you be staying in the married dorm or have an apartment rented somewhere?"

"Our eloping tonight was a spur of the moment decision. We will sit up all night in a convenience store somewhere and rent us an apartment tomorrow."

"You plan to sit up in a convenience store on your wedding night? That is a bummer. I have a one bedroom apartment. I am willing to sleep on the couch and let you crash for the night at my place if you would like. The bedroom has a door on it."

"What do you mean by crash?" inquired Hannah.

"College students do it all the time. If a student doesn't have a place to stay for some reason, he drops in on a fellow student who has a place and sleeps on the floor or the couch. He crashes for a few days. Sometimes the poorer students, who are working their way thru college, have to choose between paying tuition and the landlord. The landlord throws them out and someone like me, who has no financial problems, lets them crash till they get a few dollars ahead and able to make it on their own again. My girlfriend, that lived with me last year originally, just crashed at my place. She lost her job as a waitress. Her rent came due and the landlord threw her out. A friend of mine called and asked if she could crash with me for a few days.'

"Mr. Goldstein, I am in shock. You are the son of a man who speaks for God. Yet, you shame him by running a house of ill repute with harlot girls willing to sleep with you for room and board and men who cheat their landlords. I am not a thief, nor am I a harlot. Thank you for your offer, but I would rather sit up all night with a clean conscious!" Hannah sputtered.

Once again, David Goldstein turned briefly to stare at Hannah in disbelief while at the same time thinking she had to be the prettiest girl he had ever seen. Her blue eyes twinkled and her dimples were fascinating.

"Now Hannah, we have our beliefs but you must remember that David is English. Who are we to judge?"

"I am not judging. I am speaking the truth of God and my mouth will not be silent! You are a sinner, Mr. Goldstein, a big nosed abomination in the sight of God."

About that time, David turned his jeep into the parking lot of an all night convenience store by the campus and slammed on the brakes a little pissed. "Here we are! Your convenience store motel room for the night awaits you. Enjoy. I think I am retracting my kind offer of lodging. Goodbye Mrs. Zook. If I were you Uziah, I would take her back where I found her. You are going to regret your marriage to her. She is quite mouthy, slow in school, and definitely homely in comparison to college coeds. You should have chosen more carefully."

"I may be homely, Mr. Goldstein, but I am respectable. You prefer harlot girls and thieves for companions. I believe I am one up on you and your harlot from last year, in God's eyes. You are an abomination, a sinful man, and definitely a child of the devil."

Once again David eyed her unsmiling as she climbed out to join Uziah who had exited and was holding her pillowcase and his feed sack.

"Don't mind her!" stated Uziah reaching back in to shake hands with David. "Thank you for the lift, I appreciate it. Perhaps we will see each other again sometime on campus. God ride with you!"

Hannah and Uziah stood in the unplowed snow covered parking lot watching as David sped away.

"Hannah we are living in their world now. We must get along with the English. Many of them will be the means by which we will survive here. You must not speak with the English like you did him. When we are in public, I think it best if you hold your opinions to yourself. He could have been a much needed friend to us. He has a vehicle. We could have rode with him to supermarkets and other places in the future. The English will not live by our values. We must accept them as they are and use what they have to offer to survive. He offered us lodging as well as possible transportation for a few days. Life here is different than amongst the brethren. You have alienated him and denied us lodging and transportation."

"He called me homely, old, and slow in school. It didn't sit well with me."

"He just told you the truth. Sometimes the truth hurts. You are old to be going to high school. You have a sin of pride just as large as his sin of fornication. I think you best pray for you and him."

"Shall I pray for his big nose to shrink also?"

"Hannah . . ." Uziah scolded. "You are acting like a two year old. Grow up. If the opportunity arises you must apologize to him. He doesn't have to apologize to you. He lives by different standards. Childish behavior will cost you. Tonight, it cost us a night's lodging and a friend."

"Alright, I will pray for his big nose to shrink!"

"No wonder your father couldn't find a suitor for you. You are a little bitch."

"That is foul language. How dare you call me that name?"

"I dare! Now, work on not being one. Friendship with everyone we come in contact with is important. The Biology professor told me to recycle everything to survive in the land of the English. That includes people who offer us favors."

"I want an education, but I am going to hate controlling my opinions and praying for big noses."

Uziah shook his head and pointed her toward the convenience store. He had his work cut out for him teaching her about survival. She was not going to be easy. She had a mouth that just seemed to open up and pour out her opinions like a waterfall and at inappropriate times. He was sure that he and David would have become friends if it hadn't been for her. He might have crashed at David's apartment for a week. The professor had explained to him the pad crashing scene.

CHAPTER TWO

Meeting a Peeping Tom

It felt like Heaven getting inside the warm convenience store. There were two booths on one side of the store near the coffee pot and soda dispensers. Uziah helped Hannah with their things and saw to it that she was seated and had their possessions on the booth bench with her. Then he made his way over to the coffee machine and prepared one cup of hot coffee. They would share it to save money. Then Uziah headed for the register to pay for it.

"Sweetie, would you mind if I sit down across from you just long enough to stir some sugar and creamer into my coffee?" Asked a middle aged petite woman with bleached blonde hair. She had on a heavy ski jacket, jeans, and snow boots.

"Yes, join me. I would welcome a few minutes of girl chat. My Uziah is in a long line at the register paying for coffee for us." Replied Hannah. "I am trying to warm myself while I wait on him."

"My name is Georgia," said the woman sitting down and reaching for a couple packs of sugar and creamer. She then proceeded to rip them open and dump them into her coffee. "I assume you are students. Is that your boyfriend, the long legged Amish boy at the register?"

"No, he is my cousin. We will share an apartment here while I finish high school and he goes to college. Our Amish community only offers an education thru the eighth grade. I will go to high school and then on to college. We have made our way here for the coming semester."

"Good for you," she replied. "Just watch out for all the young bucks running around campus. They have one thing on their mind and that is to get in a girl's you know what."

"We have that problem solved. We will tell everyone that we are a married couple and that will protect me from the English young bucks. Neither of us may date anyone other than someone from our community. A pretend marriage is a safe option for us."

"That is smart thinking! If you should ever need a lady friend, I own the Pancake Emporium which is a restaurant out by the interstate. My name is Georgia."

"That is very kind of you! I will remember where you are. You are my first new friend here." Hannah said smiling. She recalled what Uziah had said about making friends with everyone you came in contact with.

"I have got to run, when I see your cousin heading back here. Do you like secrets?" Georgia asked.

"Oh yes. I was hoping to find a friend that I could share secrets with. Do you have one?" Hannah asked grinning.

"The reason for my being cold and needing coffee is that I have been standing outside in the cold spying on a man that I am crazy about. I have been window peeping. You will never guess what I saw looking in his window?"

"What?" Asked Hannah taking the hook.

"I saw him in his underwear and they had holes in them. That is my secret for you to keep till you come visit me out at the restaurant." The petite, smiling, older woman shared giggling. "Peeping is what I am good at."

"You saw him in just his underwear and they had holes in them?" Hannah asked in shock.

"Big holes . . ." the older woman replied. "They were not little finger tip size holes. They were the size of lemons."

"Did you see anything that is a sin for a single woman to peep at?" Hannah blurted out in a shocked questioning voice.

"I will only tell you what I saw when you come for a visit." The older woman stated laughing.

"My father called me his curious cat. I will not be able to sleep thinking about your peeping. I will definitely come out to visit you and hear about what you did or did not see. I have never peeped. Was it fun?"

"Haven't you ever peeped thru the hole in a wooden fence at anyone?"

"I once peeped thru a hole in the barn wall and saw my mother and father in the hay. They caught me peeping and I had to paint the whole wall of the barn outside for peeping. I didn't see anything exciting. They were just taking a nap in the hay." Hannah replied.

"If you had seen a good looking Amish boy with his shirt off thru that hole in the barn wall, would that have been exciting and worthwhile?"

"I see what you mean. It is what you choose to peep at that makes it fun." Laughed Hannah.

"You have got the picture. It was what I saw thru the holes in his underwear that made the peeping fun!" Georgia laughed. "You come out to the restaurant and we will girl talk and become friends. I learned many years ago that you can't be friends with your employees. They will stab you in the back."

"Do you have many holes in your back?" Hannah questioned giggling.

"It looks like Swiss cheese," Georgia replied giggling in response to Hannah's girlish laughter. "I will look forward to our chats." She then got up and left waving goodbye from the door as she exited the store.

Hannah was pleased that she had made a new friend. She would tell Uziah about her tomorrow when she wasn't so tired and could be excited about sharing all the details of her encounter and the story of the underwear peeping. Then she decided she had better not mention the underwear part. Uziah would probably tell her she had sinned listening to Georgia. She had only heard about the fun of peeping and hadn't actually done it. She was sinless. She would only peep, if her new friend asked her to go along.

Starting to become comfortable in the booth, Hannah removed her hat and gloves. Then she loosened her cloak to let her body absorb the heat of overhead vents blowing warm air. There was a man seated in the other booth, a very odd looking stranger. He had a white piece of cloth wrapped around his head and he had beautiful golden brown skin. He wasn't an Indian. She didn't know what his race was. He was dressed in a white shirt as well as white pants. She was totally fascinated with him and couldn't keep her eyes off of him.

Suddenly, the man with his head wrapped in a white cloth, looked up and discovered her looking at him. He smiled at her seemingly equally as fascinated. She reached up and straightened her white cap thinking it might be on crooked. It had been hidden under her heavy winter hat.

The man suddenly kissed his fingers and pointed to her cap. Hannah blushed and straightened it thinking that was what he meant. Then she pointed to her head and then his and grinned. He smiled back and straightened his own. For some odd reason, she was attracted to him and had a serious case of butterflies in her stomach. She hadn't expected to be attracted to a man. She had decided to never marry or have children. However, this stranger with his head wrapped in a white piece of cloth pleased her. She watched as he drew something on a white paper napkin that he pulled from the dispenser in his booth. Then he got up to leave putting on his coat. As he walked past her booth, he placed the napkin in front of her. It had a beautiful bird drawn on it. He pointed to the bird and then pointed to her and kissed his fingers. Then he waved bye to her from the door just as Georgia had. She wondered if his expressions and the drawing meant that he thought she was a beautiful bird. Whatever he meant, she was pleased with her experience and would treasure it always. She quickly tucked the napkin away in her dress pocket. It would be the first item to go into her a memory box, when she found a shoe box to start one in.

Uziah seemed to be doomed standing in a line of customers at the counter waiting to pay for their coffee. She relaxed into the booth. She had experienced two fun people. Perhaps her life in the land of the English was going to be a good one. Perhaps

Uziah was right and she needed to work at thinking, but not saying. She had thought the bleached hair of Georgia was like molded straw. However, she had held her tongue and not said it. In her self control, she had made a new friend. There was nothing about the man in white she disliked. He caused her to have butterflies. She was proud of herself. She would survive in the world of the English and make friends.

Uziah Meets a Witch

Uziah stood patiently waiting as a long line of college students paid for their various purchases. He eyed the strange looking girl on the register. She had black fingernails and black lips. He wondered how much licorice she had eaten and sucked on to get her lips so black? Her long black straight hair hung way down her back and she was dressed in a black sweater and jeans. He was familiar with the witch's star emblem that she wore around her neck. He had seen one like it in the many books of the Biology Professor who had home schooled him. The Amish bishop had spoken once on the witch of Endor from the Old Testament and the wicked witches who lived in the land of the English and came out on Halloween to play. He, however, had never encountered one before. He was fascinated with her and glad to stand in line to get to eye her.

Finally, it came his turn and he stepped up to the register to pay.

"Well aren't you a cutie," the witch stated winking at him and then taking his money to pay for the coffee.

Uziah blushed. "Would you know by any chance where I might find a cheap room or apartment? I start classes after new years and I need shelter. I will be sitting up tonight because I do not have housing yet."

"How about coming to my room and crashing. My bed is big enough for two. My uncle might yell in the morning, but that is a small price to pay. I like the looks of you." The witch replied.

"I . . . I just got married about two hours ago. That is my wife sitting in the booth. I thank you for the offer, but I am taken." He replied not knowing what to say and blushing as she handed him his change.

"Darn, the good ones are always taken. If you ever dump her for any reason, come look me up. I don't mind being second in line." She said winking at him again.

Again he blushed. English girls were so bold. He wasn't sure that he would have turned her down if Hannah hadn't been along. She was pure temptation and a witch. It would be a sin to associate with her according to his Amish faith.

"About shelter, could you suggest anything?" He asked again.

"Actually, my uncle owns the apartment house we live in. There is a vacant studio apartment on the third floor that has been vacant for several months. The stairs are on the outside and no one wants to climb the three flights of snow covered stairs in the winter. If you are interested I could take you over to talk with my uncle about it when I get off work in fifteen minutes. He waits up for me on bad nights like this to make sure that I am in. He will be up and possibly thrilled at the idea of finding someone to possibly rent the dump to. Offer him half what he asks! I guess, by looking at the two of you, that you need cheap shelter."

"That is very generous of you. We would be most grateful for a ride and the opportunity to see the apartment. We would love to rent something tonight and have a place to sleep."

"Well, sweetie, I wish you were sleeping with me. She is one lucky girl. What is her name?"

"Hannah," he replied. "We are Amish. My name is Uziah."

"Well, Uziah, my name in Endora and I am Wiccan." She replied waving at Hannah.

Uziah eyed her for a moment as he stepped aside for another customer to pay for his purchases. He was shocked at the girl's words. He had just met a witch and she was open about it. Also, he was in shock because he was attracted to her and had a stomach that was doing flip flops. God was not going to be happy with him. He knew he was going to have to resist the spell she was casting on him. The spell was coming from her black lips. He wanted to lick them like they were licorice.

When the customer was gone he asked, "Do you cast spells like the witch of Endor in the Old Testament?"

She grinned and replied. "I plan to cast one on you. Mark the words of this witch's mouth. You will fall madly in love with me! Do you want to make a little wager that I can do it?"

"I do not gamble. How hard should I pray to keep you away from me? I have never come face to face with a witch before. Just tell me up front."

Endora went to laughing. "Don't pray! That will get you nowhere with me. Give in to my spell, come home to my gingerbread hut, and we will make wild pagan love."

"I am in trouble!" He replied. "I will tell Hannah about the apartment and we will wait for you in the booth. However, I must turn you down on the night of wild love, although I am tempted."

"Drink all the coffee you want! Refills are free." She laughed thinking that she would sleep with him for free. She was a call girl and used a couple nights a week at the store to meet men with money who came and went buying gasoline. She could peg the rich ones and was building herself up a clientele for the weekends.

"Thank you, I will." He stated and made his way back to the booth to Hannah.

"You looked flustered, Uziah. Is something wrong?"

"I met a witch, a real live witch at the register and she has cast a spell on me. I have a racing heart and now must pray hard to overcome her curse. If you hadn't been along, the witch would have seduced me and taken me to her bed. I wanted her to." He stated with big eyes.

"Well, at least she is a pretty witch." Hannah stated while eyeing the girl at the register. "I really don't think witches exist, Uziah. I think they are fairy tales or Bible stories written to scare us and keep us in line. What is her name?"

"Her name is Endora and she is definitely the witch of Endor." He replied. "She has cast a spell on me and I can taste the licorice on her lips and I have never kissed her."

"God has sent you a temptation on your first night of life amongst the English. It is better to get temptation over with and then you don't have to worry about it. I will probably be next and meet a devil man wearing red."

"You pray for me and I will pray for you!" He replied. "The witch knows where there is a third floor apartment that we can possibly rent for half price. We will ride with her after she gets off from work. Do you think we will be safe? You must ride in the middle. If she touches me, I may turn into a frog or a locust."

"You told me to make friends with everyone that comes along. We will ride with her and be her friend. We do not have to embrace her ways to enjoy what she can do for us. I have thought about what you said about thinking, but not saying. To me she looks like the black ashes from our wood stove back home. I hate cleaning up black ash. To you she looks like licorice. I will not tell her she looks like stove ash. I will concentrate on smiling and the free ride she has offered us to look at an apartment. I have learned my lesson tonight. I will befriend the people we encounter and zip my lip."

"You are right, I am being silly. She is transportation and the key to shelter tonight." He replied sharing the cup of coffee with her. "Do you think that the black she puts on her lips is some sort of witch's potion. I actually thought that I would like to lick the black off her lips when I was standing up there. I could hardly force myself to step away from the counter. She has done a number on my heart and has cast a love spell on me."

Hannah grinned but didn't mention her encounter with the golden skinned man. He was her secret that she wanted to dream about. She didn't want to share him. In her thinking, every girl needed a fantasy to think about when the winters got long, especially if the girl lived on an Amish farm. She was delighted to have a new secret someone to think about. His drawing of the bird would go in her Bible till she got a shoe box to store her memories in. The bird was a graven image. However, she wasn't a firm believer in all the Amish taught. She considered herself to be a modern Amish, whatever that meant. She had heard the term used by one of the community's mothers describing her son who had moved to the city and was living there. The Bible said not to make a graven image. She had not drawn the bird. She only owned the napkin with the bird on it. There was a difference in her thinking.

When packing her things earlier in the day, she would have loved to of had a photo of her mother and dad and her siblings to bring to the new world with her. However, there was not one due to the graven image belief. She secretly wanted a camera. Once when she was about ten, an English neighbor took a snapshot of her and gave her a copy. She never told her parents about it because she knew they would have burned it. She had it hidden in her bible. She had decided one day, when she was thirteen, that she would get herself a camera someday. She would ask a friend to take photos of those she wanted a picture of. She would not sin, because she wouldn't be taking or making the graven images. She would just own the film and the photos. She was sure that she was indeed modern in her thinking.

Uziah refilled their cup of coffee that they were sharing and put a lid on it to take with them. They could use the cup to put water in wherever they ended up. They needed to save everything and recycle till they had what they needed to survive. Then, he and Hannah rode with Endora to the apartment house and followed her to her front door.

CHAPTER THREE

Fifteen Day Old Pizza

David Goldstein unlocked his apartment door and was surprised to find his lights on. As he stepped inside, thinking he had accidentally left them on, he spotted his friend Mooch Martin standing in front of the refrigerator clothed only in his boxers. He was retrieving a piece of cold pizza from the refrigerator and a can of beer.

"Hope you don't mind man, I am a little strapped for cash and need to crash with you for a few days. Is that alright?"

"Better you than the female jerk I just dumped off at the convenience store." He said sitting down on a chair by the door and removing his black lace up Army combat boots. His father had given the black, lace up, combat boots and several pairs of military fatigues to him when he left for college. His father had told him that girls were attracted to military men and that the Israeli Army fatigues and boots were girl magnets. His father had been right. At the same time he wondered how his mother felt about his father giving him the items and stating why in front of her.

"You had a date with a female jerk tonight? I thought you

went home for the holidays." Questioned Mooch plopping down on the worn out couch with his refrigerator finds.

"You wouldn't believe the mouth she had on her. Do you think my nose is too large?"

Mooch grinned, "She insinuated you had a large nose?"

"She insinuated more than that and I only knew her for an hour or so. She chewed me a new ...." He stated trailing off in speech thinking about her dimples and blue twinkling eyes.

"Was she a blind date that went bad?" Mooch inquired as he watched David strip off his wet snow covered, heavy, winter Jacket and throw it on the back of a kitchen chair to dry out.

"I picked her up on my way in. She and her husband were hitchhiking in this blizzard. They eloped and had only been married for about an hour. I only picked them up because I could see that it was a girl in a dress on the highway shoulder with the guy. I wouldn't want my sister in a dress out hitchhiking on a night like this." He replied mad at himself for giving her a ride.

"She must have been one cute chic to get you all riled up. Is she a student?"

"The guy was okay. His name is Uziah and he is pre-med starting his freshman year at the university. Her name is Hannah and she will be attending the high school down the street. She is seventeen and a freshman in high school. She must be a real dumb ass!" He stated knowing better. He had caught her story of the eighth grade education. He was just blowing off steam.

"Not all of us are 4.0 like you, David. I am struggling to maintain my 3.8. Maybe she is a little slow or has been sick for some reason and is behind in her studies."

"She is definitely a dumb ass! However, you should have seen her dimples. God they were gorgeous. I could have sworn they winked at me every time she smiled." He replied thinking back how the warmth of her body felt as she sat squeezed between him and Uziah.

"Oh . . . I get it. You met a pretty girl tonight who was already married and you were attracted to her. What did you do, make a pass at her and she told you to take a hike?"

"Can it Mooch? I am serious. She was one of the most opinionated, mouthy bitches I have ever run across. She had the nerve to infer that my apartment houses harlots and thieving students who use me for free housing and utilities."

"Apparently, she was just being honest with you. I do use you for free housing and utilities when I am strapped for cash. Right now, I have enough money put back for this semester's tuition and books, but I might starve if weren't for your three day old pizza." He replied taking a bite of a piece of dried out, cheese pizza he had gotten from the refrigerator.

"It is fifteen day old pizza, Mooch. I ordered that thin crust beauty just before I went home for Hanukkah."

"Damn!" Mooch blurted out and then jumped up from the couch and ran to the kitchen trash can spitting and then throwing away the remainder of the piece of pizza. There was no other food in the apartment except for a couple of stale bags of chips in the cabinet with their tops open.

"I meant to take it with me on my long drive home and went off and forgot it. Throw it out to the birds tomorrow. They will eat it." David stated as he watched Mooch spit and gag.

"We are going to have to get some food in this place. I will rifle thru Georgia's and bring home a few things tomorrow. There is a bag of Hot Mama's popping corn in the cabinet. Do you want me to pop it and we will share it to hold us over till morning?" Mooch asked.

"Fix it for yourself. I ate just before I picked up the female jerk."

"She has really done a number on your psyche and you are in one piss poor mood. Was she that number ten that you have always claimed was out there that one day would waltz into your life suddenly?"

"Cool it Mooch. I have had a bad night and yes she was a ten. She was also mouthy and married. God must have wanted a good laugh at my expense tonight. I am going to take a quick shower and then I will watch some television with you to wind down. Chances are I will never bump into her again. They will probably end up in the married dorm or a cheap apartment over in gutter row the other side of campus. The apartments here are out of their league."

"Why didn't you invite her and her husband to crash with us for a couple nights?"

"I did. She said she was an honest woman who didn't sleep in the houses of harlots and thieves. I was so pissed that I swung into the nearest convenience store and dumped them. I hope she has to sleep in the snow and cuddle up to some street bum for warmth. It won't be my utilities warming her ass."

"You have got it bad, man. I can tell by the look on your face you fell in love with her at first sight. It is kind of humorous." Stated Mooch grinning as David stomped off to the shower.

About twenty minutes later, David returned barefoot and

wearing a pair of gray sweat pants and a T-shirt. He plopped down on the couch. "Have you seen Ohm while I was away?"

"No, but I bumped into his servant, the turbaned man out by the dumpster. Why?" Mooch asked.

"I asked him before I left if he would loan me his servant for a day. I was hoping that his turban man would clean this apartment while I was gone. I offered to pay." David replied.

"Give the turban dude a break, David. Ohm bosses the poor guy around and treats him like he is a slave. Pay me and I will clean the apartment."

"Not a bad idea, Mooch. However, I am paying you with free rent and utilities. Perhaps, I have my own slave."

"I can't clean if you don't own a mop, broom, and a toilet bowl brush. If you want to invest in the items, I will clean up around here once a week. What did you do before I came along, anyway?"

"I usually hire some girl who has an ad on the student bulletin board looking for some extra cash." David replied.

"Forget about Ohm's servant. He doesn't speak English and Ohm treats him like he is a dog. Don't add to his misery. Mrs. Begley tells me that the turban guy is a really sweet man who likes birds and paints in his room on the third floor at night. She says Ohm is insistent that he not learn English."

"Are you thinking what I am thinking?" David asked.

"Ohm's rich parents have bought the turban man and he is a slave. As long as he can't speak English, he doesn't know that he could walk away here and be free here. Mrs. Begley has been teaching him a few words when she sees him. He is only allowed out of Ohm's apartment to take the trash out and once late in the evening to walk down to the convenience store, have a cup of coffee, and then bring back whatever Ohm is sending him for."

"What do you see in that old Mrs. Begley, Mooch? Couldn't you find someone younger and prettier to spend your Sunday nights with?"

"It isn't the young university coeds that have money, David."

"I see your point. However, I don't think I could do the wrinkles and dentures." He stated rising and walking to the window to watch for a pizza delivery man. He had ordered a fresh pizza while he was in the bedroom dressing.

Peeping out of his front window which had no curtains, he yelled, "Oh Shit. It is her!"

"Her who?" Inquired Mooch turning from his sack of popcorn that he had just retrieved from the microwave.

"The Amish bitch. She is down there with Endora who looks like she is fumbling for her apartment keys."

"Really?" Stated Mooch hurrying to the window to get a peep at the girl that had David flustered. David Goldstein was considered a hunk on campus and had more dates and women than he could handle.

"Looking out, Mooch was taken back. There was a spot light over their landlord's front door. He could see the Amish girl very plain and she was indeed a dish. "Damn, David. No wonder you are in such a foul mood. She is one pretty girl. She is out of both of our leagues."

"Rub it in why don't you. "David spouted in a pissed voice'

"It it wasn't so late, I would put my clothes on and head down to Endora's place to meet her. I would like to get a close up look at that eye candy." Mooch stated watching the Amish couple enter their landlord and Endora's apartment. "Why are they with Endora, do they know her?"

""Endora has probably just rescued them for the night. I offered to let them stay here and have the bedroom. She turned me down." Stated David irritated and getting madder by the minute. Endora was a call girl and they accompanied her home. He was just a good old boy who took in strays like Mooch.

"Maybe I will saunter down to the Sergeant's apartment in the morning for breakfast and get a chance to meet her." Stated Mooch. He was used to dropping in on people at meal time when he was between sugar mamas.

Mooch's parents died in a house fire and had left him nothing. After their funeral expenses were paid and what little his parents owned sold off, he had ninety-seven dollars left. He finished his last year of high school living and sleeping in a beat up wreck of a car that his mother had drove and it was hardly a chic magnet. However, there were more important things in life than having a girlfriend back then. He had always wanted to be a doctor. So, he hung in there finishing high school and then applied for college.

His senior year he applied for a part time job at the Pancake Emporium. That was where he met Georgia and she introduced him to the world of being a man of the night, a male escort. He first went to work for her as a dishwasher and she started picking up minor bills for him in return for sex. That was when he secretly started taking on other older women and scraping together from all of them college tuition. His two morning's of being a waiter kept him in gas money to get to his female clients and that was about it. College was expensive and it took everything he made as a gigolo to pay his tuition and books. He had his freshman year of college in and was now getting ready to face the second semester of his sophomore year. When he was out of medical school, he never wanted to look at a woman again. His opinion of women was tarnished by the type of women that paid for his services. He saw all women as users like Georgia.

However, Georgia was a God send and was promising to pay his way thru medical school. She said by the time he entered medical school, she would be coming into a trust left her by her father. She would then take over his medical school bills. So, for now, he was servicing Georgia and several other older clients that she knew nothing about. Georgia was his ace in the hole and he wasn't going to rock his boat with her. However, he needed the money from the others to survive. Georgia had given him a couple thousand towards the coming semester with the understanding his services were free for that period of time and when she wanted with no questions asked. He agreed to her terms. Without the two thousand, he would have been hurting. He needed her money long term as well as Mrs. Begley's and the others.

David plopped back down on the couch with Mooch to watch TV. It wasn't but about five minutes when he heard footsteps on the stairs outside.

"Are you expecting anyone?" Mooch asked.

"I did order a pizza, but that sounds like multiple people coming up the stairs. I hope it isn't the door knockers this time of night."

"They dropped by this morning leaving their literature under the door." Mooch replied not getting up.

"We are the last apartment on second and the third floor studio is vacant . . ." David stated trailing his voice. Then he watched as Endora, Uziah, Hannah, and their landlord passed his window heading for the stairs to the third floor studio. "Damn it all to Hell. They found their way here without me and sure as I am Jewish they are going to rent that dump on the third floor above us. That is just my luck."

"You might not like the idea, but I don't mind a little eye candy passing in front of our window. She is hot!"

"She is not!" Shot back David who then turned out the overhead light so the Amish couple couldn't look in and see him if they came back down the stairs.

"My friend," Mooch began and then paused eyeing his friend who was now hiding in the shadows of the apartment and peeping out the window. "I think you have met miss right and she has a mouth to keep your Jewish backside in line."

"She is married, Jackass. I don't want to hear another word about her from you."

"Well, then why are you peeping and waiting for her to walk back by?" Stated Mooch laughing.

The Recycling Project

Hannah and Uziah followed Endora and her uncle, Sergeant Pepper, up three flights of stairs to check out the small studio apartment that was for rent. The stairs were snow covered and the climb a wee bit treacherous. After reaching the top, the pair entered and looked over the one room apartment. On one end was a vacant area under a window where a small bed could be placed. The kitchen cabinet, stove, and refrigerator were in the other end with a bathroom behind it. I it was one long room with a door on the side leading to a fairly large closet under the eve. In the end of the closet was a tiny window that looked out onto the alley.

"It is pretty small," stated Hannah as she watched Uziah as he looked about the room. "I think I prefer the apartment across the alley that we looked at yesterday. It does not have all of those stairs to climb." She stated giving Uziah a reason for bargaining.

Uziah grinned at her knowing that she was setting him up to ask the landlord to come down on the price of the rent. Hannah's dad was a barterer and known for getting good deals on whatever he purchased from the English. He could see that talent coming out in her. He was amused and pleased.

"I think you are right Hannah," Uziah stated checking out the window in the end overlooking the dumpster. "The view across the alley is better also. This one looks out at the top of a dumpster."

"You don't want that roach infested place across the alley. You will fight bugs constantly." The wimpy little landlord quickly threw in the conversation. "The landlord there does not exterminate. I spray my units twice a year."

"I really want the other unit, Uziah. It is furnished and has a washer and dryer hook up for the same amount of money." Hannah stated running her finger across the top of the refrigerator to see how much dirt was up there. She couldn't wait to get to the cleaning. She was going to love the place. It would be as though they were birds living high in a tree. You could see the far city from the window.

"You are right, Hannah. This apartment is worth only half of what is being asked. Also, it has no laundry facilities, is very small, and has a very bad set of stairs to climb." Uziah replied adding to Hannah's comments. "Should we decide to have a baby, you would have to tote it and our groceries up and down those stairs. You are a little woman. I am not sure you could manage it. Plus, we must commit to one apartment for three and one half years. Our Amish family will move us in their buggies only once."

"You are looking for a three and one half year lease?" The landlord asked in shock. He was plagued with nine month move in and out students who sometimes ran out on the rent and left the apartments in shambles.

"Yes. We will not move out till the month after I graduate college. We will be long term tenants." Uziah replied. "It costs money to move and we are very frugal. We will not even go home to our Amish community until the month after I graduate for a visit. We are not frivolous or dirty like your last occupants of this apartment. Cleanliness is next to Godliness."

"There is no washer and dryer, Uziah. How will we do our laundry?" Interjected Hannah. "We do not drive and it will be almost impossible for us to get our clothing to the Laundromat across town."

"You are right, Hannah. We need laundry facilities because we cannot keep our horse and buggy stabled here. We must have laundry privileges."

"Take the apartment, sign a three and one half year lease, and I will include the once a week use of my private washer and dryer as a bonus providing your wife does one load of laundry for me while she does hers. I am a busy man and really need a housekeeper. However, I have problems that prevent that."

"That is reasonable, Hannah dear." Uziah stated grinning at

her again. "Perhaps you and the Sergeant could come to some future term or barter for cleaning his apartment once a week."

"Now, Uziah, we must have at least a bed. This apartment is unfurnished. We cannot sleep on the floor. The other apartment has a nice big bed and curtains."

"I have a storage room downstairs and have two twin beds. You could set them up, push them together, and make one nice large bed. I am willing to pull some curtains from one of my other units."

"And will these curtains be at my disposal to wash in your facilities first. My apartment will be clean. No trace of anyone else's filth will be allowed. Should we take the apartment, you would be required to remove your shoes when entering it? I am surprised you treat your units so disrespectfully. You should make everyone entering and looking at one of your units take their shoes off. I could teach you a few Amish ways of cleanliness that could improve your life style. I can see you have not had a wife or a mother to train you." Hannah stated looking the little landlord straight in the eye and purposely intimidating him. She could easily look directly into his eyes. Her father had taught her to use the eye when bartering or needing to get the upper hand.

"I always take my shoes off when I enter my own apartment. I am not thinking tonight. Of course you would not want the water and snow from our shoes to clean up. What am I thinking?" The landlord quickly shot back crouching under Hannah's eye. "Take the apartment and I will come up tomorrow and personally mop up this mess that I have tracked in."

"Will you bring tea, two cups, and a kettle to heat water so that you and I can have tea after the two of us clean the whole apartment, not just the floor?" She replied looking into his hazel eyes. She was going to be crazy about that little man and have him jumping thru hoops. Perhaps, she might marry him. She wanted a man that would let her wear the pants and be boss. She would never let a man control her. He was a possibility. However, she didn't smile but continued to give him the eye.

"You and I clean the whole apartment and then have tea?" he asked surprised. Every woman he ever met, hated hot tea. They were coffee or soda drinkers. Also, he hadn't offered to clean the whole apartment, only the floor.

"Yes, we will have tea. The cleaning will go faster if I help you. After cleaning the whole apartment, I will show you what a great cup of hot tea is. I am a sassafras or East India Cinnamon tea drinker and it must be made exactly a certain way to bring out the beautiful aroma of the exotic land the tea come from. Do you know anything about tea, Sergeant Pepper?" She then asked turning from him so she could grin.

Sassafras root was a treat on the farm. Her father dug up the root and her mother boiled it. She recalled how her father had been given a box of cinnamon tea by an elderly neighbor as a Christmas gift one year. One cup was all she had been privileged to have of it, but she had read the exotic looking box till it was worn out. She had used it for a pencil box in the seventh grade at their Amish school.

"I have a feeling you are going to teach me!" He replied not being able to take his eyes off the dimple winking face of a simple girl with no makeup that was making his heart do handsprings. "At what time would we do this whole apartment cleaning? I work and have a full schedule of business appointments tomorrow." He shot back trying to give her the eye. He knew what she was doing. He was a negotiator himself.

"When you get off from work would be appropriate. Bring a chair up with you when you come. If we take your apartment, we do not have a place for you to sit. Should we take the apartment across the alley, you may still come for tea and help me clean." Hannah grinned.

He grinned back. He was a realtor and had pulled off a lot of big deals. However, this seventeen year old Amish girl with dimples was twisting him around her fingers and getting what she wanted. He was on her hook and he knew it. He would clean and have tea with her. Something inside told him he was going to be crazy about her, as well as a pushover. He would just have to make sure that his friendship with her was on the quiet. He wouldn't want Mrs. Zook plagued by the relentless nastiness of his stalker, Georgia Macon. She had run off numerous housekeepers as well as dinner companions. He would need to keep Mrs. Zook and their friendship on the quiet and not tell anyone, not even Endora.

"Tea it is, Mrs. Zook, after work tomorrow. After work, I will change into my jeans and be right up to help you, should you take my apartment."

"Do you know how to boil water, Sergeant Pepper?"

"Of course I do, Mrs. Zook. I am a tea lover."

"Good, I like a man who shares in the tea making, the setting of the table, as well as the cleanup."

"I wouldn't have it any other way." Sergeant Pepper stated eyeing her dimples and her lips. He wondered what it would be like to just kiss her one time. She was bringing out the man in him that he thought was dead. His nightmare as a boy being used by his predator, Georgia, had left him almost impotent. His psychiatrist said that would change when he met the right someone, fell in love, and got his head on straight.

As Hannah turned from eyeing him, the landlord stared at her. He was sure that Hannah Zook was the most gorgeous young woman that he had ever met. She wore no makeup or displayed long painted, manicured nails like the women on his staff. She was naturally beautiful where the women in the office got their beauty out of bottles and lipstick tubes. He was having a serious butterfly stomach moment that he was sure he would never forget. However, at seventeen, she was way too young for him and he would never take advantage of someone so young. He had barely turned fifteen when Georgia had started using and abusing him. He couldn't do that to anyone. If Mrs. Zook was fifteen years older, he might make a pass at her. Her husband could only half kill him. It might be worth it, if she were older.

He had been the victim of Georgia his stalker till he was seventeen years old. All of his youth had been stolen from him as he tried to live in the grown up world of twenty-four year old Georgia Macon. She was a predator of runaway boys. Georgia was forty-eight now and still stalking him. He had her under a court ordered peace bond, but that didn't mean anything. She purposely harassed any woman that had anything to do with him. He wanted a female companion, even if he couldn't perform. He was lonely.

"I think you should throw in a coffee maker, Uncle Pepper, and enough coffee for the first day or so till the snowy weather moves out and they can get to a store to buy what they need. I just imagine Uziah is a coffee drinker, not a tea nipper."

"I have an extra one downstairs in my apartment and I will throw in a can of coffee provided you pay first and last month's rent and a cleaning deposit up front."

"Absolutely not," Hannah smirked. "My hand is filthy from running it across the top of the refrigerator. I will have to clean and definitely paint the rooms. If you wanted a deposit, you should have cleaned it before you every showed it as available to rent. This apartment is dirtier than our chicken house back home. I might also add, our outhouse back on the farm is cleaner that the inside bathroom of this apartment. A cleaning deposit is out of the question."

"First and last month's rent and no cleaning deposit. . ." Uziah said in firm agreement. "Plus Sergeant Pepper, we really need a bed and curtains. All the apartments across the alley come with those amenities."

"I believe we are coming to terms." Sergeant Pepper replied eyeing Hannah's black socks and ugly, black, old lady shoes. She was absolutely stunning in spite of them. His heart was racing big time. He wondered what her feet looked like. He bet they were just as beautiful as her face. He was a feet man and loved to look at women in their spikes and summer sandals. Her feet were like hidden Christmas presents. He wondered what the two gifts were like in the old lady, nicely tied, black boxes called shoes.

"Uziah, we must consider the weather. The landlord across the way kindly offered to feed us one meal a day till the weather breaks. It will be a few days before we can get to a major shopping center to purchase food and other items. It was a kind offer and I really think that she and I could be really good friends."

Endora interjected. "Quit the song and dance, Pepper. Throw in a can of coffee, a loaf of bread, a jar of peanut butter and an invitation to breakfast for the next three mornings. I am sure they are early risers and will eat with you before you leave for the office. Remember when you last rented this unit?"

"The landlord across the alley is a terrible cook and I think she occasionally makes sandwiches from dog food. You definitely do not want to eat her cooking. You and Uziah must eat breakfast with me for three mornings till you are settled. I make a marvelous pecan waffle, scrambled eggs, and bacon."

"I am sure that I make a better one Sergeant. It takes an Amish woman to show a man how to cook. If we take the apartment, I will cook. I wouldn't want you to think that we were taking advantage of you. I make homemade biscuits and sausage gravy that could put a little meat on your bones. You are much too skinny. Should I live here, I will make it a point to fatten you up a little."

"Mrs. Zook, I would be pleased to let you cook breakfast in my kitchen the next three mornings. To be honest, I am tired of eating my own cooking and would welcome eating something new as well as have guests."

"Will we take the apartment under all of the terms specified?" Uziah asked totally amused at Hannah. She had the landlord eating out of her hand.

"It is the charitable thing to do, Uziah. Sergeant Pepper needs me and He will be my first patient. He needs fattening and I intend to see that he does so in order for his health to improve."

"What do you mean, see that my health improves?'

"We are both pre-med. We will be doctors." Uziah quickly added stretching the truth. "You will be getting hands on attention from me as well as the future Dr. Hannah Zook who intends to go into gene research." Hannah had not decided what occupational field she wanted to go into yet. She had only one day's experience at being a midwife. Uziah was stretching the truth.

Sergeant Pepper turned to Hannah, "Will I be the one you practice your bandaging on?"

"Every doctor has to have his skeleton and you will be mine. You are so skinny I can see your bones." She replied reaching out with one finger and poking his arm.

"Well, Uncle, I always knew there was a woman out there somewhere who would one day make a rollover, pet dog out of you. I can see your tail wagging." Endora laughed.

"Be nice, Endora." Thirty-nine year old Sergeant Pepper stated glaring at her and hoping that his wagging tail wasn't that obvious.

"I think we should take the apartment Hannah. The landlord could use our caring. He looks like he might be suffering from depression and a possible eating disorder." Uziah replied hooking on to her assessment of the little man.

"I have mental problems and an eating disorder?" Sergeant Pepper asked with big eyes. That was what his psychiatrist had inferred.

"You need me," stated Hannah. "I will personally make sure that you are prayed for every morning, every night, and that I train you and improve your health till I am happy with my handiwork."

"Endora," whispered Sergeant Pepper, "Have I just been had?"

"Yes, I am afraid you have, Uncle. You may be a shrewd dealer in the world of real estate, but you have met your match in the future Dr. Hannah Zook. I think she is the one for you." She whispered back and then giggled.

Sergeant Pepper grinned to himself. He was in love with her already and he had only known her possibly twenty minutes. How often do you meet a woman and know instantly that she is the one that you have always dreamed was out there somewhere. It was a bonus her wanting to be a doctor. However, her having a husband was a disadvantage.

"There is one other Item that must be considered before I personally agree to take the apartment." Hannah stated.

"And what would that be Mrs. Zook?" Questioned the landlord smiling at her.

"When I do your basket of laundry once a week, there better not be anything in that basket that I might find offensive. I am referring to soiled underwear in case you are not thinking too clearly this late at night. If I find any soiled underwear in your basket, I will throw them away. There will be no perversions in the shorts in my laundry."

"Absolutely, Mrs. Zook, I will change my underwear every day," he quickly answered and then realized what he had said and blushed.

Hannah grinned at him. He was wonderful. She was going to train him and make him her best friend. She would just love to cuddle him up in her arms like a big lap dog and love him forever. However, she must train him first.

"Now tell me Sergeant Pepper, do you have any allergies? I plan to bleach your underclothes till they are suitable for me to look at. I do not wish to use my midwife skills to treat you for rashes." She asked eyeing him and giving him her best flirty grin.

"I think I have just developed an allergy to an Amish woman chasing me with a fly swatter. I don't like fly swatters so this fly will try to not do anything that you might find inappropriate. Bleach away, Mrs. Zook."

"What will you be putting in your tea tomorrow, Sergeant Pepper?" She asked to zing him again. She loved the fact that she had the little man flustered.

"What do you take in yours, Mrs. Zook? I prefer honey."

"You are a man, Sergeant Pepper. You should be drinking a tablespoon of Molasses in your tea. It will get you up and get you going. Honey is wimpy. Only sick women drink honey in their tea. Do you spend a lot of time drinking honey tea with sickly women?"

"Er . . . uh . . . I drink it with Endora and Mrs. Begley who lives behind me. Yes, I guess I do"

"Oh Sergeant Pepper, I have three and one half years ahead of me to make a man out of you. I have my work cut out."

"Just make a list, Mrs. Zook, of what you think we should be drinking in our tea and I will pick up the items and stock my kitchen. I have an electric tea maker. I will show it to you tomorrow morning when you come for breakfast."

"Oh no Sergeant Pepper, a prime cup of tea must be steeped with boiling water poured over it. The bag, if you use one, must be dunked exactly six and three quarter times." She stated keeping a straight face.

"You are absolutely right, Mrs. Zook. I have grown lax and have been taking the easy way out with my electric tea brewer. For our teas we will go all out. I will drive out tonight and purchase some molasses. I have been thinking my tea needs a little punch to it. I have never tasted Molasses. Does it have a nip to it?"

"Do you like a nip in your tea?" She asked totally amused.

This little wimpy man suited her.

"I do like it to bite me back a bit. Along with the honey, I usual put a squeeze of lemon. I like the sourness of lemon and the way it makes me pucker." He said and then blushed again because it sounded like he was speaking of a kiss.

"You are absolutely right, Sergeant Pepper. That is how I caught Uziah. I put lemon in his hot tea and he puckered. One stolen kiss in the Amish world and you are engaged." She shot back knowing that she had him.

"I would say your husband is one lucky man, Mrs. Zook. A lucky man knows when to put lemon in his tea. Does lemon and molasses go well together?"

"They do complement each other if you wish your tea to do spring cleaning. On those special tea drinking occasions, please do not put your shorts in my laundry basket." She replied knowing that she had got him again.

"I have a lot to learn about tea and you don't I, Mrs. Zook?" He asked grinning and knowing that this seventeen year old girl with dimples had led him down a path of conversation and then zinged him.

"You and I will be friends, Sergeant Pepper. I am sure of that."

"I am agreeable." He replied gazing into her twinkling eyes." Also, I am open to trying new tea concoctions with the exception of the molasses and honey. I wouldn't want to upset my laundress with a doggie accident."

"When you go out for the molasses, you might consider some orange marmalade. I like it on my biscuits in the morning."

"That is my favorite too. I love it on toast and it goes so nicely with tea."

Hannah grinned at her new little dog. She would have him trained to her wants and wishes in three months. She had trained her two mentally challenged brothers to say grace, bathe, and act appropriately in public. Just because they were challenged didn't mean that they couldn't be agreeable little rollover dogs. Sergeant Pepper had his mental faculties and he would train easily. House breaking the landlord, Sergeant Pepper, was going to be fun. She would have him sitting up and begging. He might even roll over a time or two on demand.

After shaking hands, Uziah and Sergeant Pepper headed back down the treacherous stairs to sign a lease agreement. Endora went with them.

Hannah sat down by the floor register to warm herself. When she felt comfortable, she removed her cloak and winter hat. Then she took her white Amish cap off, removed her hair pins, and shook her hip length dark brown hair loose. Sometimes her hair was heavy in its bun. It was always a relief when night came and she shook her hair free.

Sitting in the floor, Hannah did not see the turbaned man in whit,e she had met earlier, looking out his third floor room across the alley. She also did not see him quickly grab a pair of binoculars, turn his light out, and stare at her thru the window. She didn't see his shocked face, wanting eyes, or his tiny studio apartment filled with drawings and paintings of birds.

After warming up and resting a few moments, Hannah rose and looked over her new home with delight. Tonight, she and Uziah would sleep on either side of the floor furnace vent which was blowing out wonderful warm air. She would use her pillow case of possessions for a pillow. Uziah could do the same using his feed sack of things for his pillow. They would use his heavy coat and her cloak for quilts. She had big plans for her new home. She was thrilled and couldn't wait till she had a rag and some cleanser to clean with. She would keep her home sparkling clean and make her tea towels and linens. Her mind buzzed with ideas.

For a brief moment, her thoughts returned to the driver of the Jeep, David Goldstein, who had given them a ride in to town. In her mind, she could see herself training him. He was like a dog that had fleas. He would have to be relieved of his blood sucking, apartment crasher fleas before she could brush his coat and teach him to stand up on his hind feet and beg. She could see him begging for scraps from her table. He would be an inside, scrap eating, house dog with an unusual snout. She liked his nose although she had inferred to him that it was big and ugly.

After about twenty minutes, Uziah returned carrying a loaf of bread and a jar of peanut butter and a couple plastic bags containing a coffee maker and other items.

"You are wonderful, Hannah. We have breakfast for three mornings and Endora sent this up for us to snack on till the weather breaks. You must take bartering and zinging after your father. I am pleased. We have our apartment for half price plus a coffee pot, coffee, peanut butter, bread, two beds, curtains, and a place to do our laundry for free. We are going to do well here. I am glad I brought you along."

"Thank you, Uziah. That is a nice thing to say." She replied taking the peanut butter from him. "This loaf of bread made into sandwiches will feed us for at least two days plus we have a free breakfast each morning."

"We have done well. I like peanut butter." Uziah stated.

"I should have asked for a jar of jelly in the deal," she replied laughing. "The peanut butter will taste pretty plain without it."

"Jelly will come. Everything we need will come. I start my dumpster diving tomorrow morning. We must rise before everyone so that I can check and see what people threw in the dumpsters before going to bed. I will find something for us to use for a cleaning rag. It may be a pair of Sergeant Pepper's dirty worn out shorts. You psyched him out, do you realize that?"

"I do like a man that can be trained. While I am at it, you will take your shoes off at the door before entering the apartment after tonight. You have tracked snow and water from the balcony all over the floor. Just because we are not in the Amish community doesn't mean that you will be allowed to abandon your indoor manners, do you understand?"

"I am sorry. My mother would have yelled at me and then made me clean it up." He replied.

"And so will I after tonight." She retorted.

"Pecked by an Amish hen, that is what I am going to be." He muttered to himself.

"We have our first home Uziah. I am so excited."

"We must be really frugal Hannah and use everything to our advantage. That is how we must think in order to survive and make it thru college. You have four years of high school before starting."

"I will take a heavier load than most students and will go to summer school. I should be able to graduate in three and one half years."

"That is good because I plan to go to college year round and graduate in a little over three years."

"We are on our way to a new life Uziah. This apartment is the first stop on our journey. I have not exactly decided what I wish my college major to be one day. However, the name Dr. Hannah Zook does please me. Did you know that I get ill at the sight of blood?"

"I think we best tell people that you are going to be a psychiatrist then." He laughed. "As soon as the weather breaks, I am going to take you with me dumpster diving so you can get an idea of how I will find our treasures. The professor, who home schooled me, taught me how to look for and recycle throw away items. We must get up early in the morning and it is very late. Which side of the vent do you want?" He asked.

"The left, I believe. I really am not sure. I shared a bedroom with three sisters and there was no choice as to where you slept. I lay my head where my mother assigned me to sleep."

"It does seem a bit strange making decisions for ourselves, doesn't it?" He asked taking his feed sack of belongings and laying them down on the right side of the floor register for a pillow.

"We have freedom to create a life of our choosing. I would have been miserable had I married one of my father's chosen suitors. This is where I belong. I want to embrace new things, new ideas, and new ways of being. My faith in God I will not change."

"Good night, Hannah. I am too tired to talk anymore. I think it is about one or two in the morning."

"Good night, Uziah. I am tired to. Did you say your prayers?"

"I will say double tomorrow night, Hannah. God will just have to understand tonight that the body he made for me is too sleepy to talk."

"I will pray for both of us. You listen as you fall asleep."

"I will Hannah!"

"Dearest Heavenly Father, Thank you for a memorable snowy, night flight into our Egypt and for the opportunity here to become colorfully educated individuals like Joseph who wore a coat of many colors. Bring to us rich Pharaohs and their servants. Make us wealthy beyond our imagination from the grains of their storehouses. Let us dine with kings and our table be always full with friends and fine food. Most of all, let Uziah and I be thinkers and turn our thoughts into money to pay for our educations. Bless us with peaceful sleep tonight and if you are willing, give us dreams like Joseph and show us the future. This is Hannah and my prayers are for me and Uziah. Good night."

She listened a moment. Uziah was snoring. She rolled over and pulled her cloak up around her face, fell asleep, and dreamed of the man in white who kissed his fingers, touched her nose. In the dream she asked him who he was. He said he was her coat of many colors and one day he would wrap and keep her safe in his arms. It was a good dream.

Dumpster Diving

Uziah rose early just as the sun was coming up and made his way down the ice and snow covered three flights of stairs and then to the back alley where the blue dumpsters were. Four huge apartment complexes shared the back alley. Sergeant Pepper owned two on one side of the alley. Across the alley were two. One was owned by a widow and the other by a rental agency. Two snow covered dumpsters on each side of the alley waited for Uziah to discover their treasures.

The English were frivolous and Uziah was happy with his finds. He retrieved the dumpster's treasures and made his way back upstairs to Hannah to share his finds.

"The science teacher who home schooled me was right, Hannah. We will be able to find everything we need, if we hit the dumpsters on a regular basis." He stated excitedly dumping out two shopping bags of items onto the cabinet top.

"What will we do with these things? You must teach me because I did not have the privilege of knowing the English farmer who taught you recycling."

First, we take these three empty detergent bottles rinse them out with a cup of warm water and pour the three together in one. There will be enough liquid to wash one load of clothes. The English as a whole do not wash out their laundry soap bottles and the excess left drains to the bottom and the container isn't really empty. The sediment from these three detergent jugs put together will make us one free cup of laundry detergent. That is about equal to a dollar bill, when you consider we are also going to use the two empty jugs. The caps are one cup measures. You can wash them and use to measure your flour and liquids for your baking and cooking."

"You are right. My first measuring cups and they are colorful." She squealed excited.

"That is not all," he replied. "The bottom of the two empty detergent jugs we will cut off about four inches up from the bottom. They will make you refrigerator bowls to keep our food in. We will use the refrigerator even though our people would see it as prideful and sinful. We will not have a cellar in the land of the

English. In some ways we must adapt to survive. The refrigerator will be our cellar."

"You are absolutely right, Uziah. As soon as we have something to cut with, I will cut the two jug bottoms off and make bowls."

"You may use my pocket knife. Just be very careful. It is really sharp." He stated pulling a worn pocket knife from his pocket.

"I will be careful." She said taking it from him.

"These plastic dish liquids bottles we will do the same," he said picking two up that contained about a quarter of an inch of liquid in the bottom of each. "Together they will make enough to wash one sink of dishes. We will cut the two containers off and make us both a tall drinking cup for the bathroom to put our tooth brushes in. They are different. You may have first choice for which is yours."

"I definitely want the one that is shaped like a woman's body. I will make my toothbrush cup a dress when I have the time."

"I am glad you chose that one. I prefer the plain green one. We will make what we need from the throw a ways of others." He replied picking up an empty bleach jug.

"What will we do with the white bleach jug?" She asked.

"Rinse this jug out and pour the contents into the stool in the bathroom for now. There should be enough bleach in the rinse to disinfect the bowl for now. We will cut off the round bottom with a half inch lip to make ourselves a plate. I also brought up a couple of empty milk jugs. Cut the bottom of one for a square plate and the other up high to make you a temporary mixing bowl. We will buy very little and save all of our money for school, expenses and rent."

"Tomorrow, if you find more milk jugs, I need one to make myself a cleaning bucket out of. The second, I will turn into a second square plate. We will use the round one from the bleach bottle for serving our bread." She replied getting into the mood of the recycling project.

"We are going to need several plates, Hannah. We will be inviting our friends to eat with us. I will bring home every larger based plastic container that I can find tomorrow. We are going to need at least eight of the milk jug bottom plates and eight sets of the plastic throw away forks and spoons from the fast food sacks. Be prepared for tomorrow. We will have a lot of cutting to do. I will take a nail and punch holes in the caps of two of those small water bottles and we will use them for salt and pepper shakers. They will be large, but at least we won't have to fill them too often."

"I need salt, pepper, flour, sugar, Cinnamon, and baking powder."

"I will find something in the dumpster that we can barter with for those items from the neighbors. Just give me a couple of days and we will have most of the things we need and they will not cost us anything. Our linens will be the hardest to come up with. My home school teacher said to watch for thrown away curtains. They can be used for quilts and sheets if necessary.

"I have a pillowcase." She stated. "What cloth you find I will sew together and make what we need. I was the family seamstress at home. I made my dresses and those of my sisters. Mother said I had an eye for detail and she trusted me with her cloth."

"Here is your first piece of cloth to recycle. I found this plaid shirt in the dumpster. It has a frayed collar and is missing a button. We must use it wisely. I thought perhaps you could cut the two sleeves apart and make two tea towels. The cuffs and Collar you could tack together and make a small pot holder. The two front panels I thought could be made into two table napkins. The back section, we could share as a towel temporarily till I find something else. One of us could bathe in the morning and the other at night so the towel will be dry for both of us."

"I will make very nice linens out of that shirt, Uziah. I will put my love into them." she replied all smiles. This is my first home. Everything is special to me."

"I have one more item I pulled from the dumpster for a special reason. I thought you could take this discarded metal cookie tin and start yourself a button and sewing can. I know buttons are thought of by our parents as proud, but I think we should save them. My mother had a secret can and she loved them. She sewed them on for eyes on my sister's dolls."

"Oh thank you Uziah. I loved my mother's button can too. We played checkers with some of my mother's larger ones. I will treasure the round tin and put my scissors and needles in it also. I will use it often in mending our clothes and making our linens. It will be my treasure!" She said looking at the round tin that was covered with red poinsettias.

"Tomorrow, I will find more items. Till then we will use what we have. Oh, I forgot! I have one more item hidden in my pocket." He said grinning.

"What is it?" She asked excited

"There was lots of Christmas trash in the dumpster. Someone threw away the box from a jelly gift set. Who ever received the gift must not have liked plum jelly and pitched the one little jar. My home school teacher said the English would throw away what they didn't want, instead of passing it on. We will be blessed from their ignorance."

"Jelly to go on our peanut butter sandwiches. Lunch is going to be wonderful."

"Today we will be a little short on what we need, but each day we will gain and be blessed by our Heavenly Father. I heard you ask God for jelly last night."

"God always answers my prayers when I have a need. This time he gave me a want," she laughed.

"We will pray and give thanks, Hannah."

"Yes, let us give thanks."

So, Uziah gave thanks for their finds and then they went about cleaning up their treasures, the blessings of God that the English didn't want.

Three days flew by. They ate breakfast with Sergeant Pepper and had peanut butter sandwiches for lunch and fasted their dinner. Uziah dumpster dived and spoke with anyone who happened up the alley trading some items he found. He pulled an old tackle box from the dumpster and traded it to a student in one of the back apartments for three boxes of macaroni and cheese. And so the recycling madness took flight. After giving it some thought, Uziah rescued several partial rolls of Christmas paper for them to cut clean pieces to put by the door to set their wet shoes on to save the floors and not waste their cleaners. Each day was a new adventure.

The only items they did have to purchase were a bar of soap, a big spoon to stir with, and a large pot to boil potatoes or macaroni in. Uziah found an old worn skillet in the dumpster and a small burnt cookie sheet. Hannah scrubbed till the cookie sheet was usable.

On the fourth morning, Uziah was standing at the corner of one of the big blue dumpsters trying to get an inside house door loose from the items piled on top of it. Someone had dumped construction items in the dumpster the night before and everything was in a tangled heavy mess. No matter how much he yanked, lifted, and pulled he could not get the door loose and he needed it.

He had plans for that door. He would make a much needed table for their kitchen. From the jumbled construction mess, he had pulled four short pieces of boards to make legs. He wanted to surprise Hannah. They had been standing at the cabinet to eat. He also planned to make a couple of simple stools from four milk crates he had found. Hannah could make square cushions for their tops as soon as he found some discarded material and stuffing of some sort. It would come. The English were frivolous and threw away items like they expected to never be broke or need anything.

"Would you like some help?" A voice inquired from behind him.

Uziah turned from the dumpster to see a male student about his age standing and watching.

"I am trying to get this door loose. I need it for my apartment on the third floor. It just won't give up its home in the dumpster. Thank you for offering, my name is Uziah."

"I am Mooch Martin. I live on the second floor just below you. I have seen you and your wife pass my window a couple of times."

"We are neighbors. I am pleased." Uziah stated sticking his hand out to shake. "I would indeed appreciate a hand."

"Then, let us show that door who is boss." Stated Mooch crawling up on one end of the dumpster to see why the door wouldn't slide out of its position. "It looks like the door knob is hung up in a jumbled mess of lumber and discarded electrical wiring. I will lift up on the lumber and you pull."

"I am ready." Uziah stated getting a good grip on the end of the door.

After about three tries and the moving of some lumber around by Mooch, the door knob came free of the construction discards and slid out.

"I am grateful for your help, Mooch. I plan to make Hannah a dining table from the door. I have already pulled enough lumber from the mess for legs." He stated pointing to four short boards leaning on the dumpster. "She is going to be really happy."

"When she sees all of the garbage and who knows what on the door, she is going to probably freak out." Stated Mooch taking a look at it. "You don't find a solid door like this now a days. Everything is made of cheap pressed board and falls apart after about two years of use. This door will last another fifty years if refinished."

"That is what I thought. I will take my time and do a good job on it. Hannah and I will use it for the years. I am going to college and then medical school. If you would carry the leg boards up, I would really appreciate it. I would like you to meet my Hannah."

"Your wife is quite pretty. I have seen her from my window." Stated Mooch picking up the lumber intended for table legs.

"Don't let her pretty face fool you. She is a Pecker Hen and keeps me in line. I once thought she was mild and gentle like a doe. I married her thinking so. Her father swore to me that she was kind, gentle, and peaceful. I should not have listened to him. You English have a ball and chain. I have an Amish Hen Pecker."

Mooch laughed. "That is why I have chosen never to marry or have a serious relationship."

"That is a good choice, my new friend. Be prepared, my Hannah may try to intimidate you a little. Just ignore anything she might say that is offensive."

"What majors are the two of you pursuing?" Mooch asked as they made their way up the three flights of outside, snow covered, apartment house stairs.

"I am a pre-med student. My wife is still in high school. She will enroll the day after New Years in the public high school."

"Are you a cradle robber?" Mooch asked as they climbed.

"Hannah is seventeen. In the Amish community we only receive eighth grade educations. I was home schooled and have my high school diploma. Hannah was not as fortunate. Although she is the age to start college, she will start high school as a freshman and most certainly be the oldest student."

"Good for her! I like women who have guts. I am a pre-med student to. Perhaps we could study together some. It takes a premed to understand another pre-med."

"I would like that." Uziah stated starting to shoulder the door. "You will be my first friend here. I am sure that Hannah is going to be delighted to meet you. She has only made friends with the landlord and Endora his niece. Would you care to eat dinner with us this evening? It will be peanut butter sandwiches and macaroni and cheese. The weather has prevented us from stocking our kitchen yet."

"I would love to come for dinner. Would you like me to bring something?"

"If you have any salt and pepper in your apartment that you could share, we would appreciate it. Till the weather breaks, we are scrounging for what we need."

"You've got it. I know right where to find some." Mooch stated picking up the four pieces of lumber for table legs. He then followed Uziah up the three flights of stairs chatting as they went.

"What time tonight?" Mooch asked as he thought about the interesting dining table that was about to be created. Recycling had been one of his loves when he was younger and living at home. He admired Uziah for recycling the door.

"We Amish eat at seven. On the farm we would have to get the milking and the farm chores done before we ate. Here the dinner hour will remain the same. I am hoping to find a part time job of some sort. If you hear of one, I would appreciate you telling me about it."

"I will keep my ears open. I do know that Mrs. Begley across the alley is looking for someone to clean house for her on Saturday mornings, if your wife is interested. Sergeant Pepper can't keep a cleaning lady either. I don't know what his problem is. He may be picky. Where I work, there is one shift open for a dishwasher on Sunday evening."

"Sunday is God's day. I cannot work on the Sabbath. Keep me in mind for anything else that you might hear of."

"I will." Stated Mooch as they reached the small balcony porch on the third floor where they leaned their loads against the railing till Uziah could open the door.

Uziah opened the door and stuck his head in. "Hannah come out and meet my new friend, Mooch Martin."

After a moment or so Hannah stepped to the door barefoot in her black stockings. "Hello, I am Hannah."

"I . . . I . . . I am Martin Mooch, I mean Mooch Martin," He sputtered with his heart suddenly racing. She was the prettiest damn girl he had ever seen. No wonder his roommate David had been in such a foul mood when he arrived home from the holidays. She was absolutely gorgeous and her dimples winked at you.

"I am pleased to meet you Martin or is it Mooch?"

"I am sorry, you surprised me. I wasn't expecting to see such a pretty girl on the third floor. Your Uziah is one lucky man." He stated sticking out his hand to shake. "My friends call me Mooch. I live in 2C."

"My name is Hannah and I am a third floor bird and not as pretty as you think. Looks can be deceiving. Ask my Uziah. He says I am now a third floor Hen Pecker bird. He says I squawk a little and that makes me a wee bit ugly. Welcome to my nest in the sky."

"It is like a bird nest up here, isn't it? He replied looking out at the view. This would be a great place for a chair and a good book on a spring afternoon; if spring ever comes again. This blizzard has run the book reading birds, like me, indoors."

"Uziah and I do feel like we are living in a tree house. The

Robins of spring will come. You remind me of a winter blackbird with your black shiny hair."

"Well, you are the prettiest gray dove that I have ever met. I doubt very seriously that you are a Pecker Hen. If you do peck, it is probably because my new friend Uziah deserves it."

"Don't forget whose new friend you are!" Laughed Uziah pleased with Hannah. She had a way with conversation and they would make lots of friends and entertain.

"Uziah has asked me dine with the two of you this evening at seven. Is there anything I can bring?"

"A folding chair if you have one. We have no furniture yet. Uziah and I will both sit to eat on two milk crates stacked. Also, I am desperately in need of some salt and pepper if you should have an extra shaker or so in your apartment. Macaroni and cheese needs pepper on top to make it palatable."

"Salt, Pepper, and one chair. I have it covered. I have got to run. I have a morning shift to cover out at the Pancake Emporium. I am a waiter there two mornings a week.'"

"We will see you tonight." Stated Uziah as Mooch left.

"What else do we need?" Uziah asked as he stepped inside to warm himself. "I will make more friends today as I check the dumpsters and invite them to dinner. What Should I ask them to bring?"

"We need some sort of green vegetable to go with what we have. Ask for a head of lettuce or some green beans." She replied.

"Do we have anything for dessert?"

"The plum jelly is the only sweet item of food that we have. If you should make a third friend, ask them to bring a half gallon of ice cream of their choice. I can serve it in my detergent bottle cap pudding and measuring cups."

"Good thinking. There will be ice cream left over and we can share it as a dessert for at least two days."

"Yes, we must think bulk items when the English offer to bring something. Our pantry will fill itself if we entertain often enough."

"We will survive in the land of the English and they will never know they are feeding us. I will have to write my home school teacher and tell him of this adventure in recycle dining. This is one that he never mentioned. Someday, I wish to return to visit him. I would not be here if it wasn't for him. I know we are not to have idols, but he is mine. God will just have to deal with it."

"Oh, I am sure that God is going to zing you for those words. However, people who give to others deserve respect. Perhaps it is respect you have for him. That is a good thing."

For the next few weeks they concentrated on the filing of their pantry. Anyone Uziah happened to talk to during the day, he invited to dinner. When they asked out of good manners if there was anything they could bring, he stated an item that could be stretched for the dinner plus two days of meals for him and Hannah. No one seemed to mind and there was a constant flow of new friends carrying folding chairs to the third floor nest of the Amish love birds as their friends started referring to them as. Hannah always welcomed anyone knocking at their door to their bird nest in the sky. They entertained every evening from seven till eight except Sundays. They told all of their guests up front that dinner was seven till eight thirty and after that they had to study because they were studying to be doctors. No one questioned it and everyone left on time when Hannah walked to the door at eight thirty and opened the door. Everyone wanted to be friends with the pair of future Amish doctors. No one rocked their boat by staying past the hour of welcome. That would get you off the future invitation list. The Zook's were strict about dinner protocol.

Practically everything in the Zook's apartment was recycled and that included the plates that were cut from the bottoms of milk and bleach jugs, Napkins were cut from the backs and sleeves of discarded shirts, and flatware rescued from discarded fast food containers and sacks. Food was served in bowls cut from the bottoms of plastic jugs, and drinking glasses were the bottoms of drinking water bottles. Their dining table was a door with the knob still on because Uziah didn't have tools yet. Recycling was part of the Zook's Mystic.

Evenings at the Zook's were interesting and you never knew what well known person would have an invitation and show up carrying a meat loaf or a sheet cake. Uziah invited everyone rich, poor, educated, or not; with the exception of God's will adults and children. Hannah's friends at the high school were considered by him as children and were not invited. Uziah was firm in his demand that no children or adult God's Will children be invited or served at their table. Since he had made a conscious decision not to have children, he saw no need to entertain those of others. The Zook's fast become one of the most popular couples on campus with the students, office staff, as well as the professors. Uziah invited everyone that said hello. He saw them as a two day meal ticket and invited them for dinner.

The college Newspaper interviewed them and ran an article about their recycling. They had an immediate following of everyone who recycled on campus. Hannah's stories about her bird nest in the sky and the making of her linens and other items caught the attention of the women on campus and she became well known and was asked to speak and tell of their projects in different lady's groups, student and otherwise.

The Zook's nest in the sky became the place to be if you wanted to be seen socially or hit the social column of the college paper. Everyone was intrigued with them and the reading about them. The Sunday newspaper editor became equally as interested in Hannah and asked to run a two month on going column about them and their recycling projects. When the well known around town started bumping into the elite of society at the Zook's third floor dinners, word spread like wildfire and people were purposely bumping into Uziah in an effort to obtain an invitation. Elite or wealthy meant nothing to him. He saw each as a bag of flour or a sack of noodles. If a rich man with a chauffeur said hello, Uziah struck up a conversation and invited the man to dinner.

The other flip of the coin was that the rich and the famous of the city returned invitations to Hannah and Uziah taking them to restaurants, movies, and whatever else was going on around the city. A couple who recycled friends in order to feed themselves shot into the social scene of the city and was on the must have list at your dinner. Uziah and Hannah always informed their hosts they would attend if there was no alcohol served. They were invited to a lot of Sunday brunches and whatever the rich and famous could dream up that was alcohol free. Everyone wanted the Zook's as guests. It was prestige to be seen with them. So the Zook's entertained five nights a week for food. Hannah and Uziah entertained their original friends on Wednesdays. They included Sergeant Pepper, Endora, Mooch, Ohm Oto a Buddhist friend across the alley, and two other students who were college classmates of Uziah. They were the heart and soul of Zook's Place, the inner circle that Uziah and Hannah bonded with.

College classes were going well for Uziah. Hannah was breezing thru her high school courses. Mooch talked Georgia Macon of the pancake emporium to let Uziah work two shifts on the dishwasher each week. Hannah picked up three dwellings to clean including that of Sergeant Pepper. Uziah was selling and bartering items he found in the dumpsters. Financially, Uziah and Hannah were bringing in enough money for their rent, but not much else. They had their feelers out for any part time work that they could work around their school schedules.

CHAPTER FOUR

Georgia's Suggestion

Two months after arriving in the city and starting their education, Mooch brought to the Wednesday friend dinner his boss, Georgia Macon. Sergeant Pepper didn't talk all evening and seemed a little agitated. Hannah, however, was delighted recognizing her as the peeping Tom woman. Mooch brought her as his steady dinner date after that. Hannah liked Georgia and they became friends and occasionally talked on the phone. Georgia had an extra cell phone that she gave Hannah to carry in case of emergency. The two women were so different, but they saw in each other something that no one else saw. No man was going to wear the pants and rule them. They formed their friendship on the fact that they were strong women and knew what they wanted out of life. Neither appreciated wimpy women who willingly let their men run over them. They had strong opinions about women being all they could be and making enough money so that they didn't have to depend on a man for their livelihood. Hannah could talk openly to Georgia about her and Uziah being cousins. She had told Georgia their story the first night she met her in the convenience store. Georgia kept her secret like a friend would.

Hannah had an aura about her that was like a magnet. Everyone wanted to know her or have a tiny piece of her. It was not having a tiny piece of her that drove men crazy. Every man wants what he cannot have. Hannah could not be had and the men in her world found her most desirable.

One Friday afternoon towards the end of March, Uziah returned from working an afternoon shift at the Pancake Emporium. While sitting and eating a sandwich at their door table he initiated a conversation with Hannah about an invitation from Georgia for her to come out to the restaurant for a chat.

"Tomorrow when you are out of school for the day, Georgia wishes you to come out to the restaurant. She said she has come up with a money making idea that could provide us with several hundred dollars a week in cash. She would not share her idea with me." Uziah stated pausing to take a few bites of his peanut butter sandwich. They had dinner guests coming later and he was having a little pre-dinner snack.

"That sounds interesting. Georgia is the nearest thing to a sister I have. I would love to go visit her and hear a story she wishes to tell me. We girl talk; things that men don't want to hear." Hannah replied.

"She is not exactly a girl, Hannah. She is older that our mothers."

"Do you see Sergeant Pepper as old as our fathers?" She asked alarmed. She secretly liked Sergeant Pepper and never had considered him old enough to be her father.

"Sergeant Pepper is at least fifteen years older than you and possibly twenty. Yes, he is of the age of our fathers; both of us being firstborns." He replied.

"Oh!" Hannah replied. "To me, Sergeant Pepper and I are the same age. We think the same." She replied.

"He is a friend. It is okay for us to have friends all ages. That being said, I accept the fact that you see Georgia as a sister. I will quit thinking of her as a mother type."

"Our mothers never had painted lips, straw color hair, or wore high heels. She definitely is not the mother type."

"I will have to admit that I have looked at her legs in her hi-heels. I agree. They are not mother legs. There are other parts of her I find most attractive also. However, it is Endora that drives me crazy with her black licorice lips. I am most shamefully attracted to her Hannah."

"As long as you have me for a pretend wife, you are safe."

"I asked Endora if she would give you a ride tomorrow afternoon to the restaurant. You must catch a lift back with Millie the day waitress. She gets off at five and has agreed to bring you home for a dinner invitation next week when Mooch is attending. I think she has a crush on him."

"Maybe Georgia has an opening for me. Our dinners are feeding us well, but they are not putting money in our pocket. I could work three or four nights a week and it not affect my studies. This may be the answer to our prayers for additional work and money. God always answers my prayers. Do you know that I pray every Wednesday for a chocolate bar and Mooch usually brings me one and slips it to me when he is helping me do the dishes?"

"You have been eating chocolate bars? Why haven't I been getting half?" He asked amused.

"I eat half and Mooch eats half. It is a friendship bar and he says the chocolate will keep me from being a Pecking Hen. He never fails to help me clean up."

"Well, don't get too fond of him, Hannah. He is a little too friendly with the women around us. Your friend, Georgia, seems quite attached to him and the waitresses at the restaurant swoon over him. He has lots of dates, paid dates."

"Paid dates? What do you mean?" She asked putting bread pudding into her detergent bottle cap pudding dishes to serve later.

"You know what a harlot is, don't you?"

"Yes. The Bible speaks of them. I have never met one." She replied.

"Mooch is a male harlot. He sleeps with women for money. That is how he pays for his education."

"Oh . . ." Hannah stated big eyed. "I did not know there was such a thing as a male harlot."

"Georgia pays him to be her dinner date on Wednesdays and also for certain favors afterwards." Uziah replied trying to not sound vulgar.

"I understand. We do not need to discuss his vocation any further. I have wondered why he visits Mrs. Begley every Sunday evening and doesn't leave till midnight."

"Just don't get to fond of him. It is Mrs. Begley's and Georgia's money that is paying for your chocolate bar."

"I understand! I will buy the chocolate bar for Wednesdays

from now on. I will tell him so next Wednesday. I must pay for his services helping me do the dishes and clean up. It is unfair for me to use his services and not pay."

"I wish I hadn't said anything," replied Uziah shaking his head and laughing. His cousin was as dumb as a box of rocks sometimes and other times smart as a whip. He never knew what was going to come out of her mouth.

The following afternoon, Hannah rode with Endora out to the Pancake Emporium restaurant to visit with her friend Georgia Macon. Inside the restaurant, she slid into a booth in a quiet corner where Georgia had instructed Millie the waitress to seat her. Hannah sat in the booth patiently waiting. She eyed Millie the waitress; whom Uziah had said had a crush on Mooch. Hannah wasn't sure how she felt about that. She tried to decide if the waitress was prettier than herself. For some reason, it annoyed her to think of Mooch washing dishes and sharing a chocolate bar with someone else. Mooch breezed by stopping long enough to set a hot cup of coffee and a piece of chocolate pie piled high with whip cream in front of her. He did not have on his waiter's uniform. She wondered what he was up to. He looked very nice and had his hair combed. He must have a lady friend she told herself and then bit her lip. She didn't want him to have a lady friend. He belonged to her. He was her Mooch.

"The pie is from me, not Georgia." He whispered in her ear. "You are my only chocolate girl!" Then he hurried to the rear of the restaurant and disappeared.

Hannah grinned as she took a fork and sampled the delight. She wondered if she should save half for Uziah. Reluctantly, she cut the slice of pie in half and saved part for him. He would do the same for her, she was sure.

"Hi, Sweetie," stated Georgia walking up to the booth and

sliding in on the seat opposite of her. "I am glad you have finally found your way out here?"

"I rode with Endora here and will ride home with Millie. I understand you wish to speak to me about a money idea. After the idea, I wish to hear the stories of your peeping. I want to know what you saw in the holey shorts. You promised one day to tell me." Hannah stated smiling.

"Honey, what was in those shorts wasn't worth looking at. However, after we discuss business I will tell you what I saw."

"Do you plan to take me peeping with you sometime? I am a little bored in my nest in the sky." She asked giggling. "There is a man who dresses in white across the alley that I would like to peep at. However, I have never seen him in shorts. He usually is fully dressed when he sits at his window."

Georgia broke out snickering. "From the third floor position you are looking from, you need binoculars. I think I have an old pair at my apartment. I will bring them to you next Wednesday."

"It must be our secret. Uziah would tell me that I should mind my own business and that only busy bodies peep into other's lives. However, I see the man doing something with his hands. I think he might be painting graven images in his third floor apartment. I would like to see what he is painting. Perhaps he paints women with holes in their under things."

Georgia snickered again. "Sweetie, you and I are destined to be lifelong friends. We think alike. I would like to see what he is doing with his hands also."

"Thank you for the binoculars you are bringing me. I will keep you informed as to what I see with them."

"It is time to discuss business." Georgia stated.

"What do you have in mind?" Hannah asked expecting an offer of a part time job running the dishwasher or perhaps a cook's helper position.

"Several years ago, I had an idea for a private supper club for the wealthy. However, I couldn't come up with a unique idea to pull it off. Your dining table is eclectic and culturally interesting. There are wealthy people in our town who seek out the unusual and are willing to pay for the experience. They are colorful people who would never be invited to an Amish home for a meal because they probably speak a little colorful and have had two or three too many wives or husbands. They are rich, but not so nice. I would like to suggest that you sell your six seats on Saturday nights as a fine dining experience. They would get to eat with an Amish couple who both are studying to be doctors, recycles, and eats whatever the crowd brings. The new rich want to be doctors but don't have the education. They also want nice. The old rich are bored to death with French restaurants. The rich are never satisfied and look for new experiences. You are the talk of the town right now. The rich would pay to eat at your private supper club."

"Sell the seats at my dining table?" She inquired looking confused."I know nothing about running a restaurant or a private supper club.

"You wouldn't be running a restaurant like the Emporium. You would be the hostess of an invitation only private supper club. Everyone wants to hang out with a movie star or someone wealthier than they are."

"They would pay too eat with me? I don't have plates or chairs. Everyone brings their chair."

"That is the beauty of it. Everyone will be required to bring their folding chair and it must be decorated. Anyone showing up with a plain folding chair won't be invited a second time. I will spread the rumors. Wealthy women spend fortunes decorating their houses. They will see the seat at your dining table as an opportunity to express how wealthy they are. I will tell them all that an oriental prince dined last week and he had his chair gold plated and the Buddha's photo hand painted on. They will fall over themselves trying to top the Oriental Prince and if nothing else desire to be on the social invitation list of someone who entertains princes."

"But Ohm and his Buddha chair is one of us, a student. He is not a prince."

"He won't be there next week sweetie. I will spread the word that you didn't give him a second invitation because he had a spot of something on his trousers that was questionable and that you are a neat freak who presses her dress ten minutes before opening the front door. They will spit shine themselves. Seeing each other in black tie, they will fight each other for the next week's six seats."

"How would I handle such a table of wealthy guests? I am just Hannah."

"Just serve and talk to them like you do the students and others on Wednesdays. Sometimes you will find that the wealthy may have less of an education that you do. They start off early making money while the average Jane or Joe has his nose still stuck in his college books. They buy the educations they need. They don't have to be a doctor or hold a degree when needed. They hire the educated."

"I see. They are like me, but they have made their money making ideas work for them."

"You've got it, sweetie. They have the money to burn and want to be somebody. They will tip big and pay well for the privilege of being seen as someone. I will make it known that no one leaves the table without leaving a twenty dollar tip if they want a second invitation to the dinner club. Ask Sergeant Pepper to provide entertainment on his sax on Saturdays. He plays some pretty cool blues. He will get whatever tips that the guests put in a glass by him for requesting certain musical pieces. Ohm Oto is wealthy to begin with, but he is studying sociology and I am sure would love the opportunity to write his term paper on the unique subculture of the supper club. Also, he is crazy about Endora. Ask her to be the bathroom attendant for half the tips left on the dining table. Let Mooch serve. He will agree to it. He is broke. The diners must bring the food just like they do on friend night. The wealthy will trip over themselves bringing their servants to see that their food is served properly.

"For two hours, Uziah and I would just sit and talk with six rich guests who will bring food and wild chairs. I will get six hundred dollars for smiling and polite conversation?"

"You will get five hundred dollars for now. My payment for helping you is one of the six places at your table. I like mingling with the rich and the famous. By my attendance at every dinner they will assume that I have more money than they do. They will in turn include me on all of their dinner invitation lists. I win, you win." Georgia replied.

"I must ask Uziah. He is head of our house."

"He will agree. The two of you will make five hundred a week plus whatever is left over of the better quality food that will be left behind. It will be a no leftovers club. No one takes anything home."

"Our invitations are our way of growing new friendships with the people we meet on campus and in our business dealings. Would we need to be friends with all the vagabond rich?"

"You will probably get as many return dinner invitations as I will. You can pick and choose who you wish to socialize with on your off nights."

"You are brilliant, Georgia. Are you sure that you aren't Amish? You would be great at bartering." Hannah replied.

"I know what I want and it is seated at your dinners. I can't catch him, if I am not in the right place." She replied thinking of Sergeant Pepper.

"Your heart races for someone at my dinners?"

"Yes, my heart races for someone at your dinners. He is an ugly man, but I want him."

"Does his heart race for you?"

"He is seeing some damn woman that he is seeing secretly. I will take care of that when I find out who she is."

"What if the man doesn't return your affection, what then?" Hannah asked. She was sure that Georgia had to be referring to Uziah. He was the most homely of all the men at her dinner table.

"That is a good point," she replied. "If he doesn't sit up and pay attention to me in a year, perhaps I will race my heart for Ohm Oto."

Hannah broke out laughing. "He is almost two heads shorter than you. You could thump him and make him mind real easy. I would like a man that I could henpeck. I am the Pecker Hen type." Hannah snickered.

"That is why you and I are becoming friends. Neither of us intends to have a man that is capable of running over us. I am the Pecker Hen type too."

"My answer on the dinner club venture is yes. However, I must present the idea to Uziah out of respect. He is head of our house hold. Also, thank you for keeping my secret that Uziah and I are just cousins." She said politely and then asked, "Who should I let my heart race for secretly?"

"Always choose money, Hannah. I have learned the hard way that young love doesn't pay for your beauty shop appointments or make the payments on your convertible. David Goldstein is very wealthy. His family is in the diamond trade. I would set my cap for him, should you ever want to divulge your secret that you are not married. A little secret flirting will keep him dangling and waiting."

"He houses harlots and thieves! I would let the garbage collecting, dumpster man call on me before I would consider him."

"He is a toot, isn't he? You are probably the only girl on campus that David Goldstein can't have."

"He is a toot!" Replied Hannah. "He toots his horn of abomination with harlots."

Then Georgia broke out in uncontrollable laughter with Hannah wondering what she was so amused about.

The Madness Began

So, the madness began. Uziah did approve after hearing how

much money they would make. It was way more than both of them could make working part time and going to school. Money was the name of the game when it came to him. They needed money.

On Saturday nights, black limos and fancy sports cars pulled in to the parking spaces of the Pepper Apartment complex at ten minutes to seven. It was made known by Georgia that it was considered rude to arrive at the door eleven minutes before seven or one minute after seven. It was also made known, if you arrived one minute after the hour, you would lose your seat and not be allowed admittance to the private supper club. There was no being fashionably late at the Zook's. When a multimillionaire manufacturer was turned away because his wife chose to be fashionably late, the ten minute admittance window was not ignored. It was months before the fashionably late couple was able to obtain another reservation.

On Saturday night, a line would form on the third floor stairs and the wealthy of the city socialized on the outdoor stairs of the third floor. An occasional flask was passed around but carefully put away before the person in the head of the line knocked. A few major business deals were made on the steps and hairdresser and designer names swapped by the women. However, no one knocked to get in out of snow, rain, wind, hail, or any sort of inclement weather till ten minutes till seven. Dining at the Zooks came with strict rules. Dress was strictly black tie and anyone arriving carrying an ordinary plain folding chair would not be given a second reservation. Plain chairs were considered lower class.

The Sunday paper went crazy writing about the social scene and who was dining at the Zook's. The mayor of the city had to beg Georgia for reservations for him and his wife and offered to pay double for the opportunity to dine with the millionaires of the city. Zook's place quickly became the in place to be.

Ohm Oto saw the opportunity to write a book about the unusual cultural phenomena and became the doorman on Saturday nights wearing a red Buddhist Monk robe and glasses like the Dahli Llama. He took coats and welcomed the guests. He didn't need the tips because he was wealthy himself. However, he enjoyed counting what he made each Saturday night. He secretly gave the money to Endora knowing that she needed money for her college expenses and he was in love with her. However, he had an arranged fiancé he was to marry after he graduated college. Ohm pretended to speak no English and wore a small cardboard sign around his neck reading:

Welcome to Zook's. I do not speak English. Bless this monk and I will remember you when I become the leader of the Tibetan chosen. $20 is the proper tip for the doorman. For an extra $20, I will kiss your gorgeous dining companion and she will not age.

The women loved Ohm Oto who winked at them, blew kisses, and folded his hands bowing to them and pretending to ogle their legs and cleavage. He had a servant of his own. However, his man would be beaten if he disrespected a woman by looking at her legs or feminine offerings. His servant had been relieved of his male hood when he was young to make him a safe servant for a house hold of girls in India. He was a Eunuch.

Sergeant Pepper, an amateur sax player, loved the attention he got as the in-house entertainment. The tips meant little to him because he was already wealthy. He secretly gave them to Hannah telling her to put them in her private purse for girl things that she needed. She always blushed and kissed him on the cheek telling him thank you. Mooch needed the hundred or so dollars in tips he made on Saturday nights for the two hours. Both men were loved by Hannah, each in their own way.

Uziah and Hannah continued to sit on their milk crates at the ends of their table and served their guests on their recycled plastic jug bottom plates and water glasses cut from the bottoms of water bottles. They prayed before meals and offered friendship and ears to listen and discuss whatever subject was on the mind of their wealthy guests. The five seats plus Georgia's sixth seat at their table were filled every Saturday night. Uziah and Hannah were really happy with the money they were making. Life was going well.

Their presentation of themselves as an Amish married couple and future doctors was paying all the bills. They couldn't afford to blow their image. In one semester, they had put back enough money for the next two years of Uziah's college expenses. By the end of three years, if they were careful, they would be able to save enough to pay for Hannah's college education, Uziah's master degree, and the tuition for him to enter medical school. The private supper club was raking in the money. Only Georgia Macon knew that the Zook's were cousins and single.

CHAPTER FIVE

Big Hands to Hold You

Hannah stood at the back door of Sergeant Pepper's laundry room waiting for the dryer to turn off. Endora was folding a few things that she had washed. Everyone hates being stuck in a laundry room watching a dryer go around, so they stepped to the back door to aimlessly chat and pass the time.

As they stood waiting for the laundry cycles to complete, they both watched the turban man, who always dressed in white, exit his back door across the alley, walk to the dumpster and toss away a black plastic bag of trash. Seeing the girls, he smiled and then kissed his fingers pointing to the sky which was dark with storm clouds.

Hannah waved back, kissed her fingers, and pointed to the sky. She could see the turban man grinning as he returned inside the apartment where he had exited.

"What do you think about the man in white, Endora? Uziah says he cannot speak and that he is possibly a God's Will child of another religious faith. He seems quite nice to me, but Uziah tells me to stay clear of him that he might be dangerous."

"What do you mean by God's Will Child, Hannah? I don't understand."

"A God's Will child is one born in our community with a deformed body, Maple Syrup Disease, or mentally challenged. Uziah says the man doesn't speak and is probably mentally challenged to go with it and could hurt me. He says sometimes God's Will children can grow up to be physically strong and mean."

"Well if that isn't straight from the dark ages in thinking! The man across the alley is a servant, Hannah. He is here with his employer who is a wealthy student. The rich often travel with their servants. He doesn't speak our language so he uses hand signals and body language to communicate. What he was just trying to tell us was possibly that he loves a stormy day or the God's were smiling on him and sending rain. He is a working stiff like Mooch. Mooch waits tables and the turban man waits on his wealthy employer's table." Endora stated giving Hannah an 'I don't believe you are that dumb' look.

"So, I have no need to fear him?" Hannah asked ignoring Endora's raised eyebrows and funny look.

"He is a hunk, Hannah, and has the body of a movie star. Did you see his hands? They are the size of plates. Imagine yourself being held in his arms and those hands on your backside. He is hot Hannah."

Hannah blushed. "I should not think of such things. I am married. Uziah is handsome."

"Don't take me wrong, Uziah isn't even in the same ballpark with the turban man. Hands man has a natural suntan and a body I would like to ravish. He is definitely hot."

"What do you mean by hot. He didn't look like he was sweating?"

Endora turned to Hannah grinning and shaking her head. "Hot means he is so handsome that you can see yourself sleeping with him and never letting him out of your bed."

"Oh . . . that is sinful. It is lust of the flesh. I must not think about your words."

"The only sin is not having him." Endora shot back. "He could sleep in my bed free anytime." Endora stated and then realized what she had said. She hoped Hannah didn't catch the free reference. No one knew that she was a call girl and not a student. Her uncle would throw her out in a heartbeat if he discovered it. He had given her tuition and book money for the last year. She had used the money for rental sports cars, jewelry, and clothing to attract wealthier clientele at night. She kept her lady of the night clothing in the trunk of her ten year old car that Sergeant Pepper had bought her. She changed in a public rest room when needed. Uziah was the one kink in her secret lifestyle as a call girl. She had not expected to meet someone and find herself falling in love. She was crazy about the long legged farm boy who was untouchable. She wanted him.

"You should never do anything free for a man." Hannah stated. "If Uziah wants me to cook supper or wash his clothes, then he must do something for me. I insist he carry out all trash, sweep the balcony, and clean the bathroom bowl and shower."

Endora grinned. "You are absolutely right, if the white turban man was my husband, I would make him make the bed, wash my car, and give me foot massages."

"I am a barterer. Nothing in life is free and that includes me. A man should be willing to work for the rights to your affection.

When I was sixteen, before Uziah came to call, I would not accept a suitor if he wasn't willing to help me pick vegetables in my garden or help me milk."

"I think we are in agreement, Hannah. A man should pay for our favors."

The two young women returned to their chores.

Later that night about nine, Hannah walked down to the convenience store where she and Uziah had coffee the first night they had arrived. She was lonely. Uziah had a lot of friends he visited. She, however, wasn't allowed to bring her high school friends to the apartment. Uziah didn't want to be seen associating with kids as he called them. He wanted their world to be filled with the higher educated and those pursuing careers. He was gone and wouldn't be home until eleven. He had been invited to a night of sports watching across campus in one of the male dorms. She just wasn't in the mood to sit and stare at the third floor walls. Her homework was done and Uziah's supper was on the back of the stove waiting for him. She just felt the need to splurge and buy herself a cup of coffee. So, she walked to the off campus convenience store, purchased a cup of black coffee, and then seated herself in one of the two booths and watched a variety of students and regular people wander in and out paying for gas and other items.

About fifteen after nine, the turban wearing man entered the convenience store and purchased a cup of coffee. Turning to walk back and sit in the booths, he spotted Hannah. His face lit up like a Christmas tree and he headed her way.

"May sit?" He asked in a choppy sentence.

"Please do." She said pointing and smiling. She had never been able to have a real conversation with him and see what he was like. Endora was right, he was a gorgeous golden brown skinned man who always dressed in white and wore a white cloth around his head.

"I . . . I . . ." He said.

Hannah could see that he was struggling for words. Then it occurred to her that Endora was right, he wasn't a God's Will man. He just simply couldn't speak her language. She could see that he was struggling and trying to have a conversation with her with his limited vocabulary. Uziah had denied her the friendship with this man for no reason.

"I am happy!" She returned pointing to her face and smiling big.

He grinned and his dark eyes sparkled. "I . . . happy!" He replied and then pointed to his face and then to hers.

About that time a stranger walked up to the booth and slid in next to the white turbaned man and they had a brief exchange of words. Then the well dressed stranger turned to Hannah smiling.

"Hi, my name is Lee. I spotted Chim in here while I was filling my vehicle with gas. I am just giving him a greeting to pass along to his employer. Chim has asked if I would remain in the booth for a moment and translate for him. Is that alright with you? Chim is just a servant of my friend Ohm Oto. I will tell him to leave, if he is bothering you. I know you are the owner of Zook's Supper Club. I have been trying to get a reservation for months.

"I would be pleased if you would translate briefly and you call me later tonight and I will fit you and a diner companion in." She stated taking a napkin from the dispenser and writing her cell phone number on it. I am Hannah. "She always kept a short pencil in her pocket because she never knew when someone would call wanting a reservation for Zook's Place.

"My wife will be so thrilled. She is the best friend of the Mayor's wife."

"Did I hear you correctly? You said that Chim is Ohm Oto's servant? I have never heard Ohm mention him."

"Yes, you heard me correctly. Chim is his name."

Hannah was shocked that Ohm had never mentioned him or asked to bring him to their dinners.

"What does he wish to say to me?" Hannah asked grinning at the stranger and then at Chim.

"He wishes to thank you for your friendship and to tell you that his life here would be very lonely without your waves and friendship. He wishes you to know that he is a faithful servant to his master Ohm Oto who owns him." Stated the stranger who cringed at translating the ownership part.

"Tell him that I have enjoyed his friendship and that I would like to invite him to dinner at Zook's Place one night."

Lee grinned. "You realize he cannot date or be social with Ohm's friends? He is a servant. You must be careful what you say to him because he doesn't have the freedoms you have. Ohm could beat him for just sitting in this booth with you. His sitting next to you at a dinner or social gathering would not be acceptable. He is an owned servant."

"I didn't realize." Hannah stated. "Tell him we will be friends from our third floor windows and be bird watchers together.

Tell him I will not tell Ohm or Uziah about our friendship and that he is safe with me."

Lee translated to Chim who spoke in a language that Hannah did not understand. Lee had to translate once more.

"He says to tell you that you that he will always think of you as his friend named Hannah Bird. He would like to know if you would be willing to teach him to speak English so that he might communicate with you better. He has one night off a month. He wonders if he could spend it with you here in this booth over coffee and you teach him the basics of the English language. He has no one else to ask and he is terribly lonely. He wishes you to know that he thinks of you as a gentle, beautiful, gray dove."

Hannah blushed. "Tell him that Uziah does not call me a gentle gray dove. Uziah calls me a Pecker Hen because I don't let him get by with anything."

Lee laughed. "That one is going to be a little hard to translate, but I will try. It may come out in his language that you are a squawking bird."

Hannah laughed. "That is okay. It is close enough."

Once more, Lee translated and laughed while doing so. Afterwards, Chim laughed looking at Hannah and bit his lip. Then, visibly amused, he spoke to Lee again.

Lee translated. "He says that every man should be privileged to have such a beautiful, squawking bird to keep him in line. He also says that if it is alright with you, he will call you Hannah Bird. He has asked and been told your first name."

"Tell him I am pleased and I will call him Chim, my friend with the great bird nest on his head. Tell him I have climbed many trees as a little girl and have peeped into many bird nests. I am curious what is in the one on his head. Also tell him that I will meet him here once a month and teach him to speak English. It must be on a Sunday night, because it is the only night I do not run Zook's Place. Tell him when he has a Sunday off to tie a piece of white cloth hanging from his window and I will know to meet him that night. I can see his bedroom window from mine. The backs of our apartment houses look at each other. I will know by the hanging white cloth that I am to meet him at nine here for thirty minutes to teach him English and drink coffee with him. I cannot stay longer than thirty minutes because Uziah would not be happy with me."

Lee translated once more, Chim spoke again and then Chim stated to Hannah. "He says to tell you that he is pleased. Also, he wishes you to know that he has great thoughts in his nest on his head that he wishes to share with you. His birds cannot leave his hat nest till he is able to speak your language. He thanks you for helping him. He says to tell you that he needs you desperately for a friend."

"Ask him if he would like to walk me home and we will start English lessons tonight."

The men exchanged words and then the translator stated to Hannah, "He is honored to be asked to walk you home. He knows his position in life and that you are like Ohm, higher class. He says to say thank you for helping him and that he knows that he is overstepping his boundaries as an owned servant. He just wants to be able to speak and understand the language so he doesn't feel so isolated. He is very lonely."

After translating, Lee got up and left.

Hannah looked at Chim. He was still as handsome as the first night she had met him many months before. She recalled that she had intended to tell Uziah about the encounter but never had. Chim would indeed be her treasured secret. There were some secrets you could not share. Uziah would not appreciate her friendship with the turban man. However, she saw Chim as a mission from God. She would teach him that no one owns another person in the United States or in God's sight. She would teach him about freedom and English at the same time.

When she stood up to leave, so did he. It would be a night and a simple walk home that she would never forget. They stopped and looked at simple things and he would repeat after her what she called them. Afterward, he walked her to her third floor door. There upon parting, he kissed his fingers and touched them to her nose as she opened the apartment door to leave him. Taking her own fingers, she kissed them and touched the tip of his nose. He grinned and then left.

Hannah entered the apartment and found Uziah studying at the table. He looked up. "I wish to ask you to do something that I feel is important, Hannah?"

"What is it?" She asked sitting down at the table with him on top of her two milk crates.

"It has occurred to me that we are long overdue in asking David Goldstein to dinner. He gave us a generous ride into the city and we have not repaid his kindness. I wish to be beholding to no one. I want you to invite him. It is you that alienated him and I feel that he will not come if I ask." Uziah stated pushing back his book for a moment.

"I have not forgotten he inferred that I am homely and unintelligent." She returned wanting to get out of inviting him.

"You have no choice in this matter Hannah. We owe him. God sent David along to rescue us from the blizzard, now we must invite him to dinner. I am sure that by now he has forgotten and possibly doesn't even remember your words. He is quite popular with the girls on campus and doesn't ever lack for a weekend companion. I am sure that he has not given you a second thought. Suck it up as the English say and invite him for friend night. I am head of our house and have the final say in matters. We owe him and we will repay our debt."

"Yes, Uziah," she replied in a peeved voice wanting to take his text book and stuff it down his throat. She controlled herself. She was the tag- a-long to the land of the English.

Bee Spit

After school a few evenings later, Hannah knocked on Sergeant Pepper's door. She had decided Uziah was right. She needed to suck it up and become friends with those she knew in her apartment complex. Uziah had bonded with and made many friends visiting after their dinners with the guests. She was always busy serving or doing dishes afterward. She didn't feel she was as close to everyone as Uziah was, with the exception of Mooch who always helped her clean up. So, she was on a mission to bond with the Wednesday night regular dinner guests and invite David to dinner when she got up the nerve.

First on her list was Sergeant Pepper because he was her favorite roll over dog. However, she would never tell him to his face that he was her cute, big eyed puppy. After expressing her opinions to David Goldstein and Uziah chastising her for it when they first arrived, she had learned to zip her thought's lips.

Still carrying her tote of school books, she knocked on Sergeant Pepper's front door. After a minute or so, he opened it with a surprised look on his face. Hannah quickly noted that he was wearing a pair of jeans with a hole in the knee. She quickly decided that she was not going to have her roll over dog running around with holes in his jeans. What if Georgia saw him? She might look at his treasure thru the hole. She would save her roll over dog from lady peepers. She was sure that all English women were peepers. Practically every female she knew had seen men's treasures and they were not married. Endora was her age and she often embarrassed Hannah telling her things about men and their bodies. She must save Sergeant Pepper from English lady peepers and maybe she would only peep a little at his knee thru the hole. After all, he was her roll over dog.

"Hannah," he stated smiling. "Come in. I was just about to have a cup of hot tea and a bagel with cream cheese on it to hold me over till dinner. Would you like to have tea and a bagel with me? Endora hates bagels."

"I would enjoy that very much, thank you. I have come to strengthen our friendship and also to talk to you about something of a personal nature." She replied eyeing the hole in the knee of his jeans. Georgia was right. It was fun to peep. He had a cute bony knee. She would have to repent at bedtime prayers for peeping. However, she would have to warn him about all the holes in his underwear and the possibility that some woman might peep at him. She had been doing his laundry and she knew he had some shorts that were beyond repair with holes as big as lemons. Some woman could peep really well. She must warn him. He was her friend.

"Come on back to the kitchen. I have the kettle on heating water."

Sergeant Pepper was a little man between thirty- five and forty years old. He was medium height, had a few gray hairs at his temples, but was always well groomed and clean. He was a realtor who wore round gold rim glasses and always had a metal whistle on a cord around his neck. The whistle was a policeman's whistle and no one knew why he wore it. His love was the saxophone and he had delighted in getting to play it for entertainment at the Zook's dinners. He loved the blues. He was a simple little man who seemed to be afraid. No one knew what or whom he was afraid of.

Hannah seated herself at the round, wooden, kitchen table in one of the four ladder back chairs. She eyed the Jazz festival posters framed and hung behind the table. The kitchen had Sergeant Pepper's personal design touch on it. She liked the kitchen, except for the one poster that had an almost nude woman singing with a band of some sort. She would have to talk to him on one of her future visits about what is appropriate to be seen by your guests. She would ask him to replace it with a singer with clothes on. She was sure that he would oblige if he wanted her to return over and over for tea.

"I am so pleased that you have come to see me. May I ask why?"

"I have decided that I haven't been a proper friend to you and that I need to straighten up my act as the English at our dinner table phrase it." Hannah stated sitting straight in her chair. Amish women did not lean back in their dining chairs.

Sergeant Pepper poured two tea cups with hot water and grinned while he was doing it. She always amused him how she put things. He was madly in love with her, only she didn't know it. "A proper friend, explain that to me!" He replied carrying the two cups and saucers to the table and placing one in front of her. It had a teaspoon on the side and a tea bag.

"You are the friend that I am the fondest of and I am sure will be my longest lasting friend of the group. Therefore, I must watch out for you as a friend would. You have a weak stomach and ulcers. I need to help you with your eating and drinking habits that are unwholesome.

Alarmed, he quickly replied, "I do not drink alcohol, Hannah. Has someone told you that I do?"

"It is not alcohol, Sergeant Pepper. You drink something far more revolting," she said putting her tea bag in her cup.

"Would you like honey in your tea?" He asked picking up a bear shaped container of golden honey and offering it to her.

"Honey is revolting, Sergeant Pepper. I absolutely would never put it in my tea and neither should you!" She said taking the container from him and setting it by her plate. "I do not want you ever tasting or putting it in your tea again. You could die from putting raw honey in your tea. I do not wish to lose my best friend. That is one of the two things I have come to talk to you about."

"Me . . .? Die? . . .? Honey . . .?" He inquired with a total look of confusion on his face." I don't understand. What are you trying to tell me? I promise you I am health conscious and do not put anything into my body that would harm it. I don't drink alcohol or smoke! I am almost Amish!"

"I guess I am just going to have to be blunt with you because I love you as my friend and you seem to be a little oblivious to your problem."

"Absolutely, just lay my backside on the line. Whatever it is that I am doing that is offensive to you; I will try to change if it is within reason!"

"Would you drink a cup of tea if Mooch, David, or Uziah spit in it?" She asked seriously.

"No, why do you ask? I am totally lost where this conversation is going!"

"Honey is bee spit. I will not have you drinking your tea with bee spit in it. It is stranger bee's spit at that. You don't know them."

Sergeant Pepper broke out laughing and couldn't stop till he had tears rolling down his face. When he was able to contain himself, he asked biting his lip. "Did I hear you correctly? You don't want me putting bee spit in my tea and definitely not the spit of stranger bees?"

"You have heard me correctly. Raw honey has parasites in it and it isn't recommended for babies till they are three years old. You have a weak stomach and ulcers. Those parasites may be what is causing your stomach ailments. You have blindly been drinking bee spit. As your friend, I will not have it. It is the same thing as being an alcoholic. You must give it up! I have shown you the light on the subject."

Sergeant Pepper broke out laughing again. "I am sorry, Hannah. You have caught me off guard with this one. Bee spit, stranger bee spit . . . I will think of that every time I hear the word honey from now on. You may indeed throw away my container of raw honey. You have ruined the pleasure of it for me."

"That is what friends are about. Now should you in the future see something that I am doing that I am blind to; you must inform me. I wish you to be my best friend because you are respectable, unlike some of the other members of our dinner group. They will be my friends also, but I wish you to be my best friend. I would like to have a lady best friend. However, I haven't met a respectable one. You will be my girl friend substitute. I would prefer a lady friend to chit chat and talk woman things with, but God has given me you. You must listen to all my woman opinions and silly things I wish to discuss! You must eat chocolate bars with me when necessary."

"Hannah, I am honored that you have chosen me for your substitute lady friend. I promise to keep all your girl and woman secrets. Will you come every afternoon thru the week after school for tea? I will clear my schedule for our chit chats and no honey tea."

"Yes, I will come. Friendship is a two way street, Sergeant Pepper. You must tell me your secrets also. We will share our intimate thoughts like girls back in my Amish community do."

"I have never had anyone to share with," he replied grinning. In his mind, he could see himself falling madly in love with her, if he were fifteen years younger. She was everything he dreamed a respectable woman could be. However, he was much too old for her and he would enjoy her as a friend.

Sergeant Pepper knew what it was like for someone that was much too old for you to take advantage of you. He would never do to Hannah what Georgia Macon had done to him. He was a week shy of his fifteenth birthday when twenty-four year old Georgia started raping him. He was a runaway with nowhere to go. She fed him and then made him pay with never ending years of being in her bed till he was old enough to have a mind of his own and walk away. Twenty years had passed. He was now thirty-five. Hannah was only eighteen. Even though he found her very attractive, he would never do that to her. He never went to high school, had friends, or went to the prom or football games. Georgia stole his teen years from him.

"I will go first. I will tell you a little secret that you must keep and then you must tell me one." She replied sipping her tea. "I told your renter, David Goldstein, that he is a pushover and houses thieves and harlots, I also told him that he has a big nose.

He hasn't spoken to me since." Hannah volunteered.

Sergeant Pepper snorted. "You had the nerve to tell the great Goldstein, one of the richest and most popular male hunks on campus, that he runs a house of ill repute and that you don't like his appearance?"

"He was so mad that he dropped Uziah and me off at a convenience store and left us standing in the snow watching him speed away. That is when we met Endora and she brought us here. We did not know that he lived here."

"I love you, Hannah. I would love to have seen his face."

"Now it is your turn. You must share with me a secret so I will have something to think about as I go about my household chores to snicker and think about and know that it is something that only you and I share."

"I have a lady friend at my Bell Ringer's Church. She has asked me to marry her, like I was the woman and should be proposed to. In my underwear drawer is an engagement ring." He stated lying. The ring actually was one he had bought off a fellow realtor who was broke. He kept it around just in case he did ever have a lady friend that he fell in love with and wanted to marry. "I do not know whether to keep it or give it back. I always thought it was the man's place to ask the woman. Can you imagine my surprise when she got down on one knee and asked me?" He replied lying. She was young enough that she would be fun to tell off the wall stuff to. He needed some humor in his dull world. Georgia was driving him crazy with her stalking and he was afraid to start a relationship out of fear for a lady friend's safety. He needed Hannah for a diversion.

Hannah snickered and then laughed. "Did she wear holes in the knees of her stockings waiting for an answer, or did you say yes?"

"Definitely holes. I lost my voice and didn't know what to say. She stuck the ring on my finger and told me to give her an answer in a few days. She also told me to not get the ring dirty. She knows that I like to garden." He replied smiling and eyeing her expression. She was absolutely beautiful and made his heart have serious butterflies.

"So, I must keep your secret till you make up your mind?"

"Yes, I am a slow decision maker."

"Your secret is safe with me. Is she pretty?"

"She is a lady wrestler with big arm muscles and thigh muscles. I was afraid to tell her no when she asked. She could have wiped up the men's room floor with me." He continued lying to see what her reaction would be.

"The men's room . . . she proposed to you in the men's rest room?"

"She is the church janitor. She cornered me there holding a great big mop handle. Needless to say, I let her speak her mind."

Hannah went to snickering, giggling, and laughing. "I am going to have to be your body guard. I would not be afraid of her mop. I would tell the witch to go take her broom and ride it."

This time it was Sergeant Peppers turn to snicker. Hannah was not the type of person to back down from anyone. She was a spit fire in some ways.

"Will you tell me more about your lady friend tomorrow? I want to know what she was wearing when she proposed to you.

I want to hear all of the details."

"I have a better idea than that. Do you think Uziah would agree to let you attend the Bell Ringer's church service with me Sunday? I play the sax in the Sunday morning church band. I thought perhaps you might like to hear me play gospel music. Perhaps the lady wrestler will leave me alone, seeing I have a lady on my arm. I am sure she wouldn't mess with you."

"Will my Sunday dress be appropriate to wear?" She asked.

"You will be the most appropriate dressed there and definitely the prettiest. I will be quite proud to have you go with me." He replied.

"I will tell Uziah tonight that I wish to go and will look forward to it very much. Won't your lady friend be jealous?"

"I have been praying for a lady friend every Sunday at church. I have asked God for one who would spank me when I am bad. I did not ask for a lady wrestler who could half kill me. Sometimes God gives me more than I ask for. The ring was a bonus." He shot back.

Hannah snickered. "Will you point her out to me on Sunday?"

"You just look for the biggest, meanest, ugliest woman in my church and that is her. You can't miss her."

Again, Hannah snickered. "Before I go home to start supper for guests that are coming, I have one more thing that I wish to speak to you about. It is more important than the Bee spit."

"I can't think what could top that subject at the moment, but lay it on me." He replied grinning. She had such a serious look on her face and she was leaning forward like she wanted to talk about the next subject almost in a whisper like it was embarrassing.

"Do you know what a peeping Tom is?" She asked seriously.

"Of course, it is a man that gets thrills looking in people's windows. You are safe on the third floor Hannah. No one can peek thru your windows."

"It is not my windows that I am referring to." She half whispered. "I fear that some woman peeping Tom is going to look thru your windows, see you in your holey underwear, and break in and rape you."

Sergeant Pepper spewed out the sip of tea he had just taken and then dropped his tea cup and grabbed for his napkin to clean up the mess. When he had regained his composure he wondered if he should ask why she was pursuing this subject. He tried to walk delicately around it. "I am going on forty, Hannah. I really don't think any woman is going to be window peeping at me. I am not a young, handsome hunk like Mooch or Goldstein."

"Not all women go for handsome hunks. You are a very desirable rich man and handsome in a different type of way. For instance, and I will have to pray about this when I say my bedtime prayers, I peeped at your knee through the hole in your jeans when I knocked on the door and you opened it. I saw something inside of your jeans that I shouldn't have been looking at. I peeped at your knee and liked what I saw. English women do not pray and ask forgiveness for such things. If one of them had knocked on your door and saw your knee, she might have raped you."

Sergeant Pepper sat back in his chair and put his hand under the table over the hole in the knee of his jeans. He didn't know what to say. She had him backed up into a corner and he was at a loss for words as to where to go with this conversation. "You think my exposed knee could get me raped?"

"Oh yes. Georgia tells me that it is okay for English women to be peeping Toms. She secretly watches a man with holes in his underwear the size of lemons. She has told me of looking thru the lemon size holes and seeing male things that I cannot say. You must be careful and keep your curtains closed at night till you purchase you new underwear. I wouldn't want an English peeping Tom woman like Georgia peeping at you."

"Georgia . . . ," He stated with the blood draining from his face. He had thought for some time that someone had been peeping thru his windows, but couldn't prove it. Flower beds outside his windows looked at times like they had been walked in. He had blamed Mrs. Begley's Doberman.

"Sergeant Pepper, you must be careful. I do not want you wearing underwear with holes in them. You are my friend and I don't want any strange woman looking. Only your doctor should look at such things. One day I will be your doctor and then I won't have to repent at night for looking." She replied seriously eyeing him. "I hate to be so blunt with you Sergeant Pepper, but there are English women peepers out there who would love to look thru your lemon holes. I do your laundry and feel it is my duty to inform you of such things."

"Do you think Georgia has been peeping in my windows or are you referring to someone else she peeps at?" He asked trying not to sound alarmed. She was genuinely concerned for him and he loved her for that. However, he was amused that she was going to have to repent for looking at his knee. He had never considered his bony knees as secret treasures.

"Georgia has told me about window peeping and what fun it

is. She has a man she says she is in love with and she peeps late at night. She was peeping the night Uziah and I arrived here with Endora. She came into the convenience store and sat down with a cup of coffee and laughed about it and told me about it that night. She peeps at someone who has holes in his underwear the size of lemons. I don't know who she peeps at, but I have washed your underwear and I know they have some serious holes in them. I do not want you getting taken advantage of. You are my friend. I must protect you and insist that you buy new underwear and a new pair of jeans. It is wrong of you to tempt me with your naked knee showing thru. It is a good looking knee and I happen to like knees."

Sergeant Pepper didn't know what to say. "You are absolutely right about the shorts. I will buy new ones tomorrow and double curtain my windows. However, this is my favorite pair of jeans. Could I please keep them and you and I come to some sort of compromise?"

"You are right. I will patch the knee of your jeans when I find them in the laundry next week. It is my sin in looking so I should pay, not you."

"I promise in the future not to seduce you with a hole in my jeans. However, I have one question, what about summer when I wear men's shorts? Will my knees be a problem then?"

"I have given that some thought. It is not the exposed items that cause a seduction. It is the hidden that entices men and women. It is their wondering what is in the hole in the shorts and jeans that is the root of sin. I looked thru the hole. When you have summer shorts on, I won't have to worry about it because there will be no hole that will tempt me to be a Peeper."

"Hannah, I don't know what I did before you come along to keep me on the straight and narrow as well as teach me the facts of life. For you and your peace of mind, I will throw away my holey underwear. Do you look thru the holes in my underwear when you do my laundry?" He couldn't help buy asking.

"Ever since Georgia told me what fun peeping is, I have had a problem with your underwear. I once held them up to the light and looked thru one of the lemon sized holes and wondered. However, I have already asked forgiveness for that time."

Sergeant Pepper wanted to laugh but he knew he had better control himself if he wanted her companionship on a daily basis for tea. She was young and curious. However, he was not happy about Georgia bending Hannah's ear with peeping stories or the fact that Georgia had been looking in his window. She was under a restraining order and wasn't to come within twenty feet of his apartment or business. He didn't push the subject with the Zook's. He just kept his distance from her when he went to the Zook's for dinner. He didn't want Hannah to know that he had been a rape victim or that he had serious issues with intimacy now. He wanted to protect Hannah. She didn't need to know about his youth spent with Georgia. He was ashamed of it.

"I am a no nonsense friend and woman, Sergeant Pepper. I know you are a good looking man and possibly want to strut a little like a rooster showing your uniqueness thru your lemon holes to possibly the wrestler lady or other lady friends. However, I should turn you over my knees and spank you for your flaunting in front of me and whatever English woman peeping Tom that might peep thru your window. I have chosen, as your friend, to just give you a good talking to this time. I do not like violence. Uziah says sometimes a woman needs hitting to keep her in line. I will not hit you. I love you too much and hitting hurts!"

"If Uziah ever hits you, I expect you to share that secret with me!" Pepper stated alarmed. The possibility of her being struck ripped a hole in his heart and it was at that moment that he realized he was hopelessly in love with her and there was nothing he could do about it. Although he wanted to take her in his arms and not let her go home, he knew she was married and that the Amish married for life.

"I will always tell you everything! You are my chit chat friend. I will expect you to do the same. I must go now. Remember, no bee spit in your tea and throw away your holey underwear. I insist."

Sergeant Pepper walked her to the door and let her out with a heart that was in his gut. Surely Uziah wasn't hitting her. After closing the door, he decided to have a little talk with the Amish man who lived in the studio on the third floor.

CHAPTER SIX

The Dinner Invitation

Once outside of Sergeant Pepper's apartment, Hannah gave her conversation with Uziah some thought. Tomorrow evening was friend night and she was running out of time to invite David. She couldn't cross Uziah. She had to ask him. Then she had a light bulb moment as her friends at school said. Rather than knock and look like the campus women who chased him, she decided to just write a dinner invitation note and stick it under his door. That would be fine with Uziah when she told him that David wasn't home. She hadn't forgotten that he made her heart race sitting near him in his jeep on the snowy ride to towns. However, she was not a man chaser or a harlot. A man must court her. Leaning on the dumpster outside Sergeant Pepper's back door, she wrote a note on a piece of lined school paper.

Dear Mr. Goldstein,

Uziah has pointed out to me that perhaps I offended you with my opinions a few months back when you gave us a most generous, snowy night ride into the city. I wish to apologize for letting offensive words out of my mouth concerning your nose

and life style. I should have just thought them.

Uziah has asked me to invite you to eat with us. Dinner tomorrow evening will be from seven till eight. After eight, Uziah must study as I will also.

At one minute past seven we will be seated. Be on time as we do not get up from the table to answer the door for late rude guests. Our Amish customs are somewhat different from yours. The guest brings a food item, usually dessert. Respecting our ways insures future invitations and our friendship. We understand college students as a whole are not prone to cook or bake. So, we have agreed English guests may bring a bag of cookies or something from the deli for dessert. I am sure the only thing in your apartment refrigerator is probably six day, left over pizza and soda. A bottle of Soda will be fine. I can add it to ice cream and make floats if necessary. The English take flowers to the hostess. We take food.

Just so you won't be disappointed, we are having macaroni and cheese and spinach for dinner. We, like most students, are on a budget. We do not have fathers to stick a silver spoon in our mouth. I only have opinions in mine.

Sincerely,

Hannah Zook

P.S. Bring your own chair. We don't have kitchen chairs yet. Please make sure your chair is clean!

Hannah was happy with her note. She had apologized and had at the same time intentionally tried to tee him off enough not to come. Uziah would be happy she had invited him. However, the secret sarcasms of her note would be hers to snicker about and share with Sergeant Pepper. She grinned sliding it under David's door and then quickly scurried away. She did not want an open confrontation with him.

The Zook's Secret

Later in the evening after Hannah's visit, Sergeant Pepper knocked on the Zook's door. Uziah answered

"Welcome friend, would you like to step in?"

"Could we speak out here, I do not wish Hannah to hear what we are speaking of."

"Is there a problem?" Uziah asked stepping out on to the third floor outdoor landing.

"There is a situation that I would like to discuss with you," replied sergeant Pepper waiting for Uziah to close the door.

"What might that be?"

"First, I want you to know that Hannah is very dear to me and I am going to be blunt. Should I ever catch wind that you have in any way mistreated, hit, or abused her; I will see to it that your male parts are cut off and stuffed down your throat. Do I make my point clear?"

Uziah grinned. He was being threatened by his two heads shorter, wimp of a landlord. He liked a man with guts. The English would say he had balls. His father back on the farm would say he was a goat with bull horns. Whatever he was, Uziah was impressed.

"Let me assure you Sergeant Pepper, you have got your point across. I assume that you have figured out our secret or you would not be approaching me in this manner? Is that the reason?"

"Yes, Hannah tells me all of her secrets." Pepper stated wondering what secret Uziah was referring to.

"We would like to keep it a secret that we are like brother and sister living together. It is safer for her if men think she is married."

"You and Hannah aren't . . .?" The Sergeant asked stumbling over his words.

"No, we are not married nor do we sleep together. We are cousins. However, your niece Endora is tempting the hell out of me. Her I would like to sleep with. That black stuff she puts on her lips brings out the worst in me. I can see myself licking the licorice black off. She is a sinful temptation that I am fighting. If it wasn't for Hannah, I would have slept with her the first night I arrived here when she asked me?"

"You and Endora?" Questioned a smiling Sergeant Pepper.

"Yes, don't tell Hannah I told you so. I am mad about the witch."

"This has to be the luckiest day of my life." Pepper stated slapping Uziah on the back. "You are welcome to my witch when you no longer need to pretend to be married. I hope Endora tempts the Hell out of you and you shout your love for her from the rooftops. When you do, I am next to howl like a wolf. I want Hannah to be mine."

"I am Hannah's guardian or surrogate father here. She is here for an education, not English suitors."

"I understand and am willing to wait till she is out of high school. After that, if she will have me, I will marry her and pay for her future college education. I have no objection to her being whatever she wishes. I am wealthy enough to put her thru medical school. I love Hannah and would like to grow old in her arms."

"Well, you better pray she doesn't think you wish to arm wrestle. You will be wearing an arm cast. A racing heart for Hannah should be thought about long and hard. She is a spit fire. I will not lie to you about that, Sergeant Pepper. She is a Pecker Hen that is driving me crazy and she is only my cousin. Bigger men than you have fallen by the way after trying to win her affections. She intimidates men."

"Perhaps the secret to winning with Hannah is always letting her be the winner. I might like a pretty little arm bender to intimidate and keep me in line." Sergeant Pepper replied.

"Neither of us can consider a mate till we are finished with our educations. Amish singles do not date at all. We only call on a girl when our heart races for her and we wish to suggest marriage. I am protecting Hannah with our pretend marriage from boys such as Mooch and David who do not understand that she may not date. Hannah is protecting me from Endora."

Sergeant Pepper replied. "I will wait for her to have the fun of her high school years. I would not deprive her of her youth like mine was deprived me. However, I wish to be the first in line as a suitor when the time is appropriate."

"You are approved of me and may call on Hannah the day after she graduates high school. However, you may not put your arm around her shoulders or kiss her. An Amish woman receives one kiss from her fiancé the night before they marry. You must ask me for that right after she graduates. Otherwise, I will send her back home to our community and you will not be allowed visiting privileges. Do you understand?" Asked Uziah eyeing the smiling wimp of a landlord.

"I want to marry her Uziah. I will play by your rules."

"She is one mouthy controlling little Amish woman. You will be sorry. She is likely to turn you over her knee and spank you like a child. You should run like hell. She has threatened to spank me and I am two heads taller than her."

"She has threatened to spank you?" Sergeant Pepper asked grinning.

"Sergeant Pepper, you have chosen one spit fire to race your heart for. At fifteen, she had so many fleeing suitors in the Amish community that her father ran out of choices for her. The men of our faith run for cover when her father brings up the subject of a suitor for Hannah. She looks sweet, but she is a force to deal with." Uziah stated stretching the truth to rib his landlord. Actually, he knew that Hannah was a sweet, naïve, and had a mouth that sometimes was open when it should be shut. She hadn't mastered the art of zipping her lip.

"I don't mind if she wears the pants in our family." Sergeant Pepper replied imagining Hannah in his jeans with a patched knee.

"I will remind you of those words three or so years from now." Laughed Uziah. He was pleased that Sergeant Pepper wanted Hannah.

Uziah knew Sergeant Pepper was respectable and faithful to his church. Hannah could adjust to his life and live well in the land of the English. Bell Ringers were protestant. That was acceptable with him. Hannah intended to live in the land of the English. The landlord would be a good choice and would be able to accompany Hannah on occasional visits to their families. He, however, had decided secretly not to return home to their Amish roots at all. He was considering wearing jeans after he graduated college. Right now, his and Hannah's Amish dress was making them money thru Zook's Place. He could not rock that boat. He and Hannah needed the money. When he went off to medical school, he would embrace the English way of dressing as well as many of their ways. He saw his family and the others of his community as willingly ignorant. He was secretly ashamed of being Amish and didn't understand the crazy wealthy who paid out the nose to eat with him and Hannah. He wanted a life intermingling with them.

"I understand that you are having a group of guests tonight for supper. I was wondering if I could beg for an invitation for myself and a lady friend. Her name is Bette and she is the food editor from the Sunday newspaper. Connections are important in life and I feel this woman could provide some good publicity for Zook's Place. Georgia Macon would give her eye teeth to be friends with her, but her hole of a restaurant is not considered fine dining class. I will bring a huge pan of pork chops and dressing."

"Sure, bring her and your pork chops! I wasn't particularly looking forward to macaroni and cheese. Will you be dating other women while you wait for Hannah to mature?"

"I won't be sleeping with them, if that is what you are asking. They will be friendship dates with no romantic involvements."

"That is good. I would hate to cut your male hood off and stuff it down your throat along with your pork chops and dressing. Do you understand?" Uziah replied intimidating his landlord. "If I hear of you sleeping with anyone, you automatically lose your chance to call on Hannah when the time comes."

"I think we have an understanding!" Sergeant Pepper replied with a serious face. "Faithfulness to Hannah is not a problem with me."

In the back of Sergeant Pepper's mind were the years he had slept with Georgia starting at fourteen. Intimacy with Hannah was frightening to him. His being raped by Georgia and her years of stalking him had emotionally crippled him. He secretly wondered if he could still perform as a man. He feared Hannah would see him as some sort of pervert and hold it against him. No one ever spoke of a man being a rape victim of a woman.

Stink Weed

Hannah's dinner invitation lay on the floor till the following day in David Goldstein's apartment. The apartment was a mess with papers and miscellaneous discarded notes from classes. The two occupants of the apartment were studying for mid-semester finals and just ignored the piece of notebook paper on the floor by the door. Now, it was three in the afternoon on Wednesday which was Friend night at the Zook's.

Mooch was busy grabbing a soda and a piece of six day old pizza from the refrigerator. He had an afternoon of serious studying to do before he headed up to the Zook's for dinner at seven. The rattle of keys in the front door sounded. The door opened and David entered and proceeded to remove his winter wear and then throw it on a chair along with his back pack. The apartment was just two blocks from the university campus, so he walked back and forth to classes.

David sat down on a straight chair by the door and proceeded to untie the laces of his black army boots. His father had given them to him the day he left for the university. They were Israeli and he was proud of them. His father had been a member of the

Israeli Army before migrating to the United States and becoming a Rabbi. As he kicked the snow laden boots off, he spotted a sheet of notebook paper on the floor with boot prints on it. Apparently he and Mooch had stepped on it several times entering and exiting the apartment. He picked it up with the intention of throwing it away. Out of curiosity, he unfolded it to make sure it wasn't class notes that he or Mooch needed for their studying. He was missing two days of notes from his Biology class. He was sure they were somewhere in the apartment's mess. Reading the note on notebook paper, he began to curse and kick the chair leg with his stocking foot forgetting he had removed his boot. Immediately, he went to yelling in pain and hopped about on one foot.

"What has got your shorts in a wad?" Inquired Mooch closing the refrigerator door and biting into a cold piece of dried up pizza.

"Has anyone knocked?' Asked David still cringing, standing on one foot, and holding his other in pain.

"I don't think so. However, I was soaking earlier in the tub and reading my sociology textbook. Is something wrong?"

"What's wrong? That damn Amish female jerk from the third floor dump has dared to invite me to dinner and insult me with her invitation. Here read this. I am going to burn her ass if I ever get a chance. I don't see what Uziah sees in her. I have run into him a couple of times on campus and he seems nice enough."

"Hannah insulted you? You are reading her wrong man. She is one of the sweetest women you will ever meet. If it wasn't for Uziah, I would trip over myself trying to be first in line to date her. Have you seen her dimples?" He asked taking the note from David and proceeded to read it.

"Yes, I have seen her damn dimples. Her damn beauty will deceive you. She is a bitch!" David retorted.

Mooch read the note and then went to laughing. "I told her at one of the first dinner parties you called her homely and a female jerk. I have got to give her credit. She is one cool female warrior. She has waited till the time was right to lay your ass low."

"She has insinuated that I don't have the sense to show up at a dinner party on time and with a gift for the hostess. She has even insulted the six day old pizza in our refrigerator!"

"It is that old? Shit!" Mooch said walking over to the trash can and pitching what was left of the piece he was eating and then spit a couple times half gagging.

"She has used Uziah's request for me to be invited to dinner to spear me with her forked tail. He probably doesn't realize he is married to an imp from Hell."

"Oh… we have gone from female jerk to bitch and now she is an imp. I know what your problem is. You are attracted to her and pissed that she is not obtainable and doesn't see you as a hunk?"

"Shut up Mooch before I throw your ass out." Then he asked sheepishly. "What is the protocol for their dinner parties?"

"You are going?"

"Damn right I am! You are looking at Uziah's new best friend. I will look for opportunities to return her insults."

"Man, I wouldn't mess with her. Uziah is a full head taller than you and has muscles from chopping wood and doing farm labor. He could snap you like a toothpick." Mooch replied.

"It might be worth getting snapped." David growled.

"Don't say I didn't warn you. However, I have already filled the slot as Uziah's best friend. I have been there from the beginning." Mooch added to annoy him.

"Where do I find a homemade pie or cake around campus? I need a dessert quick and a bouquet of flowers, stink week if I can find them."

"Give Endora a ten spot and ask her to bake you a cake from one of those box mixes. It only takes about an hour. She may have a mix in her kitchen cupboard. Just make sure it is chocolate."

"Why chocolate?"

"Girls love chocolate, stupid. They eat it at certain times if you get my drift. Chocolate calms their craziness. Hannah's note sounds like she has a current onset of the crazies."

"Oh… You think...? Never mind," he replied. "I have got to run down and see if Endora will do it. I wonder how long this note has been here."

"I remember stepping on it once yesterday." Mooch replied sitting down at the kitchen table and opening one of his textbooks.

"Damn, if I had seen it yesterday I would have had time to write a nasty note back and turn the invitation down. It is rude to call and say you aren't coming hours before dinner. The hostess is usually already preparing the food."

"Suck it up then. It is your apartment and your invitation. You should have picked up the damn thing yesterday and read it." Mooch added laughing. It was rare to see his friend David flustered, especially by a girl. He was popular and never lacked a date for any event or the weekends. His buddy was considered a hunk on campus, plus he was rich. That alone was a chic magnet. Now there was one chic that didn't cater to him. It was great.

David exited the apartment in his stocking feet slamming the door behind him.

Mooch sat at the table grinning and counting, "One . . . two . . . three . . ."

The door opened and David walked back in sheepishly stating, "I forgot my boots."

"Hannah is that number ten that you always have claimed is out there somewhere and you are flustered because you will never score with her. She is way out of your league."

"Damn you, Mooch. Don't kid me about her. She makes me curse and act like a mad man. Yes, I am attracted to her. However, she is not Jewish and I know what my boundaries are. I am a couple years away from my Rabbi studies."

"Do you, as a Jew, go to confessional like we Catholics do for lusting after a married woman? I have watched you peep at her when she passes our apartment front window."

"Damn it. I am Wailing Wall bound. Do not tell my parents about her, please. I am a good Jewish boy in my mother's eyes. She would have a cow if she thought I was interested in an Amish backwoods protestant girl."

"Forget your mother. It is Uziah that is your problem. He beat you to her." Mooch laughed loving that the campus hunk had found a woman he couldn't have.

"One hour, Mooch. They were married possibly an hour before I picked them up out on the highway the night of the blizzard. God must be mad at me or something. I haven't been to overly serious about my religious studies. Maybe He is getting even with me. It is as though God took the most beautiful woman in the world and let you sniff her cologne to the point of intoxication and then gave her to someone else. I want more than just a sniff of her."

"I can see you now, you will spend a life moaning the blues and crying over the female jerk you were once in love with who loved another." Mooch stated in a teasing voice.

"Can it Mooch?" David stated loudly in an annoyed voice.

"Don't get your feathers ruffled. I find her rather attractive myself."

"I am going to that dinner party, be the perfect guest, and wait for my chance to get even with her. I will find a way."

Finding that the conversation was losing its amusement, Mooch sauntered over to the kitchen cabinets and started searching for something to snack on.

David picked up his cell phone and called Endora and talked her into baking him a cake for a twenty.

CHAPTER SEVEN

Georgia the Predator

Whistling and excited about his future with Hannah, Sergeant Pepper returned to his apartment and entered his front door. He was going to make himself a special cup of hot tea and then call his friend Melvin who was in the diamond trade. He was going to ask him to keep an eye out for a special ring for Hannah. He was going to sell one of his rental houses and buy her an engagement ring that would let the world know she was taken. He planned on spending a hundred grand on it. The dumpy four hundred dollar ring he had in his drawer would never do.

Sergeant Pepper had come to grips with being older than Hannah. He was not a predator. Loving her was the reason he wanted to be with her. To prove it, he was willing to wait till she matured. That made the difference. He would let her enjoy all the years of her education and then marry her when she was twenty two. Age didn't mean so much, once you became an adult. He was sure she would feel the same. They were meant to be together.

After closing the front door, he headed back to his kitchen

to put on a tea kettle of water to heat. This occasion called for a little secret indulgence. He would retrieve his hidden honey bear and celebrate with a special cup of Hannah forbidden tea with raw honey in it. He would brush his teeth afterward in case Hannah showed up for any reason. He was sure she would discipline him, possibly spank him, if she caught him with his addiction. Like an alcoholic, he had to keep his bottle hidden. He was a closeted Bee spit drinker. As he stepped into the kitchen, he was startled and came to a quick halt. He closed his eyes briefly, shaking his head.

"What are you doing here, Georgia?" He asked in disgust. He had a restraining order against her for stalking.

Georgia was the owner of the Pancake Emporium, a local lower end restaurant. She was also a secret predator of young boys and Sergeant Pepper had been her first. He was fourteen when he entered the back door of her café and asked if he could work for a plate of food. He worked all right. For years she threatened to call the police and social services on him if he didn't do what she asked. She had been almost twenty five at the time and he was a young, stupid boy who had run away from foster care. He ran her dishwasher and kept her bed warm till he was seventeen. When he grew up and walked out on her, she couldn't handle his rejection and had stalked him ever since. He was thirty-five now and she was slipping over the hill towards fifty. She was a perverted female predator; a wild dog with a bone that she wouldn't let go.

"I am checking to see if there is a woman in your bed. You know that I am not going to stand for that. Another woman just is not in the cards. We are destined to be together. I am ready to retire and spend some of your money for a change. You owe me. I fed you for almost three years when you had no place to go."

"I don't know what it is going to take to make you understand that I don't want you and never intend to sleep with you ever again. I was a kid and you were a predator, Georgia. That isn't love. If I could go back, I would head straight back to my foster home and yell rape. I was a child that you took advantage of."

"You got what every fourteen or fifteen year old boy dreams about. I didn't hear any complaints back then. You were a willing bed partner."

"You used me, Georgia. I missed out on high school, being with kids and dating girls my age. You robbed me of my youth. I was a dishwasher and a victim. Now get out of my apartment before I call the cops and have you thrown out. Go play with your current boy toy. I am sure that you have one stashed somewhere. I am a grown man and no longer the age you like them."

"We are destined to be together. I knew it when I saw your fourteen year old face peeping in the back door of the Pancake Emporium. I have no intention of letting you have a lady friend. I will harass whoever she is till she dumps you." She stated not getting up from the table in a defiant manner.

"Not this time, Georgia. I have a reason to stop your interference. Yes, I have met someone and I plan to marry her. I am a rich man and willing to move half way around the world with her if I need to. Your restaurant and stalking days are about over. The cheap ass restaurant you own is bellying up and you will not have the money to follow me. If I were guessing, you might have a couple thousand dollars stashed somewhere and that is all. You have car payments and promises made to boys you can't keep. Boys are going to laugh ten years from now when you try to seduce them. You will have to pay for guys like Mooch to service your wrinkles and sags. Look in the mirror, age has caught up with you. Your reign as the pancake house queen, secret rapist is about over. I should have gone to the police when I was young. I was naïve and stupid. I am not that any more. I will burn your ass if you try anything with me or my lady friend. I am buying her a hundred thousand dollar engagement ring. Eat your heart out!"

"You will regret these words, Pepper. You are mine and will always be mine." She stated rising from the table with fire in her eyes.

"You don't want me, Georgia. You just can't stand it that I walked on you. You are used to dumping the boys when you get what you want from them or they don't please you. I am the only one that walked and didn't believe your lies of promised educations and starts in life. The bell Ringer's gave me my start, not you. I had seventy five dollars when I went to live in their mission. My will is made out leaving everything, all seven million in assets to them, should anything happen to me?"

"You didn't mind the free meals you begged off of me once upon a time."

"I worked my ass off free on a dishwasher afraid that you were going to send me back to foster care or call the police on me. I crawled in your bed and did what you wanted trying to survive in an adult world. I was a naïve child. You are a predator that will one day get what is coming to you. Now get out of my apartment and don't come back. Who I am, I have created since you, not with you."

Georgia Macon, a petite one hundred pound older woman, stood and hurried towards him to slap him. Grabbing her arm, he then took her physically by the back neck of her shirt, pulled her screaming and kicking to the back door, opened it and threw her outside and slammed the door. He was a little man, but his adrenalin was pumping.

Georgia was red faced, cursing, and angry to her core as she picked herself up off the ground. Physically she couldn't do anything to Pepper, but she would get even. Perhaps she would use her pea shooter on him. No one was wearing a hundred thousand dollar engagement ring except her. "You just think you have won today, Pepper!" She muttered.

On the third floor of Sergeant Pepper's apartment complex, Hannah took a short break at the back window of their apartment by the twin bed where Uziah slept. It over looked the alley and back door of Sergeant Pepper. The apartment window was closed preventing sound. However, she could see Georgia below in the alley shaking her fist at Sergeant Pepper's back door. She told herself that Sergeant Pepper had possibly caught her peeping. She would ask him about it tomorrow. Sergeant Pepper was a good looking man. She couldn't blame Georgia for secretly peeping.

Her attention moved to watch Chim open the back door of the apartment house behind her and take a black bag of trash to the dumpster. She watched as he eyed the sky and the tree in the yard of his unit. He was always looking for something or so it seemed. He was an extremely good looking man, but odd. Uziah had said that when he spoke to him, on more than one occasion, he did not answer back. She knew what his problem was. However, she couldn't convince Uziah of it.

Uziah was busy with a last bit of studying. They had guests coming and she was beginning to cook. She had decided to bring up the subject of Chim again.

"Uziah," called Hannah. "The man in white across the alley, do you think that we should invite him to one of our dinners? He seems so lonely and I never see anyone with him."

"He doesn't answer me when I speak with him, Hannah. He plays with his fingers and points to the sky, the trees, and birds.

I am thinking that he is a God's Will child of another religion of some sort. I am sure that he probably has the mind of a seven or eight year old child. He may be deaf. I don't know."

"We were lonely when we arrived in the world of the English. We have made many friends and he has none. I watch him thru my bedroom window. He seems to always be watching the birds thru a pair of binoculars."

"That is not good, Hannah. Make sure you close your curtain at night. He may peep at you. You are different and beautiful. He might get obsessed with you. Men get by with sordid deeds here in the land of the English. I would not want you to be a victim."

"I really think we should invite him, if nothing else out of a spirit of charity."

"The answer is no. I had my fill of caring for my little sister and brother when I was on the farm. I am not in the mood to waste my time on someone like that. I want my college years to be filled with intelligent people and intelligent conversation. Our college years will be short. There will be plenty of time for God's Will children when I become a doctor. Till then, I want a life not burdened with them. Many girls of our Amish community would not let me call because of my mentally deficient brother and sister. They saw me as less of a man. I have not forgotten. I do not want to be seen around campus as a man who hangs out with the lesser smart of the campus. It will be the intelligent and rich of the campus that will help me get where I am going. I do not want to associate for now with God's Will children. Our parents in their ignorance produced our mentally challenged siblings. Let them take care of them. I have chosen a better life for myself. You should look at it the same way. I am sure that some of the better Amish family boys never once called on you."

"I respect your decision. He just seems so lonely. I watch him at night from my window. He sits at a table on the third floor across from me and draws birds. Sometimes he will hold one of his drawings up to the window for me to see. That is something my two little brothers would do. I feel guilty cooking for so many knowing he is lonely. I am sure he has plenty to eat, but his eyes say he has no one to play with."

"You cannot take in every stray cat or dog that comes along, Hannah. He is a stray. I want a pedigreed life, not one filled with strays."

"Would it be wrong if I drew a picture of a bird and held it up to the window in an attempt to communicate with him?"

"God says we are not to make graven images. It would be wrong and a sin. I am struggling with science class where I must draw diagrams and pictures of human organs. I am torn in my belief about drawing things."

"We may have to alter our beliefs, Uziah. As you have said, we now live in their world. I cannot communicate our God to him with words. I may have to draw birds."

"I forbid you to do so, Hannah. I do not want that man in this apartment or approaching us when we are on the outside. I do not wish to be seen with him or be judged by him as I was at home. Do you understand?"

"Yes Uziah." Hannah replied sadly as she watched the man in white return into his apartment complex.

The Toe Jam Creepers

Recycling became a way of life at the Zook's and they made many friends on campus who were also interested in the Subject. By the end of two months, Hannah and Uziah had all the friends that their friend night dinner table could hold. Mooch became Uziah's best friend and helped him often when he found something in the dumpster that he couldn't get out alone. The latest was a dilapidated computer desk which Uziah desperately needed. After retightening all of the screws and bolts, Uziah painted it a chocolate brown to hide all the scrapes, gouges, and cigarette burns on it. Also, he had found and redone a small chest of drawers for Hannah that was missing one drawer. Hannah's pride and joy was a little rocker that had one arm missing. It was painted white and placed in her tiny bedroom beneath the eve for her to sit and sew in. Slowly they were putting together a life for themselves. Each piece of recycled furniture or plastic item became their treasures and heirlooms.

Mooch Pearson was standing on the second floor walkway taking a break from his studying. His grades were important if he wanted to get into medical school and he didn't slack in that department. He knew that if he had a future, it depended on him being a doctor. One day he would get too old to be a gigolo, a male escort. He heard the third floor door open above him. There was only one apartment up there so he knew that it was one of the Zooks making their way down the stairs. He waited in hopes it was Hannah.

Mooch had all the paying women that he could date between classes plus Georgia. However, the one girl he would like to have a date with was Hannah and she was married. He purposely stayed on friend night and helped her clean up and do the dishes. He just wanted to be near her. Until she came along, he hated women, especially all the ones who paid him. He had been with too many women and he was burnt out.

A regular part- time job could not pull in the money Mooch needed to pay for college and his future medical school bills. His parents were dead and had left him absolutely nothing. He wanted to try to make it as far as possible without grants or student loans to have to pay back. When he became a doctor he planned to start a new life and never look back. Someday, he would kiss the rich old hags like Georgia goodbye. He looked forward to telling them to lose his number and get lost. If he ever married, it would be to someone respectable like Hannah. She was his dream girl.

Leaning on the walkway railing, he waited. It was a snowy day in March. He needed a coat, but he was only going to be on the balcony for a few minutes. He had some heavy studying to do. He was taking a five minute breather. He had to study early because later in the day he was going to the Zooks for dinner.

"Mooch," called Hannah as she stepped down on the second floor walkway from the flight of the stairs to the third floor. "What are you doing out here on this snow laden walkway in your stocking feet? You will catch a death of cold. A runny nose and cold feet will never get you a girlfriend." She laughed eyeing his damp gray socks as she walked up. "Some day your wife is going to chew on you for blackening the bottom of your socks. Turn one up here so I can look." She stated.

Loving the attention he was getting from her, he obliged and turned the bottom of one of his sock feet up so she could look. Today was kickback day so he had on sweats and a pair of athletic socks that had a couple of holes in them. He saved his good ones for the nights he was making his living as a lady's man.

"Those are awful!" she stated pointing to the bottom. "I see crumbs of what looks like bread and I can smell an odor that has to be the Toe Jam Virus."

"I am kicking back. These are my comfortable clothes. I am only going to be out here for a moment or so. The socks will dry out. I have been careful where I have stepped and have avoided the heavy snow spots." He replied.

"I want you to bring every pair of your socks to my apartment later when I get back. You are a disgrace to me as your friend. Knowing you have holes in your socks will drive me crazy. I will mend all of them and bleach the pair you have on till the stains are out. I must insist that you buy a pair of house slippers or mop your floors. I will not have a friend of mine having dirty feet. You could catch something serious running around barefoot like that with holes in your socks." She replied.

"And just what do you think I might catch?" He asked delighted that she was taking time for him.

"The Toe Jam Creeper," she replied. "From the smell coming from your feet, I would say it has already got you. Your toes could fall off, one at a time."

"You think I have a foot disease called the Toe Jam creeper? Is it some Amish form of athlete's feet? I want your professional opinion on the condition of my feet." He stated totally amused. Her dimples were winking at him. He would love to take the tip of his finger and touch one of them. However, he didn't dare. She was married and Uziah was his friend.

"You must stop and consider where you live." She replied in a serious voice taking one finger and pointing to the open doorway and the unkempt apartment. "David's apartment is a crash pad for a sordid group of individuals who probably pick their noses, their ears, pimples, or who knows what and throws it on the floor. Then, think about the roaches running across the floor at night pooping everywhere. Also consider the dirty bottoms of crashers who have sat on the floor for the last six months or more. You could die from some other crasher's filth. I will not have you dying or getting ill from the Toe Jam Creeper."

Mooch went to laughing. "I will never sit on David's floor again or walk barefoot. You have made your point. I do not wish to die from the Toe Jam Creeper and I am lucky to have you for a friend."

"Good. Now you bring me your socks later. Be prepared to stay for an hour. I plan to soak your feet in bleach water to make sure you don't catch a creeper living in David's apartment. I can't have you, my favorite right hand man dying from the Toe Jam Creeper."

"If you weren't married, Hannah, I think I would marry you and the two of us could become doctors curing the world's Toe Jam problems. We would make wild love on the high seas and cure virus infested villages on shore. I would be Dr. Mooch Martin and you would be Dr. Hannah Martin head of the World Health Organization and captain of a huge floating hospital ship. We would make love and cure diseases."

Hannah smiled. "For now, you need Doctor Hannah Zook to keep you from dying from Toe Jam Creeper."

"I am your patient, Dr. Hannah. Love me and cure me. I am willing."

"I love you just enough to wash your socks. A loving wife might find your socks disgusting and tell you to wash them yourself. It is better to have a loving friend as a Pecker Hen. Uziah says I am a relentless one and that I am hopeless in ever having a man love me. He tells me sometimes that he does not like me."

"Uziah is wrong, Hannah. You are a loving Hen Pecker that your husband doesn't see as his treasure."

"I have never been a man's treasure. I am what I am, a Pecker Hen. I have just now pecked you. I am hopeless. However, I do care about you and will not have you being a Toe Jam Creeper man." She laughed.

"Are you really going to bleach my feet?" He asked amused.

"Dr. Hannah takes you on as a patient today. I will cure you of your sins and the Toe Jam Creeper, or die doing it." She replied with a serious look on her face. "I am also going to check your head for lice when you come for your feet bleaching."

"Head lice?" He shot back in a surprised questioning voice. "I am going to be a doctor, Hannah. I can assure you that I don't have head lice."

"David's apartment is a low class, never been cleaned, dog house for strays who have not a place to bathe or lay their heads. I mustn't let you my friend be affected by the environment you must live in."

Mooch succumbed to the power of suggestion and reached up and scratched his head. Just thinking about the possibility of head lice in David's apartment made him cringe and then scratch his head again. Hannah was right. The bachelor pad was dirty and had used furniture found on curbs. He scratched a second time. The power of suggestion had got to him. He had never given head lice a thought till she said something. Suddenly, the nape of his neck began to itch. Then, he began to itch in other hairy areas including his underarms. He started scratching like crazy.

"See what I mean? You have the creepy crawler head lice as well as the Toe Jam Creeper. You are on my list for feet bleaching and a shampoo for head lice. The way you are scratching in unmentionable places, I think I will put you in my tub like the dog back on the farm and do a thorough job. You are my friend. I must cure you!"

"What are you going to use to cure my head and feet?" He asked suddenly wanting her to cure him.

"It will take an Amish salve like mixture made from black walnut hulls to get rid of the lice. Your scalp skin might look a little strange for a few days as will your skin in unmentionable places. Walnut hulls are like black licorice. They will stain your skin. However, it is worth it. You don't need little bug insects sucking your blood and eating your skin."

"Oh God, I know I have head lice. Do you want to look now so I can take care of it?"

"I will look one hour from now when I return. I am on my way to the market. Do not scratch till I return. You don't want to get the creepy crawlers running all over your body like it was a sporting event." She replied pausing and grinning at his scratching. "I must put you on my Pecker Hen list. I insist on keeping you bug and creeper free as long as you must live in David's apartment. It is my Christian duty."

Mooch grinned as he scratched. He loved the way she expressed herself. She was different from any woman that he had ever known and she cared about him. He could secretly see himself growing old in her arms. She wasn't a piece of loose crap like most of the coeds and clients he interacted with. He was fascinated with her and wanted her. In his mind and heart, he could see her as his wife. She was the woman that every man dreams of meeting. However, she was married and Uziah was his friend. He would definitely take an hour from his studies later to have his feet bleached and his head shampooed. He would take Hannah's love in any fashion that she was willing to give it to him. He was sure that Uziah didn't realize what a treasure he was married to. He knew that Uziah was cold and indifferent to Hannah; as well as not sleeping in her bed.

Chocolate Cake Apology

It was six in the evening. David was pacing back and forth in front of his window arguing with himself about going to dinner. He didn't have a dessert. He had phoned Endora and asked her if she would be willing to throw together one of those box mixes. However, he hadn't heard back from her. He was totally pissed at himself for wanting to go and pissed with his crasher of a roommate for falling in love with Hannah. He found her first out in the blizzard. He was pissed with Uziah for eloping with her just minutes before he met her. He was in a foul mood.

Walking over to the cupboards, he opened every door looking for something that could be feasibly passed off as dessert. All he saw was multiple bags of poorly closed stale chips and microwave pop corn. He was doomed and the mouth from the third floor was right. All there was in his refrigerator was leftover pizza and beer. Soda floats weren't even an option. He should have got our earlier in the day and bought ice cream or something. He thought for sure that Endora would come thru for him. He was stewing mad.

"There is nothing in there, man. Someone needs to grocery shop or order a fresh pizza." Stated Mooch as he straightened the collar under his jacket and then started to buckle the belt in his black dress pants.

David turned from the refrigerator and was surprised to see Mooch freshly showered and wearing a new dinner jacket. "Where are you going in your monkey suit?"

"Hannah and Uziah invited me for dinner."

"Won't you be a little over dressed?" David asked eyeing his friend who had on sweats and a holey T-shirt earlier.

"You are expected to wear your best when you dine with the Zook's. Hannah wears her best dress, her Sunday one. Uziah wears his best. This is my best. Georgia bought it for me so I wouldn't look like a low class heathen on dinner invitations to the Zooks. She has a new black cocktail dress and spikes to go with it. We don't want to lose our spot at the Zook's dinner parties."

"You have got to be kidding?" David shot back in a sarcastic questioning voice.

"No, I am not kidding. Dinner at the Zook's is casual black tie on week nights and serious black tie on the weekends. You had better get the lead out and get dressed if you are going. Georgia is driving over and we will walk up together. She purchased and had us two folding chairs painted with the restaurant logo on them. Everyone is required to bring their own folding chair. It is part of the mystique."

"If I go, I will go just as I am. My dad's army pants and a black turtleneck are my dinner out duds. Campus girls love me in this outfit."

"Wear what you want. However, with that low class look, one dinner invitation will be all you probably will ever get. The Zook's are fast becoming the upper crust of campus life and the city's social scene. I feel quite fortunate to be their friend. Georgia has spent three hours in the beauty shop for tonight."

"The Zook's are no one. If I go, I will go just like I am. They are country bumpkins, not upper crust. Hannah probably couldn't hold a decent dinner conversation if she wanted to. She is an idiot."

"Suit yourself. You are the one that is going to look like a country bumpkin. How would Hannah put it, a country bumpkin with a big ugly nose?"

"You are asking for it Mooch. I have a Jewish nose and it fits well in my world. It gets me more attention from the girls than your skinny snout."

A knock came at the door. Mooch hurried to the door thinking it might be Georgia.

"May I come in?" Asked their landlord carrying a long metal pan covered securely with foil. "Look at you, Hannah is going to love that Jacket."

"Thanks Pepper, you look pretty sharp yourself."

David hurried from the refrigerator in the kitchen to the apartment entrance.

"What is in the pan?" Asked David hoping.

"This is your cake for the Dinner Party. It is chocolate as you requested. Endora says the cover is not to be taken off until it is to be served or the icing will dissolve. She was adamant about the instructions. Do not take the foil off the cake, just hand it to Hannah or Uziah to store till time to serve."

"Tell Endora she is a lifesaver." David replied reaching for the foil wrapped pan.

"That will be twenty bucks, David. I believe that is what you promised Endora. She said not to give you the cake till you paid for it."

"Right...," said David digging in his hip pocket for his wallet. After paying Pepper, he set the pan of cake down on their coffee table till he was ready to go and then turned back to Pepper. "Do you have a dinner date or something? You look like you might be headed out to that favorite Jazz club of yours."

"I have a date with Bette Jacobs, the food editor from the Sunday news."

"You have a date with the reporter that critiques restaurants and covers the social world of the city?"

"That is Bette. I have got to run. She is waiting for me down in my apartment. We have got to get the lead out. She is interviewing tonight one of the hottest new couples in the city's social scene. They are having a dinner party and we can't be late." Sergeant Pepper replied sticking Endora's twenty in his billfold.

"You look sharp. Whose party are you going to?" Mooch asked.

"The Zook's," Sergeant Pepper answered simply.

"You have got to be kidding?" Shot back David.

"I am a realtor with a wealthy client list. Since the Zook's have moved into my building, I am bombarded with the rich and the famous of the city trying to persuade me to procure them an invitation to one of their dinners. You boys see me as your lowly landlord. I am more than that. I mingle with the city's upper crust. Bette literally begged me to get her an invitation. She offered me five hundred dollars to be my date at the Zook's tonight. Can you top that, Mooch?" Sergeant Pepper asked winking at Mooch. He knew what Mooch did for a living.

"No, Sergeant Pepper, I can't top that one tonight. I am being paid a new dinner jacket worth two hundred bucks for my services. You are three up on me."

"Who is going to be there tonight?" Asked David suddenly taking an interest in the couple that he had called country bumpkins.

"The mayor and his wife, Bette and I, Mooch and his date, and Professor Ann Newberg head of the pre-med program undoubtedly will come with the men's dean. I will give up my seat at the table next to Bette and will play my sax for entertainment. Hannah will make me a carry-out plate for later. Mooch may have to give up his seat and become a butler for the night and serve. Seats at the Zook's table are coveted. We of their original group of friends realize that and step aside letting someone have our chairs if needed. We are lucky to be there."

"I will believe it when I see it!" David retorted sarcastically.

Sergeant Pepper left.

"Why aren't you taking dessert?" David asked Mooch as he was preparing to leave.

"I dropped off chocolate ice cream earlier in the day. Hannah was thrilled. Georgia sent over some hot fudge sauce to go with it. We are covered for the evening."

"Are you in love with Hannah, Mooch? I just want to know."

"I love her enough to choose her if the chips were down and I saw you hurting her. I would dump you and sleep in the Pancake Emporium's storage closet if I had to. Yes, I love Hannah!"

"She has got to you. My roommate is a traitor."

"Hannah is every man's dream girl, the one that you would like to take home to meet your mother. My mom passed away five years ago. If she were alive, I would want to take a Hannah home to meet her." Mooch replied as he took one last look in a small mirror that hung by the door to see if his hair was presentable.

"Not my Jewish mother, she would have heart failure." David replied as Mooch opened the door and then left.

There was no time to waste. It was five minutes to seven. It was either go or not go. David was down to the line of making a decision. Grabbing the foil covered rectangle cake pan in one hand, and an odd chair from his kitchen, he let himself out of his apartment and hurried clumsily up the stairs with both hands full. Once on the third floor balcony, he immediately knocked. He knew he would be late if he didn't. He took a deep breath in case it was her that opened the door.

He was surprised when Ohm Oto, a Tibetan student, opened the door and pointed the way in to him.

"What are you doing here?" He asked in a whisper to his wealthy jogging buddy who was wearing a long red Buddhist robe of some sort.

"I am the doorman tonight. There is not room for me at the table. Hannah will send me home a plate later. Senator Bailey is going to be here. He is expected to run in the next presidential election. I wouldn't miss this opportunity. I love politics. It is a rare opportunity for an ordinary man like me to be included in a dinner party with a senator, much less a future presidential candidate."

"Since when have you started running around in red robes? As I recall from our year of friendship, you are a business major not a religion major."

"When you dine with the Zook's, you are supposed to wear

your Sunday best. This would be my Sunday best if I were a religious man. I had my parents mail it to me from California. Our family is Buddhist!"

"I see," David stated sitting his chair down upon entering.

"What is your religion?" Ohm asked grinning. "Is what you have on your Sunday best?"

David looked down at himself a little embarrassed. He could tell from those present he was very much under dressed. He was going to stand out like a sore thumb in his army pants, black combat boots, and black turtleneck. He should have listened to Mooch. "I am a Jewish soldier who must work and defend God's people on the Sabbath. This is my Jerusalem Sunday look." He replied thinking quick to save himself from being totally embarrassed.

"You may have to explain your look. Everyone else is pretty much in Black Tie."

"I see they are," David replied as he glanced about the room. Sergeant Pepper had on some type of navy blue dress suit from the Bell Ringer's Army. Endora had on a long black witch's robe. He recognized Georgia Macon from the Pancake Emporium. She had on what looked like a brand new black cocktail dress. Everyone in the room was well dressed. Holding his cake, he saw Uziah heading his way.

"Welcome friend," stated Uziah. "I have hoped all day that you would come! It is time for Hannah and me to repay your generous ride on the snowy night of our flight into English Egypt. What have you in the foil covered pan?"

"Chocolate cake, don't take the foil off till time to serve, It has fragile icing on it that air will affect."

"I will tell Hannah. She is in her bedroom straightening her white cap. She swears it sits crooked on her head that she somehow starched and ironed it wrong. I do not see it. Of course women have eyes for details. She tells me if my beard is a quarter inch too long. I am Amish hen pecked!"

"You do have a hen who likes to peck!" Replied David sarcastically. "Where should I place my chair?"

"You will sit next to Hannah. You are a new guest and that is appropriate. At an Amish table, the men sit on one side and the women the other. We do not sit side by side as you English do. That would be inappropriate touching. Hannah will sit on the end and you on the men's side next to her."

"Will I be safe next to your hen on the end that pecks?" David asked grinning.

"She only annoys me!" Laughed Uziah. "Everyone thinks she is perfect who don't have to live with her. I have to ask seven days in advance if I wish to be in her bed and also not dumpster dive equally as long."

"You are kidding?" Asked David considering the odd remark.

"No, it is the Amish way. Women say when and where. Sometimes I like the where." Uziah retorted grinning and thinking about the wonderful fabricated story he had just told that had David's attention. The English were so gullible. However, he couldn't let Hannah catch him saying anything like that. He would be mopping floors and cleaning the toilet bowl for months and would be sleeping in the dumpster till she forgave him. They were just cousins, but he had learned not to cross her in the months they had shared an apartment. She was a spitfire. He felt sorry for her. He was sure that she would die an old maid and that even Sergeant Pepper would not want her, after he got to know her. She was hopeless.

"You let her get by with that?" David asked sure that Hannah had to be the biggest young bitch on the whole campus.

"She says I smell from dumpster diving and it takes seven days to air me out like a quilt." He replied lying. He had a husband image to maintain. "She is Amish and rules the house. I rule the barn, or dumpster."

"You are pathetic, Uziah. Never let a woman have the upper hand. A man should head the house as well as the dumpster. I will marry a Jewish woman who will follow my lead."

"Thank God you want a Jewish woman!" Stated Hannah walking up behind him.

Spinning around, he faced her. Just the sound of her voice behind him threatened his existence. He was like a soldier turning to confront his enemy. He quickly eyed her. She had on a neatly ironed Amish gray dress and looked the same as the first night he saw her. She was the prettiest damn dimpled angel he had ever seen. There wasn't anything about her that he didn't like to look at including her black socks and shoes. He could feel his heart racing in his chest and he couldn't make his mouth work.

"Thank God you are not Jewish." He replied.

"Thank God you are not Amish. We are a non- violent people. We do not go to war." She stated eyeing his military clothing. "Have you chosen not to wear your Sunday best to my table?"

"This is my Sunday best. It is a Jewish Soldier's pants and boots. They belonged to my father. A Jewish soldier guards Israel on the Sabbath. I am wearing my father's Sabbath best when he was a soldier. He is now a Rabbi." David quickly replied trying to give a reason for his being under dressed and the object of her scorn.

"It appears to me that you have not seen my invitation as a need to clean up or dress appropriately. A Jewish woman might let you get by sitting in garments of war at her table. An Amish woman would give you a bath, teach you not to war, and see that you were properly dressed for dinner." Hannah shot back starting a new war with him. She had hoped he wouldn't come.

"As a Jewish man, I would have to say that you are the one that is poorly dressed for dinner. One section on the back of your dress has not been ironed. Only an unintelligent farm girl would do such a thing."

"I did iron the back of my dress," she stated twisting to take a look.

"I made you look. I got you." David stated laughing. "I win this round."

"It is rude to make fun of a woman. I do hope you have washed your hands and don't have any man's blood on you. I can smell the stench coming from your clothes and hear the dirt coming from your mouth. I should take you in our bathroom, dunk you, and soap out your mouth while I am at it."

"Go right ahead if you think you are big enough!" He stated leaning in to her and whispering. "The war is on between us. I intend to make Uziah my best friend."

"Uziah can be friends with whoever he chooses. I do not have to like them, nor do I have to cook for them. Those on the dinner invitation list are my choice." She stated whispering back.

"In case you haven't looked in the mirror, your cap is on

crooked. I am the only one on your invitation list that is honest enough to tell you so." He whispered knowing he had got her. Uziah had told him she had been fussing with her cap.

"What?" She asked and then hurried off to take a look at herself in the mirror.

David watched as she checked her cap in a mirror by the door. She had to be the most beautiful woman that he had every met and at the same time the most annoying. She probably could go toe to toe with his mouthy Jewish mother and win. God forbid!

"Isn't she wonderful?" Mooch asked walking up beside Goldstein. I heard your war of words with her. Don't let Uziah catch you disrespecting her. He is a big farm boy with muscles, if you know what I mean."

"She brings out the worst in me. I don't know why." Stated David.

After a few moments of mingling, Hannah rejoined the crowd after taking off her cap and putting it back on and this time definitely getting it a bit crooked. Being flustered will do that too you.

"Hey Sweetie," Georgia greeted when she joined the group just before sitting down to dinner. "Do you know Mr. Goldstein?"

"Good evening Mr. Goldstein." Hannah said extending her hand to shake. "I don't believe I have had the opportunity to greet you properly. However, I did meet a jerk at the door earlier who looked a lot like you."

"Good evening, Mrs. Zook. I left a special dessert in the kitchen. I would have brought you flowers as well, if it were summer. I believe snap dragons might be your favorite. I also know that you are fond of stink weed."

"Perhaps we share a love of snapdragons and the scent of stink weed, Mr. Goldstein. It takes a snap dragon to know one." She replied.

"Come on you two," stated Mooch interrupting the war of flowers. "You two would like each other if you would give each other a chance."

"I apologize, Mr. Goldstein. It is not my intention to make a guest feel unwelcome."

"I apologize, Mrs. Zook. It is not my intention to give you the impression that I dislike you. I just don't have a preference for homespun. Uziah will be an educated man. I am sure he felt sorry for you when he eloped with you. My hat is off to Uziah for his charitable nature marrying an uneducated lower class woman."

"I am looking forward to you being seated next to me at dinner. I like individuals with strong and unusual opinions. Perhaps we could discuss while eating why you always smell of a mixture of molded coffee and garlic. It is an unusual after shave preferred by red necks and men like you of a white trash variety."

"I will be delighted to sit next to you. May I ask once more why your hat sits so crooked on your perfectly combed bun of hair? Do you need glasses per chance?"

"Where is my cap crooked?" She asked out of vanity. She had nervously dressed and checked herself for an hour before David arrived. "Georgia, tell me the truth, is my cap crooked?"

"Yes, Sweetie, I am afraid it is. Were you in a hurry when you were dressing?"

"I told Uziah my cap was crooked. Leave it up to a man to lie to you. He told me it was just fine. I should make him sleep in the dumpster tonight for that."

"The English have dog houses for their men to sleep in and the Amish have dumpsters. What about you David. Where do Jewish women make their husbands sleep when they have been less than desirable?" Georgia asked.

"We never let the sun go down on our wrath. We agree at dark to stop all wars. Jewish men are always in their bed at night and their women are happy to have them there. A perfect Jewish wife would never deny her husband seven days in a row or force him to sleep in a dumpster." He replied to annoy Hannah. She had to be one uptight, Victorian prude to make her husband wait seven days to sleep with her.

Uziah walked up to the group and that ended the war of words. "It is time for us to be seated." He stated.

Hannah pointed David to the table.

David took the seat at the table that she pointed him to. Then she sat down at the end next to him. His knee accidentally rubbed up against hers. She looked at him funny and not smiling. He marveled at the electricity that was shooting thru him. She was the one. Her touch was unbelievable. Just the brush of her knee to his was turning him on. He didn't move his knee against hers but just looked at her unsmiling. Then he felt her hand move to the top of his leg and suddenly she pinched the hell out of the top of his leg ending the moment of rapture. He didn't yell. How could he explain to Uziah that he had been playing knee games with her? With his hand, he tried to brush her hand from the top of his leg. She wasn't letting go and she was about to kill him. He was in pain. Reaching under the table, he pinched her leg thru her dress. Instantly, she let go and brushed his hand away biting her lip. They glared at each other.

Once more he leaned his knee on her. He couldn't resist. He had to feel that unbelievable electricity one more time, even if it meant her pinching him again. She was married and he was going to be a Jewish Rabbi. However, in the moment it didn't seem to matter. For the first time, he had to admit to himself that he was in love with her and had been so since the snowy night she crawled into his jeep with dimples that winked at him. The thought of Uziah in her bed wasn't a pleasant thought. How could God let her marry someone else? How could God let her be protestant and not Jewish? How could God let her have such a mouth?

Once again, he felt her fingers pinch the hell out of the top of his leg. He cringed. This time, he took his combat boot and placed it on top of her foot beneath the table and pressed down till he saw her bite her lip. She let his leg go. They just stared at each other and then quickly ignored each other striking up conversations with those on the other sides of them. However, David wondered if she felt what he felt?

For the rest of dinner, David kept his knee away from her. When she wasn't looking, he placed his glass of ice water on his leg where she had pinched him to relieve the pain and keep the swelling down. He knew he was going to have one heck of a bruise. The dinner hour went quick and Hannah ignored him.

Uziah stood up and stated after quieting those at the table, "I understand that our friend David has brought a special dessert with unusual icing. We will let him cut and serve." Then, he walked over and retrieved the foil covered sheet cake from the kitchen counter and placed it on the table between David and Hannah along with a knife to cut it.

David stood up and then reached over and took Hannah's

dirty plate and sat it on top of his and then placed the foil covered cake in front of Hannah. "I baked this especially for you because I wanted you to see what a fine man of gourmet taste I am. It is chocolate. Enjoy!"

"Thank you, David." She stated rising as David seated himself. Hannah quickly removed the foil. David watched grinning when suddenly he saw that there was writing on top of the cake. "Shit, I have been had," he muttered.

Hannah grinned and turned the cake and held it up for all at the table to see and read. There were red hearts in all four corners glaring on white icing and words in the center. "I AM A MALE JERK. FORGIVE ME. DAVID."

Hannah looked at him and then laughed, "Have I just won our war?"

"To the victor," he replied red faced. He couldn't deny making the cake because he had already made a big deal out of placing it in front of her with flowery words.

"Male Jerk, I raise my glass to you in a toast. It takes a big man to let a woman win." Stated Mooch holding up his water glass to toast.

"Here is to David, a real gentleman." Sergeant Pepper stated raising his glass to toast.

Hannah turned to David and held her glass up. "To my favorite male jerk and to tomorrow's bruises I raise my glass in honor." Then she felt his boot on top of her foot and she quickly added. "I was actually a female jerk to him first. We are mending fences. I raise my glass to my black booted friend."

He removed his boot from the top of her shoe, rose, and

forced a smile as he cut and served the cake.

Before leaving for the evening, when no one was looking, he leaned in to her ear and whispered. "What next? Will you leave me love notes on my jeep's window or crawl thru my bedroom window? You made that damn cake. I know it. I will get even!"

She quickly replied in a whisper, "I didn't bake the cake or know who did. I would slit my own throat and jump down an Amish well before I would write you a love note, enter your bedroom, or bake you a cake. You are the ugliest, big nosed, low class piece of Jewish trash I have ever met. You are only in my home and presence at the request of Uziah."

David bit his lip. She knew how to get to him. He wanted to reply, but Mooch walked up to speak with her. Mumbling to himself and mad, he left. Outside, he leaned on the apartment house wall and looked out over the black wrought iron railing in thought. He was going to be a Jewish Rabbi. How could he let a protestant, mouthy, unobtainable woman like her even cross his mind? He was pissed at himself because he knew that he could only marry a Jewish woman. He would have to keep his distance from her as well as never sit by her again at dinners should he get a second invitation. The innocent touch of his knee to hers was a sensual moment he would never forget.

CHAPTER EIGHT

Three Years Later

Three years passed and it was the end of May. The original group of friends bonded and became like family. Mooch and David graduated one semester ahead of Uziah but remained in the second floor apartment taking one semester off before they started on their master degrees. Uziah, by going to college year round, had caught up with them in hours and would enter the master degree program with them. Uziah had graduated college on the previous Sunday afternoon with the core group of friends looking on.

Hannah was excited about her upcoming high school graduation. The three years had sped by and the pair of cousins accomplished their goals. Zook's Place was raking in the cash, but the future of the private dining club was sure to come to an end, sooner or later. Eventually, Uziah would need to move on to Chicago and the plan had always been for Hannah to go with him and enter whatever college or university that was there. Hannah felt that she possibly had a year, or a little over, to keep Zook's Place continuing. Hannah would attend the university where Uziah did for three semesters and then transfer.

Hannah was looking forward to a two week visit with her family before starting her first college classes in the summer semester. She had kept her word to Uziah and had not gone home or wrote home during the three plus years. Now it was time. She would surprise her parents and siblings with a visit. Sergeant Pepper had taught her to drive and she planned to rent a car for the two weeks, which was cheaper than owning one. She just lived two blocks from campus and would walk back and forth just as Uziah had. They would be frugal just as they had always been. The rental car would come out of her pocket money.

Hannah had three friends that she treasured. One was Mooch who never failed to help her with the dishes on the nights everyone got together. Georgia Macon helped her create the private supper club and was the root of the huge savings Uziah and her had accumulated. She never understood why Georgia and her third friend, Sergeant Pepper, detested each other.

Hannah was now going on twenty two. She was not the naïve Amish girl that had arrived at the Pepper Apartment complex and innocently embraced everyone and started a new life. She was a successful business woman and on the way to being an educated person. Her feelings concerning having children had not changed. Her conscious decision to not produce God's Will children was written in stone in her thinking. As a result, she did not see herself marrying because no man would understand.

Chim across the alley was starting to speak fairly good English. Hannah was only able to help him thirty minutes once a month. He had about twenty or so hours of English instruction from her in the three plus years. However, he was a fast learner and she was proud of him. Uziah never gave in and let her include him in their inner circle of friends.

Uziah and Hannah were starting to feel the stress of two people living in tight quarters and were beginning to get a little on each other's nerves. Like an old married couple, sometimes they had words and non speaking moments. Hannah resented Uziah's constant insistence that he was right and as head of their house should dictate her every move. She was past needing a father or a brother to protect her. She was starting to make up her own mind about people and what she wanted out of life. The bird man was a constant source of irritation between them. Uziah wanted nothing to do with him continuing to state that he was a Gods Will child. Nothing Hannah could say had convinced him otherwise. Hannah was maturing and becoming tolerant of everyone in her world including David. After a couple of years, they buried the hatchet over the cake. Sergeant Pepper had baked it. He wanted to see the great Goldstein put in his place. However, Hannah didn't consider David a close friend. She could never forget that he had originally called her homely and unintelligent.

Hannah was a few days away from her high school graduation. She was home taking advantage of what her friends and school called a senior skip day. First on her list of many things to do was to pack a box of her special linens to take to her mother and sisters as a gift. She had made them from discarded clothing found in the dumpsters and was excited about sharing them as gifts. For some reason, Uziah wasn't excited about her adventure home and he openly asked her not to go. She had asked him to accompany her, but he had said he would not. Going home for a visit was one of the first decisions she had made on her own defying his authority as head of their house.

Uziah returned home from the college campus where he had met with a guidance dean to plan his master degree program and future beyond that. After entering the apartment, he poured himself a cup of hot coffee and sat down at the long door table where Hannah was busy working from a list packing and doing other things.

"Hannah, I have a money concern. We must talk." He stated in a firm voice as he added sugar to his coffee.

"Are our bills paid? Have we had some sort of emergency that requires our cutting back?"

"You are being frivolous with your spending money. I have objection to a purchase of yours and I feel you should take it back to the store and get your money back." He stated.

"Didn't we agree three years ago that you would take your Pancake Emporium earnings as your pocket money and I would take my cleaning money for mine and spend it how we wished? I have not touched a penny of Zook's Place money that we have saved for our educations."

"Yes, that was our agreement. However, we must also think about the purchases we make with our pocket money. You have purchased an expensive pair of binoculars which I feel is ridiculous. The money should have been spent on clothes for the two of us or possibly a bicycle." He replied.

There was going to be another fight about Chim. She knew it was coming on. "The Gods Will man across the alley watches birds with his binoculars. I watch him. He is fascinating and I will write a book about him one day. He holds his drawings up at the window for me to look at. Binoculars make my viewing easier. He holds up his drawings and I hold up my towels or other projects that I am working on."

"You constantly defy me when it comes to him. You are wasting your time with him and I insist that you take the binoculars back. The bird man will not be going to Chicago with us next year and you will have no need of field glasses." He stated sharply not smiling.

"What about the fancy pearl handled pocket knife you are carrying? Is it not frivolous and too fine of a knife to use to whittle. It is useless. Look at your own frivolities before you pick on me for mine." She retorted sharply. "I am your second cousin, not your wife, and my pocket money is my pocket money."

"Our friend, David, once called you a female jerk. I should have made a better decision when coming here and left you behind. You have forgotten your place as a woman."

"Perhaps, I should make a better decision now and leave you behind. I don't need you. I am perfectly capable of putting myself thru college. It is you that is overstepping the boundaries between us. What time will you be home to eat later?"

"What time will you be available to cook seeing that you have a new busy body need to bird watch?" He retorted mad.

"I do not have to cook. Saving money for your college education is the reason I cook. You will apologize to me for being a male Amish jerk or I may never cook again, much less save every penny I can get my hands on to pay for your schooling. I still wear the same two dresses I arrived here in. You have no reason to pick on me for the use of my pocket money or to be nasty with me."

"I have done my part in saving for our educations." Uziah shouted.

"All you do is sit at the end of the table and talk for two hours on the nights we entertain the wealthy. I do the cleaning, the cooking and the pampering of our guests. I could replace you at the head of the table with any student actor. Think about it. I am the one making and putting the money back for our educations." she sassed back.

Getting up and leaving his cup of coffee for her to clean up, Uziah stormed out of the apartment slamming the door. She returned to her list of things to do.

Thirty minutes or so later, Endora knocked on the door looking for Uziah, stating that she needed him to help her lift something down from the closet in her apartment across the alley. Hannah said she would tell him and then returned to her kitchen where she started supper. Uziah was still fascinated with Endora. Hannah wondered if he might not be secretly doing things he shouldn't be doing with her. However, it was none of her business. She and Uziah were cousins and nothing more.

The Last Friend's Night

The last friend night for the spring semester arrived. It was to be the last time that some of the friends would see each other. Ohm Oto would take his servant Chim and return to San Francisco in a day or so. He was sticking around to attend Hannah's graduation. She had attended his. The core of friends was moving on with their lives. Even Georgia had told Hannah that she would not be around possibly for many more months. Hannah figured that she had finally caught the man she had been peeping at and was secretly planning to marry or possibly be moving away with him. Sergeant Pepper had told her that he had made plans to sell the apartment complex when Uziah left for medical school. Uziah and Hannah planned to tell the group that they weren't married a couple weeks from now after Hannah returned from her trip. Tonight however, was a celebration of Hannah's high school graduation and a going away party for Ohm.

After a couple days of not speaking with each other, Uziah and Hannah buried the hatchet and prepared for the friend night. It would be the last friend night, although everyone was oblivious to the breaking down of friendships that was about to occur. Hannah was oblivious. A twist of fate was about to spin her world out of control. She would never be a naïve or trusting Amish woman again. She would see every man as a source of betrayal.

Uziah and Hannah worked together getting the table and the food ready for the celebration, Uziah decided it was time to tell Hannah about Sergeant Pepper's request to call on her. He had been patient and respectable for three years waiting for his cousin to finish her high school years and for her to mature. He felt that Sergeant Pepper was a man of honor and would make a good match for his cousin. Plus, it would get her off of his back. Down deep, he didn't want to take her to Chicago. He planned to dress as a regular man there and she would stick out like a sore thumb in her gray dresses and white caps. In the Amish world he was judged by his mentally challenged siblings. The last three years, he had been judged by what the English conceived an Amish married man was to be. He hadn't got to date or be single. He resented Hannah for that. She was a noose around his neck. Secretly, he had a crush on Georgia Macon. She was older, but he liked the way her body looked in her low cut blouses and tight clothing. Endora fascinated him, but he had come to the conclusion that she would not fit in to his world in Chicago and there was no need to pursue her once he and Hannah revealed they weren't a couple. He was older now, and the crush on her was dying. When he became a doctor, he wanted a sophisticated woman that would fit in with the wealthy like those who came to the supper club. He planned to dump his image as an Amish man. That was not going to get him where he wanted to go in life. Hannah wouldn't get him there either. She wouldn't be someone that he could go to cocktail hours and to dinners serving alcohol with. If she agreed to Sergeant Pepper calling on her, there was ever chance that she would marry him. They were good friends and that was basis enough for a marriage. Rarely did the Amish marry for love. You were matched with whoever was available.

"I need to discuss a matter with you concerning Sergeant Pepper." Uziah stated as he set the table.

"What would that be?" She returned as she folded napkins and put them by each plate.

"A few months after we arrived here, Sergeant Pepper discovered that you and I were not married. I explained to him that you were here for an education and that our pretend marriage was for your protection. He informed me that he was willing to keep our secret and that he had feelings for you. He asked for the right to call on you after you graduated from high school. He has earned that right, Hannah. He is a respectable man and I think you should consider him as a suitor. I do not see him as a hindrance to your going on to college. How do you feel about this? Also, when we go to Chicago I wish to meet and have a lady friend. I cannot do that and continue our pretend marriage. It is time that we make new decisions."

"What about Endora? Do you plan on asking her to go to Chicago with us? Is that the reason for this conversation? I know that you spend a lot of time with her."

"I am glad I had you to save me from Endora. I think that I am starting to see life beyond her. I am wondering what witch I will meet in Chicago and be equally as fascinated with. The answer is no. I will not be asking Endora to go with us. She is a passing fancy and I am indebted to you for keeping me from her. She would never fit in to the life of a respectable doctor."

"I see. Have you slept with her? I just want to know if you have broken your vow to not produce God's Will children." Hannah asked.

"I have not slept with anyone since arriving here with you three and one half years ago. I have not broken my vow or changed my thinking. It isn't that I have not thought about making love to a woman. I have had my struggles. In Chicago, I plan to seek out a woman who wants no children or cannot have children to take as a companion. I plan to end my friendship and fascination with Endora. I am telling myself to look to the future, to Chicago, and to new beginnings."

"That sounds like a good plan. I am proud of you." Hannah returned. "Concerning my letting Sergeant Pepper call as a suitor brings up mixed emotions in me. Pepper and I are such good friends and I enjoy our tea chats and all that he does for me. Calling on me might end the moments that I treasure with him. What if I kissed him and found out he didn't suit me or my not suiting him. We could not go back to being friends. One of us would be hurt. I am not sure that I am willing to take that risk."

"We have lived amongst the English for three or so years, Hannah. It is time that we lay down some of our ideas about courting and what is proper and not proper. Have you considered asking Sergeant Pepper to just practice a kiss on him? If you feel nothing, it won't matter. Tell him you are planning to take a suitor and need the experience. He doesn't know that I have told you of his desire to call on you yet. He will see it as one of the crazy things you occasionally do and say. He will let you kiss him to practice and be amused. You will know if he pleases you."

"That sounds reasonable and a safe way of deciding!" She replied turning the flame off underneath the tea kettle. "We are done here and our friends won't be arriving for an hour. I think that I might go now for the practice kiss, so I don't have to worry concerning it till tomorrow. My mother always told me to be the first one to volunteer when having to give a talk in school for any reason. She said it was better to get something over with, than be the last in line and have to worry about it. I will go pretend kiss him and see if he suits me."

"Practice a couple times on your arm before going," Stated Uziah. "I would hate for you to disappoint him."

"Me disappoint him? I don't think so. I have watched the English girls kiss their boyfriends. I will do as they do and make him know he has been kissed."

"I gather you are not going to kiss him on the cheek which is appropriate for a first kiss to a suitor." Uziah laughed. "I am thinking of wearing jeans and tennis shoes when we move to Chicago. I have come to the conclusion that our families are willingly ignorant in a lot of their ways. A zipper in pants is a convenience not a prideful thing. I am willing for you to wear jeans also, if you wish. We will continue to dress Amish because the supper club is providing the finances we need. However, I think it is time that we become part of the community in which we live. We are not ignorant in our thinking and are becoming the educated persons we set goals to be. I plan to buy myself a dinner jacket like Mooch has when we get to Chicago."

"Who are we now, Uziah? I really don't know anymore. Perhaps my trip home will help me remember who I am. I love my camera and do not see it as a tool to make graven images. I see it as a tool to save wonderful memories of you and our friends. I am on my way to being educated. In seeking to be what I have wanted, I question whether I have lost some of who I once was. Wearing jeans would be the laying down of Amish dress codes and with it my identity. I still see myself returning to the community and educating the women about genes and the silent incest. I could not return to our community wearing jeans. They would not accept me."

Our parents have chosen their lives and their marriages as second cousins. I am choosing different and to embrace the ways of the English. I have decided to never return. I have found happiness in education and those who are educated. It was not an easy thing to abandon my mother and my siblings. Time has eased my guilt and they have replaced me with more children and possibly more God's Will children. I do not wish to embrace ignorance or be a part of it. In Chicago, I will tell my friends of college life here, but nothing of my life before. I feel my life began the night we arrived here. The English world is where I belong and I do not want my past as an Amish man known.

"I understand. You are saying to me that you do not wish me to go with you to Chicago, if I don't lay down my Amish dress and past." She replied. "You don't want me in your world in Chicago, if I continue to embrace Amish ways and my memories of my childhood."

"We have saved enough money for my medical school expenses. If you go with me we will work and pay for your college expenses. However, should you not accompany me, you must find ways of paying for your years of college expenses. The Zook's Club money is mine. We saved it for my medical school expenses. If you stay here, Sergeant Pepper has agreed to marry you and pay for your future college expenses. Otherwise, should you turn him down; you must get a job and start saving all over for your future expenses."

"I see. The saved money is entirely for your medical school needs with no concern that it is I that have sacrificed to get us where we are. You see me as a woman who should be traded off or gotten rid of like a stock animal when it no longer pleases you."

"Consider taking Sergeant Pepper as a suitor. If you do not agree to dress English and be so in Chicago, you are on your own after I get my master degree."

"I will be back in an hour. I will go down and discuss with Sergeant Pepper his offer. However, Uziah, I don't need you. It is you that needs me. You have shamed me with your words." She said throwing down her tea towel. Then she left the apartment and slammed the door which was a first for her.

CHAPTER NINE

The Kiss

Sergeant Pepper was in his kitchen preparing to have a snack of toast and tea to hold him over till dinner at the Zooks. He heard a knock at the front door. He knew who it was. He had learned to recognize the sound of her knock. He was pleased and knew that he was only days away from being able to tell her that he was in love with her and wanted to marry her. He hurried to the front door and opened it smiling like a Cheshire cat with a secret. He was ready to move past the friend stage. It had been a long three years or so waiting for her to mature and get her high school education.

"Hannah, come in! I have the tea kettle on. Head back to the kitchen." He said holding the door open for her.

"Make us a stiff black tea, with molasses in it. I have something important to ask you that might shock you. You may need the extra caffeine and the nipping bite of the molasses."

"You sound intriguing!" He replied. "Could this possibly be a raw honey moment?"

"Have you been using raw honey in your tea? If you have, I am not going to be happy with you. It will be over my knees for you, if I find you have a honey bear hidden."

Sergeant Pepper grinned following her to the kitchen. After they were married he would let her find his honey bear bottle of honey occasionally just so he would get the pleasure of her disciplining him. He could see himself turned over her knees begging for mercy.

They entered the kitchen and Hannah sat down at her usual spot.

"I have need of a favor, Sergeant Pepper. I am not quite sure how to ask you for my favor. I am a little bit embarrassed about it."

Sergeant Pepper grinned and got down two tea cups from the cabinet. The last time she asked for a favor, she wanted him to teach her to drive. That was an experience considering that she had never ridden in a car over four or five times. Everything in the car had to be explained and demonstrated for her. He survived that one and was only thrown upon to the dash three or four times when she braked.

"Do you need me to teach you to dance?" He asked not sure of where to go with the conversation. He was waiting on her to chart the course.

"It is not dancing that I need to be taught. That is why I have asked you to make a strong tea. I need you to practice on."

"Practice what?" He asked bringing two cups of hot black tea to the table and setting them down.

"When I graduate high school, I have decided that I am going to date. Uziah has informed me that you know of our pretend marriage. He wants me to take a suitor that he like my father, would choose."

"Has Uziah told you who he had lined up to call on you?" He asked hinting to see if she knew yet that he was the suitor who had asked to call on her.

"I am sure he will get around to telling me what suitors he thinks are appropriate. However, I will choose who I want to date when I am no longer a pretend wife. Uziah is not my father. In my opinion, at my age, my real father no longer has the right to choose suitors for me."

"Do you have someone in mind that you have chosen to date after you graduate?" He asked with a somber face. He was not happy about the thought that she had possibly got out and met someone defying Uziah.

"I have met someone that I am quite fond of. Now, I need your help."

"What is the favor you want from me?" He asked cringing on the inside. He feared she was going to ask him to help her slip off into the night with someone other than him.

"I am twenty-two years old and never been kissed. I have a great fear that I will be a disappointment to the man I wish to date. All of the English girls kiss openly and often. I do not know how to kiss like crazy as they do. I wish to speak with you about kissing."

"I am sure you will do just fine in the kissing department. What do you need me to teach you?" He asked fearing what she was going to ask.

"I know this is a lot to ask of a friend . . ." she said biting her lip and searching for words.

"A friend . . . you want to ask something of me as a friend?"

"Yes. Would you let me practice one kiss on you? I need to know if my kiss will be appropriate for a first time one."

Sergeant Pepper, caught off guard, got choked and spewed out the sip of tea he had just taken. "You want to do what?"

"I know it is a lot to ask. I need you to be my practice lips and tell me if my kiss is good or bad."

"May I ask who you are planning to date after practicing a kiss on me? Do I know him?" He asked irked believing it was someone other than him. He had waited patiently for her.

"Yes, you know him. That is all that I will tell you for now. Will you let me practice one kiss on you? You can wash your lips afterwards." She stated with a serious look on her face.

"Do you want me to hold you in my arms like a man would or are you planning to do just a peck him on the lips and run thing?" He asked thinking it had to be David Goldstein. Mooch had told him that David was secretly in love with her and that he would marry her in a heartbeat if it weren't for Uziah.

"What kind of kiss do you have in mind for the first time?" He asked trying not to lose his cool.

"I would like the man that I want to date to think I kiss like crazy. Can you teach me?" She replied.

"You want to kiss the man you want to date like crazy?" He asked realizing that it was not him that would be calling on her after graduation. Someone had slipped in and stole her away before he had a chance to call on her.

"Yes, I want to kiss this man I care about like crazy. May I practice a kiss on you, a crazy kiss?"

Sergeant Pepper stood to his feet with a broken heart. He put his hands behind his back and locked his hands. He wanted her and he was afraid that when she kissed him he wouldn't be able to control himself. He had to control himself or he could lose her. He would figure out how to win her away from Goldstein or whoever it was that had came between them.

Hannah stood and faced him walking up to inches between them. Her heart was racing. She could feel the heat from his body. He was her number one choice. However, she wasn't sure that he had feelings for her. He had never offered to be anything but a friend to her. She wondered if Uziah had asked him to call, trying to rid himself of her. Perhaps Sergeant Pepper was innocent and didn't have any racing heart feelings for her. The practice kiss would decide the matter.

"How long should a first kiss be?" She asked looking into his eyes that she had always been crazy about.

"In your case, and being Amish, I would say on a scale of one to twenty seconds, maybe seven or eight."

"Alright, we will set the timer on your stove when I am ready." She replied.

Sergeant Pepper bit his lip. In spite of her breaking his heart, he was amused about the timer bit. He had never kissed to the tick of a timer before. "That is logical." He said with his hands tightly locked together behind his back.

"Should I kiss with my eyes open or closed? I kissed my father on the top of his balding spot at times with my eyes open. I have always kissed my little brothers with kisses and they were with my eyes open. Should I kiss my date the first time with my eyes open or closed?" She asked unsmiling.

"Well, it depends, Hannah. A kiss isn't as sensual if you kiss with your eyes open. You could get distracted by the color of your date's eyes or the pimple on his forehead."

"That makes sense." She replied. "Go on."

"If you want to feel the uniqueness of the kiss and get lost in it, closed eyes would be the way to go. How do you think you would like to experience your first kiss?" He was so jealous of whoever it was that she had a serious mind to kiss.

"I think I definitely would like a closed eye kiss, so as not to look at his nose." She replied. "Does he pull away first, or do I?"

"If he is kissing more than seven seconds and his hands suddenly get involved, I would say you should pull away first." He replied pissed about the big nose comment. It had to be David Goldstein's Jewish nose.

"That is good to know. I feel this man's hands could be a problem." She replied watching Sergeant Pepper with his hands clenched behind his back. Alarmed by her own racing heart and body heat, she stepped away and retrieved the timer from the stove, set it for ten seconds, and returned to her position facing him.

"Is there anything else I should know about a first kiss?" She asked.

"Sometimes they are disappointing. For instance, David Goldstein has dated hundreds of girls the last four years. The girls he dates are experienced in the kissing department. He might not appreciate a first kiss and tell you that your kiss is less than desirable. I wouldn't want you disappointed." He replied.

"Oh, I hadn't thought about that. Will you give me an honest opinion when I kiss you whether I am a good kisser or not. I really need your opinion?"

"I definitely will tell you the truth." He said intending to tell her she was a bad kisser so she wouldn't kiss David Goldstein. He was jealous and would do anything to undermine David Goldstein's chance with her.

"I will set the timer for ten seconds. When I push the button down for the clock to start, you close your eyes. I want you to feel my kiss so you can give me your best opinion. I will do the kissing. You do the feeling. Understand?"

"I understand!" He said anticipating her kiss. He had waited for three and one half years for a first kiss with her. This wasn't exactly how he planned the moment to be, but at least he was getting her first kiss. David Goldstein would have to settle for the second.

"Ready?"

"Ready," he replied with his hands clenched behind his back. His palms were sweating and his heart was racing out of control with her standing so close to him.

"Close your eyes. I must make full use of my seven to ten seconds to prove myself in the kissing department."

Sergeant pepper closed his eyes and suddenly wished he had taken the time to throw a breath mint in his mouth. He hadn't brushed his teeth since morning and he remembered the onion slices he had put on his burger for lunch.

"One . . . two . . . three!" She counted and then quickly pushed the timer down and pressed her lips to his, put her arms around him, and kissed him like she had seen the English girls did.

"Oh God …. Help me!" Sergeant pepper thought as he felt her arms around him and her lips on his. He was having a reaction and one that he didn't want her to see. She was turning him on to almost the point of no return. He wanted to throw his arms around her and recline her on the kitchen floor and make frenzied love to her. There was definitely nothing wrong with her kiss. She was curling up his toenails as well as bringing out three years of wanting her to the surface. He didn't know whether he could control himself. The timer buzzed and she immediately removed her lips from him and stepped back. He didn't open his eyes for a moment. He was in a state of sensual splendor and desire for her. He didn't want the moment to end. She had taken him to Heaven and back in seven to ten seconds.

"Well, open your eyes and tell me how it was. Will I please the man I have chosen to date? I need to know before I let him call on me."

Sergeant Pepper opened his eyes and quickly sat down at the table to control his urges. He could see himself being all arms, lips, and out of control with her. "Let me catch my breath and think about it a moment, Hannah." He stated.

Hannah didn't sit down but looked at him a little funny. "You are my friend. I want to know the truth. How was it?"

"You are my friend and I hate to disappoint you, but you are a dud in the kissing department. I would not go out with the man you have chosen. It would be better not to disappoint him. I am willing to teach you to kiss and let you practice on me. However, you are definitely a dud." He lied knowing that his words were going to hurt, but he didn't want her dating anyone but him.

Hannah's eyes filled with tears. "My kiss was no good?"

"No, I am sorry. Would you like to practice a kiss every afternoon till you improve it?"

"I am sorry that I have made a fool out of myself in kissing you badly. It is you that my heart has raced for and that I have dreamed of being with. I will not be coming for tea anymore. I have been a fool." She stated and ran out the back door in tears.

"Hannah, wait . . .!" Shouted Sergeant Pepper who was momentarily shocked by her words. "I'm sorry, I didn't mean it." He yelled but it was too late, she was gone.

He was so pissed at himself he picked up one of the tea cups and threw it across the kitchen, a first for him. He had dreamed of this moment for three years and had blown it out of jealousy. Now, what was he going to do? He was in a dog house that he wasn't sure how to get out of. His mouth and jealousy had put him there.

Georgia Confronts Pepper

Just as Sergeant Pepper was about to run after Hannah, he heard a voice from the hallway.

"Why is she leaving in such a hurry and what was the breaking sound I heard?" Georgia asked entering the kitchen.

He spun around to see his stalker, Georgia Macon entering the kitchen. He closed his eyes for a moment and bit his lip. She was always showing up when he least expected it and at moments when he didn't have time to deal with her. He wasn't a child anymore and she could no longer physically abuse him, however she was relentless with her appearances and verbal assaults.

"She was paying her rent if it is any of your damn business! How did you get in?" He stated annoyed. He needed to chase after Hannah, not fool with a confrontation with his lifelong stalker.

"The front door was unlocked." She replied walking into the kitchen and leaning against the cabinet.

"Whatever it is you want, spit it out and then get out. I have somewhere I need to go."

"Word has it that you are seeing a bell ringer down at your church. It is not going to happen, Pepper. She will find herself with a broken leg in an alley somewhere. I am the only woman that is going to be in your life."

"I am tired of your threats, Georgia. It is bad enough I have to put up with you at the dinners at the Zook's. Here, I don't have to put up with you and I am going to throw you physically out just like I did once before. What are you, a sadist wanting physical abuse?"

"I only want you. Someday, you will see that it is me that loves you."

"I don't want you, Georgia. You have no morals and face it; you are hitting middle age and everything you have got is starting to sag or wrinkle. You should have settled down with someone your age years ago."

"We have a history together and that is something that cannot be replaced."

"Get out, Georgia. I have something more important to take care of than argue with you. Just so you are not caught off guard, I am seeing someone and I have bought her a hundred thousand dollar engagement ring. God willing, I will be married by this time next month and off to live in Hong Kong or maybe Australia. Your song and dance stalking me is over. I have already purchased my airline tickets and the wedding license." He stated lying to annoy her.

"It isn't going to happen, Pepper. Take the ring back or save it for me." She replied pissed.

At that point, Sergeant Pepper grabbed her by the arm, took her to his back door and threw her out slamming the door behind her and locking it. Then he walked to his front door and locked it.

Leaning on his front door, he considered his ass hole moment with the one woman he had ever wanted. "How am I going to apologize to Hannah?" He muttered asking himself.

Outside, Georgia fuming mad and stood in the alley kicking at a rock that just happened to be in her path. Uziah walked up unexpectedly. He was headed over to Endora's to un-invite her for friend night and tell her that he no longer wanted to be her friend, he was moving on to Chicago without her, and that he and Hannah were not married. He felt he owed her the truth about that. He had turned down her seductions for the last three and one half years stating that he was faithful to Hannah. He didn't want her just suddenly showing up in Chicago thinking she was going to be a part of their new life.

"May I ask what is wrong?" Uziah asked seeing how mad

Georgia was. He thought perhaps she had words with Endora for some reason. Georgia and Sergeant Pepper never talked at the friend night dinners.

"I was visiting Sergeant Pepper to warn him that a wrestler lady that he is seeing is actually a gay woman with a lover across town. He was insulted. The wrestler isn't his lady friend but a client. I have meddled where I shouldn't have. He is a mad at me for offering advice that he didn't want. Have you met the woman that he is dating? He told me that he has purchased her an engagement ring." She asked hoping to pump Uziah for any information as to who Pepper was seeing. "I think I am going to have to invite Pepper and his lady friend out to the restaurant for a free meal to smooth this over with him."

"That is an easy one, Georgia. You and Sergeant Pepper have always known that Hannah and I are not married. Hannah will be able to have a suitor when she graduates high school. Sergeant Pepper has asked to call on Hannah starting the day after her graduation. He has been in love with her for three and one half years and is patiently waiting till we tell our friends tonight that we are not married. I am moving on to Chicago, possibly alone. He has not approached her, yet. I have never heard her say that she has feelings for him, but the Amish don't always marry for love."

"I must be a blind fool." Georgia stated biting her lip. "This one I didn't see coming."

"He asked me three years ago to call on Hannah once she was out of school. We don't date like you English do. I have presented to Hannah the possibility of having a suitor starting Saturday night, but she doesn't know who with. She graduates high school Friday night and then he will call for the first time. He will take my place at Hannah's table, if she chooses to let him call."

"You have definitely sprung one on me. Hannah doesn't know that he wants to call?" Georgia asked with her eyes tearing up. Somehow, she had to convince Uziah to send Hannah back to the farm or on to Chicago and fabricate a reason why Sergeant Pepper should not be allowed to see her. She had some quick decisions that had to be made.

"I am sure she thinks it is Mooch wanting to date her. He always hangs on the end of her dish towel on Wednesdays. He is in love with her also."

"Mooch, huh?" She questioned getting a double dose of mad. Mooch was her boy toy. She owned him, or so she thought.

"Also, David Goldstein and Dean Jackson from the Premed program at the college have crushes on Hannah. Hannah has never wanted for suitors. She had thirteen proposals between the age of fifteen and seventeen before coming here."

"So there is a possibility she will turn Pepper down?"

"Possibly," he replied. "She is a spit fire with a mind of her own."

"Who is Mooch seeing?" She asked fishing to see just how far her pup was straying.

"Mooch isn't picky. He dates anyone and everyone." Uziah stated. "You do know that he is a male escort?"

"I have heard that. Is he escorting someone special in the neighborhood?"

"Mrs. Begley who is sixty five and seventy two year old widow Perkins a couple blocks down are what he calls clients. Recently, he has been seen a couple times with Bette the food columnist friend of Sergeant Pepper. He is a male harlot, Georgia. I dare say he sees ten or fifteen women a week. I don't judge him because he needs the money for school and expenses. He told me that, one ugly old dish as he called her, gave him two thousand to go on his master's degree and that he has to work out the money by sleeping with her when she wants. I don't approve of his lifestyle, but he is my friend. Chances are, he will catch something and give it to every woman frequenting his bed. One night with the wrong woman and he could catch aids or who knows what. He tells me that he is in love with Hannah. He has been very open with me, even though he thinks she is my wife. I am sure that Hannah will turn him down if he asks to call. He has no morals."

"Thanks for the information, Uziah. I better understand the two men now."

With that said, Georgia slipped away into the evening, got in her car and drove away doubly pissed. She had two men to deal with by tomorrow night

Endora Tricks Sergeant Pepper

Sergeant Pepper made his way to the bedroom where he changed from his office clothes into a dinner jacket and dress pants. He had to hurry. The dinner celebrating Hannah's high school graduation would be starting in fifteen minutes. He didn't know what he was going to say or do to make this up to her. He had been one jealous ass hole.

Opening his front door to exit in a hurry, he was surprised to find Endora standing there about to knock. She was crying.

"What is wrong?" Sergeant Pepper asked glancing at his watch. He had nine minutes to make it to the Zook's third floor studio apartment.

"Uziah has strung me along for three years with his flirting, using me for transportation, and getting whatever else he could get out of me. Thirty minutes ago, he had the nerve to come to my apartment and tell me that he didn't want to be friends with me any longer. He made it clear that I was uninvited to Hannah's graduation party and going away dinner for Ohm. I have been dumped by the Zook's." She stated with tears rolling down her face. "I was their first friend here!"

"You cannot make Uziah love you, Endora. As I recall it, you chased and flirted with him behind Hannah's back. He is getting older and is probably realizing that one day he will return to his Amish community. It would be impossible for you, as a witch, to fit in there."

Trying to calm Endora down, he temporarily forgot about the fact that he had nine minutes or less to get to the graduation dinner. The Zook's were sticklers about not answering the door one minute after seven. They didn't tolerate late guests or those who didn't know when to leave. If they said dinner was from seven till eight-thirty, that was what they meant.

"Would you like a cup of tea?" He asked. "I have a bear of honey hidden that Hannah hasn't found."

"Do you have anything stronger?" She asked trying to smile thru her tears.

"Actually, I have molasses for the tea. Have you ever tried it?"

"I was thinking more in the line of half a bottle of vodka or whiskey." She replied.

"I don't drink, Endora, you know that." He stated with a disappointed look. Then he followed her to the kitchen in the back.

"I am asking you a favor, Uncle Pepper. I want you to make the Zook's move." She stated sitting down at the round kitchen table still in tears.

"I cannot do that Endora, they have a lease." He replied. There was no way he would make Hannah move.

"Well . . ." she said drying her tears. "At least you and I will be boycotting her high school graduation party."

"Oh shit!" Stated Sergeant Pepper looking at his watch. It was two minutes past seven. He closed his eyes for a minute and took a deep breath. He realized that his niece had tricked him into missing Hannah's party. "You purposely pulled this little crying jag to make me miss her party, didn't you?" He asked watching her tears disappear and a smirk grin cross her face.

"Pay backs are Hell, Uncle Pepper. I remember three years ago when you threw me out. Tonight has been my chance to get even. Try to explain this one to her or Uziah."

"Get the Hell out of her Endora and never come back. I should have listened to my sister. You are exactly what she has tried to tell me you are. You are a manipulative, self-centered, and a heartless piece of crap that should have never been born. I told your mother to get an abortion after her rape. You have to be like your father, whoever he is. Now get out!"

Endora got up laughing and left by the kitchen door half shouting, "Onion juice on my tissue, in case you wonder how I made myself cry."

Glancing again at his watch he saw that it was five minutes after seven. He would have to wait till all the graduation party guests spilled out onto the third floor balcony after dinner before he could go apologize to Hannah. Missing her graduation party would be a serious matter and not taken lightly. Endora had definitely compounded his problem.

CHAPTER TEN

Hannah's Graduation Party

The party had gone well. However, there were people missing from the party. Endora had not bothered to come or Sergeant Pepper. David Goldstein was missing. David had called to say that he had an emergency and he would make up for it as soon as he got back. There was sickness in his family and he had to make an emergency trip home. Hannah had forced herself to smile. Thru her poorly attended party, she was secretly a little upset about it. She had never failed to bake Endora a birthday cake or any of the friends. Tonight was her turn and she felt slighted. Even Georgia was missing claiming to have sprained her ankle suddenly.

Before anyone arrived, she had told Uziah about the kiss and what Sergeant Pepper had said about it and asked Uziah if he was playing some sort of game with her to break up her friendship with Sergeant Pepper. She told Uziah that Sergeant Pepper had showed no interest in her and that she had made a fool out of herself. Uziah wasn't happy at her accusation swearing that Sergeant Pepper had asked to call on her.

When she burst into tears, Uziah called her hopeless and not to blame him if she couldn't interest a suitor. She was sure that Uziah had fabricated the story about Sergeant Pepper wanting to call on her. Kissing Pepper had cost her the best friend she ever had.

Mooch was a little tense when he took a dish towel from her. He never failed to help her on Wednesdays with the cleanup. The guests were wandering outside for their usual last minute discussions and farewells.

"May I ask what is wrong?" She asked. "I have known you long enough that I can read your face."

"The question should be what is wrong with you. I have watched you bite your lip and hide your tears all evening. Has Uziah done something that I should beat the hell out of him for?" He asked putting his hands on her shoulders and turning her from the sink towards him.

Uziah has ended my friendship with Sergeant Pepper. I have barely made it thru the party without bursting into tears. My world here is falling apart, Mooch. My future, that I thought was so well planned, is not going to be." She replied with a tear rolling down her cheek. "I may not be going to Chicago with Uziah."

"Damn that Endora," Mooch muttered thinking that it was an affair between Uziah and her that might be the problem. I wondered why Endora and Pepper weren't here."

"Uziah says that I am a Pecker Hen and that no one will ever love me." She stated crying. "Hen pecking is my way of loving you and the others. I want to see all of you do well in life. I realized tonight that everyone here is Uziah's friends, not mine. I will be starting over alone. Look outside on the balcony, there is no one in here talking with me or saying goodbye. Everyone out there is his friends."

"Well, my chocolate girl, that isn't exactly true. I have been on the end of this dish towel with you for three and one half years. You are first with me, not Uziah." He stated pulling her to him and putting his arms around her holding her to his chest. It was a first. No one touched Hannah. It was an unwritten law. He held her tight. "I love you Hannah. I can't see my life without you in it in some form. If there is a showdown, I belong to you."

"Thank you, Mooch." She said pulling back from him after a moment or so. "I am not sure that I can get this mess cleaned up. I am too upset." She said throwing her dish rag into the sink and gripping the edge of the cabinet fighting her emotions.

"For three years we have cleaned up after Uziah's friends. To hell with the kitchen mess, we are going to take a little climb down from the third floor and go for a walk. We both deserve a night off after all the mess we have cleaned up over the years. Come on!" He stated grabbing her hand. "We need a little something to tell when we are old and in a nursing home about a night we climbed out on a roof, down a tree like monkeys, and ran away from our troubles. It is disrespectful for all of those balcony jerks to not help with the weekly cleanup. Make new friends Hannah, those of your choosing and don't invite to your table anyone that has disrespected you for three and one half years. You have sacrificed for Uziah and now your Amish mule is kicking you. I have always wondered why none of your high school friends were ever invited to dinner or the man across the alley. I know you are secretly teaching him English. I have been doing what I can do holding conversations with him at the dumpster once a day. Between the two of us he is learning English. One day he will walk away from Ohm, when he realizes a man cannot be owned."

"You are right, Mooch. I will let Uziah rule me no more. I

was a good tree climber on the farm when I was young. I used to sit high on a limb and try to see the English world from there. We had a neighbor who was English and she would spoil me with candy, coloring books, and glimpses in her catalogs which she would leave by the fence for me to slip off and look at. I loved her. My parents never knew. I would sit in the tree on our side of the fence and try to look into her windows to see what her world was like. My parents would have whipped me had they known. She gave me a dream and it has brought me here and to you my only friend."

"Come on my tree climbing, chocolate loving girl. We are going to enjoy this little bit of time that we have left together tonight. All of us are going to be busy this summer with new goals to attain. After that we will scatter across the United States into different lives. Let us make this a night to remember. We deserve one night that neither of us will ever forget. I am not ashamed to say that I love you and always will."

"You are right." She said letting go of her death grip on the cabinet edge. "I want a pleasant memory of my graduation party to write about and put in my memory box. The rest of tonight I will not put in. It has been a nightmare."

"Have you got your climbing shoes on, my tree climbing chocolate girl?" He asked and started pulling her towards the window by Uziah's bed.

"I am ready to peep into a new life from this third floor limb. I have my traveling shoes on."

So, they climbed out the window and onto the second floor roof of the apartment complex. They scooted down the roof on their backsides and grabbed hold of a limb overhanging the roof. He helped her onto it so she could straddle it like it was a horse. Then he climbed on the limb and sat like he was riding a horse behind her. He had never seen her dress above the calves of her legs. The limb had her dress hiked up and her legs in black stockings were showing. His heart skipped a beat. He knew that she would not want him looking. She had gorgeous legs. Uziah was a fool.

He thought of Endora as they started to scoot towards the trunk of the huge oak. She was shaped like a pear with a big butt and heavy thighs. Not only that, she was a cheap twenty buck call girl. His friend, Uziah, had to be blind as a bat. Hannah had a rare beauty inside and out. She was every man's dream.

"I will go first." He sated starting to climb down from the limb when they reached the trunk of the tree. They would climb down the limbs like they were a ladder. She followed him.

When they reached the last limb, there was about an eight foot drop. He hung by his hands and dropped to the ground first and then caught her when she let go of the last limb. Together they lost balance and ended up on the ground. Out of breath from the climb, she lay on top of him laughing. Securing her in his arm and holding her flat against him, he rolled over two or three times on the grass like the two of them were a rolling pin. She squealed and laughed. When he ended the rolls, she was on top of him with leaves on her and she was giggling like a school girl. He had never heard her giggle. He was amused. Rolling her over onto the ground, he began to tickle her to hear more. She squealed again and went to laughing fighting his fingers away.

"What is going on out there?" A voice yelled from the apartment house across the alley.

Mooch quickly jumped up, extended his hand to help her up, and then pulling her along they ran down the alley toward the campus green. Once there, they stopped under the shadow of a tree to catch their breath.

"You are one heck of a tree climber my Amish chocolate girl." He stated laughing and putting one of his arms around her and pulling her to him and hugging her.

"You are one heck of a tickler." She replied laughing. "I will have to repent tonight over your hands on me."

"You have nothing to worry about. I am Dr. Mooch, remember? Doctors are allowed to touch, feel, mend bones, and tickle when necessary. Tonight, it was necessary to give you a night to remember. There will be no need to repent."

"You may not tickle me again till I have my chance to tickle you. You must play fair." She laughed as he released her from the hug.

Taking her hand, he started pulling her along. She didn't resist but ran with him. Stopping near a fountain, he picked her up and twirled around with her till he was dizzy and they fell into the grass. This time she went for his ribs and it was his time to laugh.

"Help, help . . ." he yelled. "I am being tickled to death by an Amish tickle machine."

After a little fighting of hands to get her to stop, Mooch sat up and pulled her to him and she sat between his legs with her back to him and he held her in his arms with his head rested over her shoulder.

"Did you know, that I have never seen your hair down?" He stated and removed his arms from around her and proceeded to take off her cap and look at her bun of twisted hair.

"My hat," she squealed reaching for her head. "I cannot be without my cap. A woman is supposed to keep her head covered."

"God can blame this one on me and I will repent for it," he said and proceeded to pull hair pins from her bun of hair releasing it down her back. Her hair was below her hips. "Stand up Hannah. I want to see how long your hair is. You have never cut it have you?"

"No, we do not cut our hair and I am in trouble with God letting you fool with it. Undoing my hair is a ritual belonging to a husband, although I seem to be a little short in that department."

He finished taking the pins out and then stuck them and her white cap in his pocket. He straightened the long hair out and watched it flow across her hips. Her hair was below her hips and mid thigh. He had never seen such a head of hair.

"My God, Hannah, you have to be the most beautiful woman that I have ever come across. I am stunned with what a gorgeous creature you are. You take my breath away." He stated.

"Beauty is only skin deep, Mooch. You must always judge a person by what is inside them. Beauty will let you down. Being a smart man and knowing what is inside your lady friends will keep you out of lots of trouble. I am an uncontrollable Pecker Hen. Ask Uziah."

"I don't need to ask Uziah anything. I know who you are inside and out and you are a beautiful woman. I fell in love with you when I helped Uziah carry that door to your apartment. When you stepped to that third floor apartment door, you took my breath away and it was love at first sight for me. I am not ashamed to tell you that I am in love with you and have always been. Now, you are almost twenty two and you have just become remarkably more beautiful. I know that you are Amish and married for life, but it doesn't stop my heart from loving you."

"I have a secret to tell you." She said turning around so she could see his face when she told him.

"You have a secret?" He asked looking her in the eye and grinning. "Lay it on me."

"Uziah and I are not married. We are cousins and here for educations. It was for my safety amongst the English that it was decided that Uziah and I should pretend that we were a couple till I was out of high school. We planned to tell everyone tonight, but I was too upset to approach the subject and we let it slide. Uziah sleeps under the window because he is my cousin. We both do have the last name of Zook." She stated looking at the shock in his face.

He grabbed her, picked her up, and twirled her around laughing, and then set her feet on the ground. "I am claiming you as my Hannah Banana. I am glad you didn't tell. Goldstein might have beaten me to the punch asking you out. Will you give me a chance to make you love me?" He asked laughing.

"I already love you, Mooch. You have been the one on the end of my dish towel, not David." She replied grinning at him. "Yes, you may be my suitor. I wouldn't have it any other way."

Mooch suddenly turned serious faced. "Do you know what I do to make money to pay for my college expenses?"

"I know that you are a male escort. I know you sleep with English women for money. I have always known. Uziah told me long ago."

"I am not innocent like you, Hannah. I also need the money to pay for medical school. My parents are dead and I don't have rich parents like Goldstein to fund my education. Do you understand what I am trying to say?"

"Do what you have to do to survive, Mooch. I will not ever hold it against you. Bodies are just goodies. It is with the heart that two people love each other. My friends all have owned one beat of my heart each. To you, I give two heartbeats and one kiss that you may claim when you really need it. I am giving you my heart, not my body. Do you understand?"

"I would rather have your two heartbeats and one kiss than all the sex in the world. I love you Hannah." He said taking her in his arms and holding her tightly. "I understand."

Afterward, they took a long stroll on the campus green just enjoying being together. It was a night of magic for two friends who found each other.

Trying to Apologize

At fifteen minutes after eight, Sergeant Pepper hurriedly climbed the stairs spiraling upward to the third floor balcony where the Zook's party guests were outside with their usual Wednesday evening discussions of anything and everything. He spotted Uziah above talking with Ohm Oto. He was going to have to spill his guts and ask to see Hannah in front of everyone. "I deserve the embarrassment. I am an ass hole." He muttered to himself hurrying his assent up the three flights of stairs.

Once on the third floor balcony, he was pissed to see Endora there winking at him from the far end. She must have made her way to the third floor balcony and waited to see the show after the party. He swallowed and headed straight for Uziah who was having a conversation with Ohm.

"I have come to apologize to Hannah." He nervously stated.

"No apology is necessary, Sergeant Pepper. She told me what you said about her kiss. She has turned you down as a suitor." Uziah replied.

"I want to see her, Uziah." He stated firmly. "I want to see her now. Hannah and I love each other."

"She is angry, Sergeant Pepper. If I should let you in the apartment right now, I am sure you would be coming out with her rolling pin wrapped around your ears. Was her kiss that bad?"

"Damn it! She told you?"

"You must be a fool Pepper. After waiting all this time to court her, why would you insult her like that? Just so you know, I told all of our friends just now that Hannah and I are second cousins and not married. She is old enough to choose suitors on her own now. You were her last arranged suitor. Every man at our party has asked in the last five minutes to call on her including Ohm here!" Uziah said stretching the truth a little. Ohm hadn't asked.

Going along with Uziah's deception, Ohm grinned real big and then lied, "I have a dinner date with her on Monday." He was actually crazy about Endora, although she never paid him any attention.

"You will go out with her over my dead body!" Sergeant Pepper shot back.

"Believe me Sergeant," stated Uziah jumping between his landlord and Ohm to prevent an altercation, "She is one angry Pecker Hen right now. She was so angry before the party that she couldn't cook. She ordered in Pizza. We have never ordered in Pizza in the three and one half years that we have been here. You are one inside dog that has been thrown out in the cold. Not only have you insulted her kiss, you didn't show up for the most important night of her life since we arrived here, her graduation party."

"I can explain that if you will let me."

"You are on her jackass list. She called you that thru tears before our guests arrived. Go in there and you are going to get rolling pin thumped."

"Out of my way Uziah, I deserve her rolling pin."

Uziah stepped aside. "Don't forget that I warned you."

Once inside, Sergeant Pepper was alarmed to find that the apartment was empty. The table was arrayed with dirty plates and there was a sink of abandoned dishwater. Where was she? Where was Mooch her helper? He checked the bedroom as well as the bathroom. She was gone and Mooch was not there either.

"Oh God help me," he muttered thinking suddenly of Mooch and who he was. He hurried back outside to see if Mooch was on the balcony. He wasn't. Stressed, Sergeant Pepper grabbed the third floor hand railing and held on for dear life. It was possible that he had pushed Hannah away and right into another man's arms. He was in total fear of what Mooch might do to her. He knew that Mooch was a male escort and that one woman was just like the next to him.

CHAPTER ELEVEN

Night Tears

Chim Cho who was returning from the convenience store, cutting across the campus green, stood in the shadows of the campus trees watching Hannah and a man called Mooch chase each other in the shadows of the falling night. He was sad of heart. He had never had a lady friend because he was a lower cast servant from India and had been relieved of his maleness when he was fourteen to ensure the safety of the women he served. He knew that he was half a man, one that no woman would want. He could never perform or produce children.

At twenty eight, he was now owned by Ohm Oto whose father had purchased him in India. He had been Ohm's owned servant for four years. His master's college days were over and they would return to San Francisco any day now. He had all of his miniature paintings of birds stored in a cloth grocery tote he had purchased at the supermarket. He did not want to return to the land called California. He was in love with the Hannah Bird across the alley that had taught him English. He had prayed for her to come to him. She was the gray dove he had asked for, a sign and gift from the Gods. He just didn't know how to stuff her in his tote bag along with his bird drawings. He knew that he could not leave her behind and he was praying for a miracle. He needed her to survive in the land of the Americans, when he walked away into the night abandoning his life as a servant.

He watched with sadness as his friend Mooch ran and played with her in the night shadows. He wished it was him that was laughing, holding her, and kissing her like crazy. However, he would not hold tonight against her or Mooch. Just as the gray Dove had taught him English, Mooch had taught him about freedom, telling that in the United States no man could own another and that he was free to walk away. He was considering it. Mooch had given him hope and he was planning now for his escape. He knew enough English now to order food and ask for work. He would leave tomorrow night after dark. He was asking the Gods to make a way for her to go with him. He wanted her in whatever way he could have her. If necessary, he would be her lifelong servant, although he wanted to kiss her like crazy and love her forever as a wife. He knew that she was the one, the only one. He also knew that he was not a man.

When his master Ohm went out in the evening, he spent his time at the third floor window hoping for glimpses of the gray dressed bird named Hannah. He used to just watch birds and animals with his binoculars. Now, Hannah Bird was his nightly television show. He watched her thru the windows with his binoculars. His heart had beaten for her ever since the first time he saw her in the off campus convenience store over three years before. She was different from the trashy American college girls that paraded their naked bodies up and down the alley smoking and drinking. The gray bird was respectable.

Watching her run and play in the shadows of the green reminded him of his position in life. He was a servant and not a man that a woman would want. He was not capable of making physical love or planting seed for children. He was what men had made him, a eunuch or servant. In India, he had been fixed like he was some sort of animal when he became the servant to a rich family who had many girls. His heart wanted Hannah, but he knew he could never have her as a man because he was not a man, or so he had been told. He stood teary eyed in the shadows. He couldn't bear the thought of returning to San Francisco without her. He wanted to tell her how much she meant to him. All he knew were simple words from the English language. What was in his heart could not be said in simple words.

He felt like his heart was in his shoes as he watched the man he knew as Mooch take the gray bird in his arms and kiss her passionately. He wanted to go rip her out of the young man's arms, yelling that the gray bird was his. He bit his lip and a tear rolled out of his eye and down his golden brown skinned face. He had never wanted anything like he did the dimple faced bird named Hannah. He had never considered being free till the gray dove and Mooch had befriended him. He had always been owned. If he could choose, he would choose a life with the gray bird and an occupation having to do with art and birds. He could see himself writing a book about birds and painting all of the illustrations. He could also see himself sitting at the head of her table and helping her entertain. His employer Ohm had explained the dinner club to him. He would be willing to be a servant in her dinner club, if she would let him. He would do anything she wanted, if she would let him be hers.

Chim had the silent crying of the heart, the wanting of someone you can not have.

The Promise

Somewhere around midnight, Mooch walked Hannah to her third floor door. He felt like the luckiest man in the whole world and had asked Hannah if she would marry him once he was out of medical school. She had said yes. He was in a state of bliss and thinking about a ring for her. He would come up with the money somewhere for one.

"You are mine." He stated as he held both of her hands hating to let her go. She was not like one of his other women who would invite him in for the night. Don't let Uziah push you around. I will study hard and try to get thru school as quickly as possible. We will leave everything behind once I am a Doctor. I promise you that one day I will be totally faithful to you. I don't sleep with these women because I want them, Hannah."

"You don't have to explain to me, Mooch. Do what you have to do to survive. I have four years of college ahead of me. Even if we are apart, one day we will find each other again and we will indeed forget what is behind us. Survive, Mooch, for me. Survive. I will do the same."

"You have to be the other half of me, or you wouldn't understand who and why I do what I have to do."

"I think you might be right. You once laughed at me when I was doctoring you for the Toe Jam Creeper. You said you could see us as Dr. Mooch, MD and Dr. Hannah Zook Mooch head of the World Health Organization. Perhaps you are psychic. I have decided to go into the premed program and also become a doctor."

"I knew you were the one for me. We will be good together. I love you Hannah and I will never love anyone but you. Did you know that you kiss like crazy? I want to die when I am old with your lips pressed to mine."

"You will never know what those words mean to me. Thank you for tonight. You were here for me when I emotionally was at the bottom of the barrel and slipping into a pit of depression. I won't forget it. You have made my graduation party night worth remembering. I was disappointed that several didn't come to celebrate with me. My mother always said that the proof is in the pudding. The party tonight was my pudding. I will cut from my heart those who were not in my pudding cup tonight."

"I want to always be part of your cup. I am really sorry that I have to do what I do to survive."

"Survive, Mooch, I will never hold it against you."

Mooch took her in his arms and kissed her one last time passionately and then the door opened with Uziah standing there.

Thinking quick, Mooch kissed Hannah behind the ear with Uziah looking on marking his turf. He had heard Uziah speak of courting rituals and knew that the bridegroom kissed his bride to be once behind the ear the night before their wedding. He could see the shock on Uziah's face. Then he squeezed Hannah's hand, winked at her, and turning to Uziah said, "Looks like you and I just might be cousins when I get out of medical school." Then he slapped Uziah on the back. Hannah grinned knowing that Mooch was giving Uziah a hard time.

She was promised. There was no reason now to consider any man other than Mooch. Sergeant Pepper, Uziah and everyone else could go to Amish hell. They were all Jackasses and deserving of it in her book.

CHAPTER TWELVE

The Obituaries

It was a little after midnight, but Hannah hadn't gone to sleep yet. She was so excited about her promise to Mooch that she was just about to burst wanting to tell someone. Uziah had acted totally uninterested once Mooch was gone. He had crawled on his twin bed by the widow stating he wished to go to sleep. She retreated to her bedroom and closed the door. Then the cell phone, lying on a tiny table next to her bed, rang. She picked it up and checked he caller Id. The incoming number was that of Georgia.

"Good evening, Zook's Place," Hannah answered. She always answered the phone appropriately.

"Hi sweetie, it is Georgia. Where in the heck have you been? I have been calling since about eight-thirty trying to get a hold of you and apologize for not being there. I have a black eye and I am embarrassed to show my face."

"What happened?" Asked Hannah suddenly alarmed. She had wondered why Georgia hadn't come. They were friends.

"First let me wish you the best for your future and say, Happy Graduation." If you will look in your tiny chest in the top drawer, you will find a present from me. I dropped it off earlier in the day and hid it there. I let myself in with that key you gave me years ago. I hope you like it. I am not a seamstress, but I did my best to pick you out the perfect gift. I gave it a lot of thought."

"There is a present for me?" Hannah squealed in a questioning voice. Then she jumped out of her bed and hurried to the little chest and pulled the top drawer open. There lay several yards of gray dress material and a couple yards of white cap material. Hannah was pleased. She had been wearing the same two gray dresses for three and one half years and they were getting thin. "Georgia, I am so pleased. It is a very thoughtful gift. I can tell that there is enough to make two dresses and probably ten caps. Thank you!"

"Look between the two pieces of material. That is where you will find your real present." Georgia replied.

Hannah separated the two pieces of material and a very tiny package fell out that was very nicely wrapped in silver metallic paper with a black bow. "I am going to lay the phone down a minute while I unwrap it. I am so excited."

"Take your time, sweetie. I am laying here in my pajamas. I am not going anywhere."

Taking great care, Hannah removed the gift wrap. She wanted to preserve it for her memory box. When she got the wrapper and the bow off, she saw that it was a tiny jeweler's box. She opened it and there found a gold thimble. She held the thimble up with tears in her eyes. It was a thoughtful, expensive gift. Turning the thimble in her fingers, she saw that it was inscribed: Hannah, Happy Graduation, Georgia. 14 K Gold.

"Thank you, Georgia. I will use the thimble with pride for a lifetime and hand it down to someone in my family with the story of my graduation to go with it when I am old and about to pass on. You know me and what I like. Thank you."

"That is the crazy thing, Hannah. We do know each other. We are as different as daylight and dark but accept each other for who we are. What did the all the Wednesday night assholes give you for graduation?"

"The men all gave me money except for Mooch. He gave me a giant chocolate bar and a card. Candy bars are a thing between us. He brings me one every Wednesday night. Sergeant Pepper and Endora gave me nothing. I was hurt by that. They didn't even come to my party. That I will not forget. I have made them three years of birthday and celebration cakes for their special moments. David Goldstein sent me a bouquet of red roses from the florist with a card attached signed male jerk. Uziah gave me nothing. Perhaps he is waiting till Friday night when I actually graduate. Mrs. Begley from the apartment house behind sent over a pink comb and brush set. I thought it was awfully nice of her. Your gift, however, tops them all and is my favorite. I will never forget how beautifully it was wrapped and how it made me feel when I opened it."

"You hinted earlier that Mooch gave you something beside a chocolate bar and card. What did he give you?" Georgia asked expecting Hannah to say tea towels or something of that nature.

"He asked me to marry him and I said yes." Hannah replied and then heard her friend gasp on the other end of the line.

"He asked you what and you said what?" Georgia shot back in a shocked voice.

"He asked me to marry him once he is out of medical school.

I said yes."

"Sweetie, this has been one day of surprises. I was led to believe that Sergeant Pepper was interested in courting you."

"Uziah said that Sergeant Pepper wanted to call on me after I graduated. However, I have seen no indication of it. Sergeant Pepper said terrible things to me concerning it. I had the most embarrassing day of my life today and it was some sick joke that Uziah apparently dreamed up. I will tell you about it when I have got over being angry about it. It may take me a few days."

"Back to the subject of Mooch, do you know how Mooch gets his money for college, etc.?" Georgia asked thinking she was going to have to inform Hannah.

"Yes, I know he is a male escort. He goes to see Mrs. Begley every Sunday evening and the widow down the street that I clean for on Sunday mornings."

Again, Hannah heard Georgia gasp as though something were wrong.

"He was honest with me. I told him to do what he needs to do to survive till he is out of medical school and that I will not hold it against him. Mooch and I love each other. We learned to care about each other as we shared tea towels on Wednesday night cleanups."

"I can understand his wanting to wait. He isn't going to rock his money boat. I will congratulate Mooch tomorrow in my way."

"All of our worlds are changing and moving, Georgia. I will keep Zook's Place open possibly another year. The plan has always been for me to go to Chicago and transfer to a college there. It may be as many as six years before Mooch and I marry."

"What about Sergeant Pepper, you and him have always been close friends?"

"He is a jackass who embarrassed the hell out of me today, demeaned me with his words, and didn't come to my graduation party. He is history in my life."

"Men use us and then abuse us. I have two men on my list that are going to get some pay backs tomorrow." Georgia stated.

"How did you get your black eye, Georgia? We got off of the subject." Hannah asked looking at her gold thimble in one hand and holding her cell phone with the other.

"You might as well know, Hannah. You know everything else just about. Years ago Sergeant Pepper and I lived together. We were lovers. He left me for the Bell ringers."

"Oh . . ." Hannah gasped. "You are a secret he has never shared with me."

"It is okay, sweetie. You are innocent in all the madness that goes on around you. You seem to be the center or hub for some reason."

"I think I am called to love all of you, and I do." Hannah replied

"Before I forget, are you still planning to take a few days and go visit your parents? I know that you didn't go home when your two little brothers died. I have never brought up the subject because I felt you would talk about it with me when you were ready. It took years for me to talk about my father's death."

"Why would you think my little brothers are dead, Georgia?"

"I sent the obituaries from the paper home with Uziah a couple of years ago along with flowers. Don't you remember?"

Hannah was in shock and didn't know how to answer. Had Uziah with held such an important thing from her?

After a brief silence, Hannah spoke. "I am sorry, Georgia. I was not thinking straight for a moment. I have tried to pretend that the deaths didn't happen. Can you recall when you saw the obituaries in the newspaper? In my grief the originals got thrown away. I really would like to pull them up on Uziah's computer and put a copy of the notices in my memory box. I haven't wanted to face it till now." She stated lying.

"It was the week before St. Patrick's Day, two years ago. I remember because I had a broken bone in my foot and I was housebound for about six weeks. I didn't come to friend night during that time."

"What color were the flowers and what kind. I was so grieved that I don't recall and I wish to now write about them for my memory box."

"It was a bouquet of yellow roses. Something was said in the obituary about one of the boys liking yellow roses."

That settled it for Hannah. Georgia was telling the truth. One of her two little mentally challenged brothers had a fascination with yellow roses. She would wait till Georgia hung up, then she would slip into the main room and get Uziah's lap top to search for the obituaries.

"My mother grew yellow roses in front of our farm house. It is time for me to go home and make my peace with their passing." Hannah stated trying to remain calm. "I am closing down Zook's Place till after my trip home. I have no reservations for the rest of this week or for the next two."

"Will you take a photo of your mother's roses to share with me?" Georgia asked.

"Yes, I will take one when no one is looking. My parents do not believe in graven images. How did you get your black eye? You still haven't told me."

"It is unimportant Hannah. However, I am going to do you a favor tomorrow. You may not understand it for a few years, but it is an act of love."

"Do you think that Uziah is capable of deceit, Georgia? I have questioned lately some of the things he has done that I don't understand."

"People wear masks, sweetie. Everyone wears them at one time or another to hide flaws and shortcomings. I wear one with everyone but you. I am a scared little girl looking for the love and security that her father never gave her. I now wear the mask of a seductive woman and search for love in men looking like my father. You are the only one who sees the Georgia that is seven and scared."

"Be honest with me, Georgia, do I wear a mask?"

"Oh sweetie, your pretend marriage to Uziah has been a terrible mask to wear. You have had no life of your own. You have missed out on dating and such things as men sending you flowers. You have hid behind a mask that has the words written across it: I am on hold till Uziah says it alright for me to be me."

"I chose my mask when I was seventeen because I do not want to marry or have children. I feared having mentally challenged children like my brothers. My parents are cousins and I have bad genes. My mask was safe for me. I knew nothing about birth control and I chose what I thought was a safe mask. Uziah was just as dumb."

"We all do things for stupid reasons. I am going to do something tomorrow that is probably stupid, but I feel that it is necessary for your and my survival in the land of men."

"Do you wish to tell me about the stupid thing that you are going to do?"

"Perhaps I will tell you someday when I am old. You need to think about all of these things we have discussed tonight. You need to ask yourself if Mooch is wearing a mask or does he want something from you? You need to ask yourself what Uziah wants from you. If an individual doesn't want anything, then they love you and want to be with you because they like you and for no other reason."

Hannah cringed at her words which struck a nerve.

"I have got to go sweetie. Happy graduation and I am really sorry about tonight. I didn't expect to get a black eye just before your party was to start."

"I understand. Thank you again for being my friend and the graduation gift that I will always treasure. You are the great gift to me. I will always treasure you, our friendship, and our midnight talks for the last three years."

"Good night, Sweetie," Georgia stated and hung up.

After hanging up the phone, she tip toed quietly into the main room to get the laptop. To her surprise, Uziah was gone. She wondered where in the world he went at one in the morning, however, she wasn't married to him. They were just cousins.

Perhaps he and Endora were enjoying his new found freedom.

Returning to her room and sitting down in her little one armed rocker she opened up the laptop and logged on. Then she pulled up the newspaper obituaries for the week Georgia had indicated. In shock, she burst into tears. It was just as Georgia had said. Her little brothers had died over two years before about the time that Zook's place was starting to become quite profitable. It did mention in the obituary that one of her two brothers had a fascination with yellow roses.

Jelly Bean

Hannah had a fitful night of sleep. She had nightmares of Sergeant Pepper telling her over and over that she was a bad kisser and then she would dream of her two little brothers in wooden Amish coffins. Then she would dream that Mooch was dead and in a coffin. Her night was filled with nightmares.

On Thursday morning, she climbed out of bed at five and got dressed. She had some serious thinking to do and decisions to make. She was not in the mood to confront Uziah just yet. So, she decided to slip out of the apartment quietly and walk down to the convenience store to have coffee and a doughnut. She would sit there until time to go to school for her last day of high school. It would be a short day. The seniors would get out at noon. She needed the afternoon to carry out whatever plans she made this morning. A time of running away had once more arrived. Uziah and their Amish life together was the cold, icy, snowy existence she was going to leave behind.

Her world had turned completely upside down in one day's time. Sergeant Pepper had broken her heart with his comment about her kiss. Uziah had betrayed her by not telling her of the deaths of her two little brothers. Georgia was the secret lover of

Sergeant Pepper. A small amount of money was missing from the savings beneath the loose board underneath their table. What else could go wrong in her world?

The walk to the convenience store was a pleasant one in spite of her grief. The birds were waking up and starting to sing. She thought of Chim and knew that he would enjoy the moment she was experiencing. She regretted having not befriended him. Uziah and his friends had been the mask she hid behind. Now she didn't have a mask of friends of her own to turn to. She would be entering her new life alone. Mooch had to do what Mooch had to do. Plus he would be going off to Medical school in another state shortly. As she listened to the birds sing, she vowed to never let a man rule her again or strip her of friends of her own.

Today was her last day of school and she would be turning in all of her books. The teachers had told the seniors to bring a book to read to pass the morning till they were dismissed at noon. She had brought her Bible. She wanted to get back to some of the basics of her Amish faith. She planned to read the Bible thru twice in the next year. That would be her first goal for her new existence.

Uziah would be working an afternoon shift at the Pancake Emporium for pocket money. Going with him to Chicago was no longer feasible. He was using her to make money to send him thru school. She could see now that he did not have her interests at heart. He had denied her friends as well as the knowledge of her brother's deaths. He was trying to control her. She was young and stupid at seventeen. However, that was no longer the case. She credited Georgia and their midnight talks for the opening of her mind.

At the convenience store, she purchased her cup of coffee and doughnut. After paying, she took the last booth and sat facing the register so she could watch people enter and exit as she contemplated what she was going to do. The thought of leaving everyone was breaking her heart, even if they were Uziah's friends. She had loved all of them. She had been focusing her world around what Uziah wanted. Now, she must start over.

Time passed and the sun came up as she sat in the convenience store booth sipping a cup of coffee very slowly. A familiar male walked in with a girl about seventeen or eighteen who was a God's Will child. Hannah recognized the Downs- syndrome look. The girl was a little on the plump side. Her two little brothers didn't run and play like other children. It seemed that everything they ate turned to fat making them a little round. She pictured her two little brothers older with the seventeen year old girl's face on them. It was not a pretty picture. Her brothers would not have been pleasant to look at. They would have had limited lives of not marrying or having children. When her parents were gone, they would have been rotated between their siblings to live out their existence when they were old. In her mind, even though she was grieving, her brothers were better off deceased.

David Goldstein was with the girl. Hannah ignored him and didn't look up. She was there to think and plan her future. This wasn't a social hour for her to once more entertain one of Uziah's friends.

She had made two decisions for sure. She would have to put off her trip home for a few weeks. She needed a time to grieve. She wanted her trip home to see her mother to be a joyous trip, not one of sorrow. Number two, she would definitely be moving from Sergeant Pepper's apartment complex Saturday morning. For now, she just wanted to get thru graduation Friday night. Afterward, she would confront Uziah and then move out. She had nothing going on Friday morning. She would use it to find and rent herself another apartment. Today, Thursday, was a turning in books to school day and a walking trip to the post office where she would mail the box of gifts home to her mother. She was sharing all of the tea towels and linens she had made from discarded shirts. She was afraid if she waited till the last minute, something might go wrong and she wouldn't be able to take the box with her. She had left the farm with a pillow case of belongings. She might have to do it again. When school let out at noon, mailing the linens would be first on her list.

A sharp voice caught her attention. She looked up and saw David as he tried to control the girl who seemed to be touching everything in sight as he tried to pay for a bottle of soda and a cup of coffee. Then he turned and spotted Hannah and looked a little flustered. She could see that he had his hands full trying to coax the girl toward the booths. Biting his lip, he forcibly took her by the arm with his free hand making her carry her soda and headed for Hannah and the booth.

"May my sister and I sit with you for a few minutes or are you meeting someone? I will understand if you don't want us sitting with you." He stated red faced...

"Sure sit down." Hannah stated turning her attention to the girl. "My name is Hannah. What is yours?"

"Martha Jelly Bean," stated the girl sliding into the booth across from her. David started to slide in next to her when she threw a little hissy fit slapping at David and said loudly, "No . . . this seat mine. You sit there with the ugly gray dress. My seat . . .!"

"It is alright, Jelly Bean. You can have the booth seat to yourself. Do you mind if I share your side Hannah. Jelly Bean is a little territorial about some things. She is like a two or three year old who doesn't want to share a toy. In this case the booth is her toy."

"Yes, I will be happy to share my seat with you." Hannah said sliding towards the wall. She had most of her thinking done, so she would be nice and visit.

David slid in beside her a little flushed. "Why are you here? Aren't you usually cooking Uziah's breakfast about now?"

"It is my last day of school and I am treating myself eating breakfast out. I just had a doughnut. Before I forget, there will be no more Wednesday night friend dinners."

"Ouch. Are you starting a new war with me and the others this morning? Have I or them done something?" He asked grabbing the napkin container from Jelly Bean to keep her from pulling them all out.

"No war is intended. I will tell the others also. I am leaving Uziah after graduation."

"What?"

"I am leaving Uziah and moving out into an apartment of my own."

"I had to leave last night. My parents were in a minor car wreck and I had to go pick up Jelly Bean and bring her home with me. Did something go wrong at the party?"

"You weren't there when Uziah told the others on the balcony. Uziah told everyone our secret."

"Secret, I don't understand." He stated removing the salt shaker from Jelly Beans hand and placing it on the table of the other booth.

"Uziah and I are not married. We are second cousins who

have come here for educations. We do share the same family name of Zook. We felt it best for me and my safety if Uziah's friends thought I was not single. Our pretend marriage was for my safety. In our thinking, when we first arrived here, I could not marry anyone but an Amish man. My thinking has changed since then. Uziah wants to date Endora and it was time last evening to lay down our image that we created for my safety. It had become a burden to both of us. We are both adults and it is time for us to walk forward and create separate lives for ourselves."

"You have to be kidding me?" He retorted in shock. "I have been infatuated with you for three and one half years and you were single the whole time?"

"Uziah was running away from the farm to start classes here at the university. He had secretly enrolled not telling his parents. When I found out, I begged him to bring me with him. He said he would do so under one condition and that was to pretend that we were married, so he would not have to deal with English men who might want to use or abuse me. The agreement was that we would keep up the pretense till he was out of college and I was out of high school. I kept my promise."

"You and I are going to have a talk about this as soon as I have Jelly Bean out of my hair." He stated laughing.

"Why have you never told me about your sister?" She asked as Jelly Bean started fooling with the ketchup container and shaking some out on the table. David grabbed the container and cleaned up the mess.

"I don't want to be judged by her. All thru elementary, middle, and high school, I was judged by her. Girls wouldn't date me, assuming I was defective or challenged because she was. The university and freedom from her has been a God send for me. My parents and Jelly Bean live three or so hours away. No one knows her here and I have lived a normal life for a man my age and have dated and enjoyed being normal. I was forced to go pick her up last night. My parents were in a minor car accident. Social Services from the hospital called me to come get her. I drove home last night and back this morning. We have stopped in here for something to drink. I knew there wouldn't be anything but beer and pizza in the apartment."

"Uziah and I weren't the only ones running away that snowy night years ago." Hannah replied eyeing him and his frustration with his sister which was visible in his facial expressions.

"I have worked hard to have friends here. I am a grown man and I fear once more being judged as different or challenged because of her. I love her, but I have suffered a lifetime of ridicule because of her. My childhood and teen years I would never want to repeat. I am pissed that my parents just expect me to put my life on hold to care for her. My family is not poor. They could have hired a nurse for her for a couple of days till they got out of the hospital. I love her as my sister, but I don't like her very much as human."

"To be honest with you, I can see why. A two year old can be taught to sit in a booth and color a picture while adults talk. A two year old can be taught not to call a lady ugly or say inappropriate things. I don't like your sister as a person either. I have two deceased little brothers who were mentally challenged like Jelly Bean. They were taught appropriate behavior with strangers as well as what can and can't be done when sitting at a table. She is undisciplined and that makes her ugly and it reflects on you. Your parents have sinned in God's eyes not correcting and disciplining her."

"You are pushing all my buttons, Hannah. However, you are speaking the truth. What tees me off is that my aging parents expect me to take her when they are gone and care for her on a permanent basis. I never had a life till I came here to the university. Now, they want to spoil that for me by insisting I care for her and that she never go to a nursing home of any sort. I don't want her these three days much less for a lifetime. She is my sister, but I can barely tolerate her."

"I understand, believe me. I also was judged by my brother's craziness and refused by some suitors for that reason. Maple Syrup disease and mentally challenged children plague the Amish community. It is a gene thing that could be prevented in some instances. My two challenged siblings are the result of my parents being second cousins and sharing grandfather genes. When the wrong gene combination gets together, there are problems with the children that are born. That is why I left the Amish community. I am related to most everyone amongst the Amish families. I have made a conscience decision to not have children and carry on bad gene lines."

"Damn, that is exactly my thinking. I am afraid of my parent's genes and the possibility of producing more Jelly beans. As bad as I hate to admit the shame, my parents are first cousins. I am not taking any chances. My mother has had a miserable life caring for her plus being looked down on. People aren't always nice with what they say or insinuate."

"Believe me, I know all about it." Hannah replied.

About that time, Jelly Bean took her bottle of soda and started pouring it out on the table. David grabbed the bottle, scolded her, and proceeded to wipe up the soda with paper napkins. She screamed to high Heaven because David took the two thirds empty soda bottle from her. The clerk came running with a cleaning rag to help. Jelly Bean reached over and attempted to bite the arm of the clerk who jumped back.

"Get her out of her when you finish your drinks. I don't have to put up with a biting retard. She belongs in a cage." The clerk said throwing the rag down and leaving it for David to do the cleanup.

"I am sorry, Hannah, I really am. I know this has to be embarrassing to you, it is to me!" He replied. "I don't know how I am going to survive the next two or three days. The only way I can half way control her is to strap her in my jeep and ride around the city with her. She doesn't have the mental ability to get the seat belt undone. I may be sleeping in my vehicle with her."

"There are many hard decisions in life David. I made a hard one abandoning my family to become educated. I knew my mother needed me to help with my brothers. However, it is our turn to make decisions and live our lives. Our parents ignored genes and married shamefully. I have made a decision to have no children. Jelly Bean is your parent's responsibility. Personally, if it were me, I would put her in a home where she is fed and bathed regularly, a place where she is safe. You have a life and talents to share with society and the world about us. You cannot do that tied to Jelly Bean. You do have the responsibility to pay for her care as does your parents. However, sometimes we must make decisions that are not always comfortable in making. You cannot take Jelly Bean with you to Rabbi School or to the advanced degree classes. You must choose what is best for you, because you are the one that is going to have to foot the bills as well as live your future. Jelly Bean is not capable of being a latch key child or to be left alone for any reason. I see no need for you to be forced to care for someone that is impossible for you to care for. Jelly Bean would be much better off in a nice warm bed with nurses to watch over her. Some say it is love to keep children like her at home. I say it is love to let them settle into a permanent long term home. I could not run the Zook's Place Dining club and have my two little brothers under my feet crawling in and out of my kitchen cabinets or them stripping off naked and suddenly appearing at my dinners thinking it was okay. I have my life to lead and something to give back to society. I have decided the last week to become a doctor. I am giving back to society in my way and not in the fashion my family expected me to. In my opinion, you should commit Jelly Bean and let her get used to a new home for the future when your parents are gone. She is visibly spoiled and should be taught like a two or three year old that you don't pour stuff out on the table or demand to sit in a certain position or tell ladies that their dresses are ugly. When your parents are gone, she will find discipline hard and a spoil free environment hard to live with. She needs routine and that which will always be there. Sleeping in a vehicle seat belt is a disgrace to her and to you. Your parents, being older, should have made decisions for her long ago. You should not be saddled with their sins of slothfulness and neglect. They had her and should have made the decisions for her."

"You are harsh, Hannah!" He said a little red faced.

"Harsh, perhaps I am. Decisions are not easy sometimes and the fallout from them may make us look like we are uncaring. However, it is your life now to live and you should not be required to feel guilty for making decisions your parents should have made years ago. They are passing the buck as the English say. I am choosing not to have children. You must choose what you want out of life and what to do about Jelly Bean, since your parents are slothful in their duty to do so. You can take on full care for Jelly Bean, but in the end it is a no win situation. You abandon your right to live a life and become who you want to be and in the end she will still have to go into a nursing facility anyway. You, being a man, will not always be able to care for her. If I were you, I would turn my jeep around and take her back to where she is from and sign her into a facility there. Your aging parents will not always be alive. You and I will not always be alive. When I am your parent's age, I will look back and know that I have made the right decision and not produced sick children with no wings to fly. You should look back when you are old and be happy with your decisions. You shouldn't look back and see a life that was wasted caring for your parent's choice. Marrying your cousin is a choice. They should have known better.

"I am not sure I like you at this moment, Hannah. However, you are right. I can't care for her and really don't want to. I see my parents as taking advantage of me and trying to steal my new life here from me. They could care less what I want. I am a dumping ground for them."

"I don't like myself sometimes, David. However, I am a decision maker and that is a God given right. We have free will choice and no one should take that away from us. I cannot live my parent's life or care for their sins. I must live my own life and be all that I can be and try to add something to the overall grand scheme of things, instead of mindlessly producing sick children and making them a drain on family members and society. I am harsh in my thinking. However, I am realistic concerning what I feel my life is to be about. That does not mean that I won't go see my siblings and make sure they are cared for when they get older. However, for as long as my parents are able, my brothers are their responsibility and they should make the decisions for their futures." Hannah stated, knowing her little brothers were dead.

"Come on Jelly Bean, it is time to go," stated David rising with a red face. She grabbed the edge of the booth to brace herself and started screaming and refusing to leave the booth.

"No!" She screamed. "I want stay. Play! Get rid of gray ugly lady. Give me my soda!"

"Come on Jelly Bean," stated David trying to coax her out of the booth.

"No," she yelled and reached over and picked up Hannah's almost empty cup of coffee and threw it at David which glanced off him and ended up in the floor leaking what remained of the coffee on the floor.

Finally after no success in coaxing her to leave the booth, David grabbed her by the back neck of her dress and dragged her out of the booth and ushered her towards the door with everyone staring at him.

Hannah could see that he was mad, embarrassed, and wanted to shut his sister up. He was facing his need to walk away. Walking away from relatives isn't always easy, but sometimes it is a necessity.

CHAPTER THIRTEEN

Mooch Chooses Georgia

It was just after lunch when Mooch's cell phone rang. He had been up late with Hannah and he had slept in. He didn't get that chance during the school year. He always took early morning classes so he would have time to study in the afternoons and do his thing with the ladies in the evenings. The caller ID number was that of Georgia. He closed his eyes a minute and then answered. Georgia was someone that he couldn't ignore. Her money was his meal ticket to medical school. He had his master degree tuition and books covered. However, medical school was a whole new ballgame and he had to play his cards right to come up with the kind of money he needed. She was the only one of his older women that could afford it. Mrs. Begley and the widow down the alley each paid him a hundred dollars each for services rendered. However, that was far from being the type of money he needed. He had to keep his boat afloat with Georgia because he didn't have another sugar mama to replace her.

"Good Morning, my pancake queen," he answered. He really wanted to tell her to go to hell and then turn over and put the pillow on top of his head and go back to sleep.

"Congratulations, Mooch. Hannah tells me that the two of you are planning on getting married. I gather that means you don't need me or my money anymore. Come out to the restaurant at two to pick up your final paycheck. I hope she is worth it!" Georgia said sarcastically.

"Who told you we were going to get married?" He had wanted to keep it on the QT for the next four years. He needed Georgia.

"Hannah did, sweetie. I called her late last night and she was just bubbling over with excitement. I will leave your check on the time clock. I hope it is enough to get you in the door of the medical school." She replied.

"Now, Georgia. Hannah had to be telling you a fabricated story of some sort. I am not engaged to her. I will get this straightened out and be out to the restaurant after two as soon as I shower and shave."

"It is no fabrication, Mooch. Uziah told me the same thing when he came to work this morning. No one plays Georgia for a fool." She stated and hung up.

Mooch was immediately up and dressing. Why had Hannah done this to him? He thought he had made it clear to her that he needed the money from his tricks to pay his way thru school.

Hurrying, he dressed, opened the front door and started to climb to the third floor apartment when he spotted Hannah returning from somewhere with three tote bags on her arm. That was strange. However, that was the least of his interests. He scooted down the stairs to meet her just as she was about to step on to the first stair.

"I want to know why you chose to tell Georgia that we are getting married. I made it very clear to you that I need the money from the women I am with to make it thru medical school. Why would you tell her?"

"Why wouldn't I tell her? We did make plans and she is my best friend. We talk every night for about fifteen minutes or so before I go to bed. We have done so for three plus years."

"You are going to call her and tell her we are not getting married. Georgia is my main source of income. I need her. Surely you have known that I am her paid escort?"

"Georgia has never mentioned a relationship with you to me. You want me to lie to my best friend for money?"

"Yes, damn it. I need her."

"Your words have painted her as number one with you, not I. You need her more than me?"

"Yes, at the moment, I need her more than you." He stated angry and scared of being penniless facing medical school.

"I guess that says it all. You are a jackass like the rest of the men who attend Wednesday night dinners at my table. Don't knock on my door. Your invitation to my table has been withdrawn." She stated and headed up the stairs.

"Will you tell Georgia it isn't true?" He yelled after her.

She didn't answer him.

Creating a Plan of Safe Escape

Once inside her apartment door, Hannah leaned against the closed door and burst into tears. Not only had Sergeant Pepper told her that she was a bad kisser, Mooch had chose Georgia and money over her. She went to her bedroom and took down her memory box and removed every chocolate, candy bar wrapper from it and threw them in the trash. Then she allowed herself a ten minute cry. She couldn't afford to cry longer than that because she had too much to think about and do. She had stopped and purchased grocery carry totes to go with her school tote to move in. She felt that three bags would be enough. Earlier, she had mailed home the box of linens she had made as gifts for her mother and sisters. She was covering all the corners and creating for herself a safe path out.

After crying and being mad at herself, she wasted no time in packing her Bible, camera, binoculars, memory box, and some tiny perfume bottles that the ladies from Zook's Place had given her occasionally. In one bag she put her second dress, under things, and the cloth and thimble from Georgia. In the third bag she put all of the receipts and clients lists etc. from Zook's Place. The only things she left unpacked were her tooth brush and comb. She would wear the dress she had on for two days. Under her graduation gown, no one would know that she had on a two day dirty dress. When she took off the gown and had her diploma in her hand, she would just walk away and start over. She had done it once and she could do it again.

In her head, she checked off every little detail that needed to be done between now and graduation. She had mailed the box of handmade linens home. She had written a letter to Mrs. Begley and the widow explaining she would not be cleaning for them and why. Also, she had written and mailed thank you notes for the gifts that she had been given of which most were money. The graduation money was in her memory box. All she had left to do was carry the three totes to the university campus and lock them in her rented locker. She would split the money from Zook's Place with Uziah tomorrow night after graduation. She was fair and would give him half. However, she knew that he was getting more than half because Zook's Place had already paid for his college and master degree tuition. She had gone to a public high school which required no tuition. He had already used close to twenty thousand of the earned education fund. However, she was fair. She would split their savings. She was not out to hurt Uziah, she was just going her separate way.

A knock came at the door. She didn't answer. It had to be either Mooch or Sergeant Pepper and she was not in the mood to listen to either of the two jackasses. When the knocking ceased, she waited twenty minutes and then made her way down the stairs and just missed bumping into Sergeant Pepper who she saw entering David's apartment. Ducking low, she sneaked past David's window and scurried down the stairs carrying her load.

On the way to the campus, she had to stop and rest a couple of times. She hadn't anticipated how long the walk was and how heavy her three totes were. She would have to consider that on Friday night after graduation. She would need to rent her an apartment and then make three plus trips instead of one labored one moving the totes. After some tiresome tote lugging, she managed to get her three sacks of items stored in her rented university locker. Now all she had to worry about was her own well being, the one set of clothes she had on, and getting her share of the money tomorrow night. Her toothbrush and comb in the bathroom she could replace, if she needed to. Underneath her graduation robe, no one would know that she had on a two day dirty dress. She had to do what she had to do to survive.

In her physical education class in the tenth grade, her instructor invited a speaker to come from the women's shelter. Hannah remembered her speech and how she told the girls how to plan a safe escape if they ever needed to and what to take. At the time, Hannah never believed it would be her having to make a plan. However, here she was and she was proud of herself. She would leave the jackasses behind that had used and abused her. She had a dining table full of abusers, not just one. She was leaving them all behind. She had better things to do with her time and love than to give it to jackasses. She would start a new life and dump the lot.

Georgia was right. From now on, she would look behind the masks of men before she let her heart get attached and then broken. If a man told her that he loved her and wanted to marry her from now on, she would laugh at him and ask him why? Mooch had really disappointed her. He tried to make her second in line to another woman with money. She would never be second best again. Sergeant Pepper had demeaned her telling her that her kiss was bad and Mooch had put her in second place. If the two men she loved the most out of the group had been so unkind to her, there was no need to consider another suitor. A good man just wasn't out there in her book. English men were all jackasses. In her mind she would never let herself love any man again.

Happy with her afternoon, Hannah returned to the apartment. She would spend the rest of the afternoon cooking a good meal for dinner. It would be her going away dinner, only Uziah wouldn't know it. She had shrimp in the freezer that she had been saving for a special occasion. Tonight was the night. It would just be her and Uziah eating at the long door table that she had come to love. She would miss it and her life in Apartment 3C. However, it was time to move on. She would eat a good meal because she might not be able to cook for a few days till she got settled. She didn't want to get ill from bad eating.

It was about one thirty on Thursday afternoon. She would now walk home and perhaps take a nap. She was just putting in time waiting for the day to pass and then tomorrow evening till she donned her cap and gown. She remembered how long the day seemed when she was waiting to run away from home with Uziah. Here she was again. Instead of hiding her pillowcase of belongings from her parents, it was Uziah, Sergeant Pepper, and

Mooch she had to watch out for this time. The sun would have to go down on her graduation day before she could leave. She had worked hard for her diploma and the right to wear the cap and gown. All the friends had been there to see Uziah graduate college the week before. It was her turn.

CHAPTER FOURTEEN

The Seduction of Uziah

It was after lunch on Thursday, the day before Hannah's graduation. Uziah was working an afternoon shift at Georgia's Pancake Emporium for pocket money. While filling the dishwasher, he was eyeing a long legged waitress named Millie as she scurried about. Recently, he had become attracted to her and his fascination with Endora had lessened. The waitress was a year or so older than him. He didn't see that as a problem. He was free to date now. He had told all of his friends on the balcony on Wednesday that he and Hannah were not married. It was such a relief. He was no longer Amish. He wanted to live the life of an English adult his age and that including dating. David Goldstein was the only one who didn't know. He wasn't on the balcony Wednesday evening. He had left early for an emergency of some sort. He would tell him the first time he ran into him.

Eyeing Millie long legs run back and forth, Uziah decided to ask her to have dinner with him. He had taken money from the stash underneath the table and had bought himself a dinner jacket, dress pants, new shirt and shoes like those of Mooch. He had them hidden in his rented university student locker. He could change in the university men's room when he needed to and then change back again as needed in order to hide the fact that he had been spending part of the education fund. He eyed once more Millie's beautiful long legs as she passed thru in her short waitress skirt. He liked tall girls. He was tall. He would ask Millie when she took a break about two in the afternoon.

Thinking about his new dinner jacket, he smiled. He was sure that Hannah would never miss the amount from the money beneath the floor. Occasionally he took a ten or twenty when he needed it. A man had more needs than a woman. He would slip out a hundred dollar bill to take Millie out.

The breakfast rush had just calmed down. As he loaded the dishwasher, which was a never ending job, he thought about Hannah and their disagreement. He knew that he needed her, but at the same time he was pissed that she was always right as well as brought in their major income. He would dump his cousin in a heartbeat if he could. However, she had pulled in all of the money for his college expenses as well as his master degree program that he would begin in a couple of weeks. Without her, medical school was not a possibility. That irked him. The man should be head of the woman in all things. His father never let his mother get by with anything.

He thought of the secret he had been keeping. Hannah's two little brothers had died from Maple Syrup disease two days apart a couple or so years back. He had intercepted some flowers and two obituaries sent over by Georgia when they first had Zook's Place up, running, and pulling in the big bucks. At the time, he feared that she would return home and not come back. Zook's Place was not something he could run. He wasn't a cook nor did the guests come particularly to see him. He had kept the death of her two brothers a secret because he couldn't take a chance on upsetting his applecart. He had it good and didn't have to hold down a full time job while he went to college. He had been a smart man. However, Hannah was now returning home for a visit. He was a little antsy about her finding out. He still needed her. Once he entered medical school and became an intern, he would make money and then she was history. She was a Pecker Hen that was driving him nuts. She controlled him, not him her.

"Uziah," called one of the waitresses passing him "Georgia wants to see you in her office. Go now! She seems edgy for some reason."

"Thank you," he stated removing his water soaked white kitchen apron. Running his fingers thru his hair, he headed for her office just beyond the kitchen in the rear. The door was closed. He knocked.

"Come in," came the familiar catty voice of his woman boss who was also Hannah's friend. He couldn't win for losing. "Shut the door behind you!"

"Yes, Miss Macon," he replied softly closing the door so as not to annoy her.

"I have sad news for you and Hannah. Zook's place on Saturday nights is coming to an end. My wealthy friends are finding new dining experiences to try. Have you saved enough for college, your masters, and medical school?" She inquired rising from behind her paper laden desk.

"We have saved every penny possible. I have enough to at least finish my masters and the first semester or so of Medical school if we are frugal. I am shocked to hear you say Saturday Nights at Zook's is ending. Have you informed Hannah?"

"I have a proposition for you," she stated straightening up and leaning over the desk towards him so that he could look down her buttoned too low blouse.

"What would that be?" He asked turning red.

"How would you like all of your expenses paid for medical school and a nice apartment twice or three times the size of the one you now have? Suppose there was thrown in two or three hundred dollars a week in pocket money?" She asked looking him directly in the eyes.

"What would I do for this windfall, open a new business or restaurant of some sort?"

"I am a single woman who wants no children or marriage but likes a man in my bed when I call. I want you to become my sleeping companion!" She stated fingering a button on her blouse that would reveal her bra if she undid it.

Uziah turned really red. I am young enough to be your grandson, Miss Macon." He sputtered nervously. "Why would you think that I would consider this?"

"You can take the easy road to medical school as my lover, or continue to run dishwashers and dumpster dive. I am sure that Hannah is willing to continue cleaning houses to put you thru medical school. I can see the two of you going back to eating macaroni and cheese. A smart man would take my offer."

"I am astonished at your request. I am not an experienced lover or male harlot."

"Either accept my offer, or your job here ends this afternoon. The wealthy will start dining at a place called the French Connection in two weeks. The big money is over for you and Hannah. I do not need you or Hannah. However, you need me and it comes with a price!" She said rising and circling the desk and coming to stand within an inch of him. Then she put both of her hands on the sides of Uziah's face pulling him to her and kissing him and rubbing her body against him.

"I . . . I must go." He stated not knowing what to do. Then she ran her had down his chest and onto his Amish no fly front pants.

"Why are you tempting me? I must go home to Hannah." He muttered but secretly enjoying her touch.

"No, you will make love to me here and now telling me you accept my proposal or I will tell Hannah that you and David Goldstein are lovers."

"I am not a Sodom and Gomorrah man. David and I are friends. He is not one either." He replied in shock.

"Then proved it to me," she said kissing him again as he backed up against the closed office door.

"I have no protection," he sputtered.

"You won't need it with me, because I will be the only one you sleep with."

"You don't understand . . ." He sputtered trying to object thinking of his bad genes.

"You have always looked down my dress at dinner parties, now do something about it. Otherwise, I will know that you ate gay and I will tell everyone."

"Please, Georgia, don't do this to me. I am an honorable man. My community would shun me for being gay." He said as she started undoing his shirt and pushing his Amish suspenders down.

"I . . . I . . ."

Then Georgia's hands were all over him in places they should not have been. Then he gave in to the heat of the moment and took her in his arms. He kissed her with all the passion he had fought and stuffed down staying away from girls because of his genes.

Georgia unleashed the beast in him. She was his first. He picked her up and then reclined her on the office floor and started to rip off her clothes enjoying his first sexual encounter with a woman. He was pleased with all that she did to him and he forgot Millie, Endora, and Hannah.

When they were finished, she smirked, "I gather being my lover is a yes?"

"I do not know how I am going to manage this without Hannah knowing," he stated laying his face in her bare bosom.

"If you want more of me and your expenses paid thru medical school, I want you to make Hannah mad and send her back home to the farm or where ever. You will move in with me and sleep in my bed. Send her home tomorrow night after she graduates high school. I will wait for you till then. I expect you to move in with me the day after. Zook's Place will be history in a month and you will be dumpster diving again. Send Hannah away and move toward your future."

A tear rolled out of Uziah's eye. He had just sold himself for sex and money. Worse, he had thoroughly enjoyed the sensual encounter and wanted more of her. He didn't realize being with a woman could be like that.

"What will it be, Uziah. I want an answer now. If your answer is yes, I want Hannah gong home the day after her graduation."

Georgia had one thing on her mind, protecting her future with Sergeant Pepper. She knew that he wouldn't give up till he convinced Hannah to marry him. She needed Pepper's money. Getting rid of Hannah was a must.

"My friends will dump me because of you. Hannah is loved by all of them."

"Everyone is going their own way, Uziah. Mooch, Ohm, and David will soon leave for other parts of the country. Sergeant Pepper told me that he is going to sell the apartment complex and move to Australia. Your cheap rent will end. Zook's place and your life are ending." She stated knowing that her goal was to prevent Sergeant Pepper from asking Hannah to marry him. Uziah was the tool to do it secretly and before anyone knew what was happening. She knew that Pepper had told her that he intended to ask Hannah to marry him on Saturday. This was Thursday afternoon.

"I will take your ticket to medical school Georgia. Why do you want me? Mooch is far more handsome than I? He wishes to be a doctor!"

"I knew the minute I first laid eyes on you that I wanted you. I have just had to wait till the timing was right. I want you to love me!" She replied lying.

"After having you, I cannot return to my old ways. I enjoyed your body and already want more."

"Get rid of Hannah and you can have me. However, I will not give myself to you again till you take Hannah back home. I want her out of our lives, is that understood?"

"I understand. I will take care of it the night of her graduation."

"You come to my house as soon as you see to it that she is gone. I promise you a night that you will never forget."

"I am glad you are forcing me to get rid of Hannah. She has been driving me crazy with her hen pecking."

"There will be no hen pecking from me, only hot nights of sexual pleasure." She said sitting down at her desk half nude and lighting a cigarette.

Mooch gets Dumped

Mooch hurriedly entered the restaurant to seek out Georgia and soothe her ruffled feathers. His short one day secret engagement to Hannah was over. Hannah had messed with his money ticket. A fiancé was not going to get him to medical school. It was a hard choice, but it was one that he had to make. He was in love with Hannah, but he chose Georgia. There was no other choice to make. He was going to be a doctor and that meant he had to be Georgia's boy toy for at least six more years. He hadn't expected Hannah to announce their secret engagement to her. He didn't know that Georgia and Hannah spoke every night on the phone and were friends. Georgia had never mentioned it to him.

Heading back toward the restaurant office, Millie the waitress stopped him briefly by grabbing his arm and asked, "Where are you going?"

"What business is it of yours?" He shot back continuing to walk and forcefully pushing her hand off of his arm.

"Well, pretty boy, Georgia has replaced you and has her new boy toy back there in the office." She retorted in an irritated voice.

"She has what?" Mooch asked spinning around and stopping briefly in shock.

"You heard me. Georgia has a new boy toy and you have been fired. Your final paycheck is on the time clock." She replied in disgust with him.

All the blood drained from Mooch's face. His main source of income was Georgia. He headed back for the time clock. Sure enough, there was a pay envelope with his name on it taped to the time clock. He opened it. She had written him a check for twenty hours. Mad, he headed for the office just in time to see Uziah back out of the office with his shirt undone and one of his suspenders down. When his Amish friend turned around, they were nose to nose.

"You fool!" Shouted Mooch. "What did she promise you, your tuition to medical school?"

"Er . . . uh . . . Oh God, please don't tell Hannah. She will think the worst of me!"

"Get out of my face you Amish piece of shit. Thanks to you and Hannah, my future is in the trash can... You have just made a pact with the Devil that you will regret. She promised to pay my way to medical school and the pair of you has stabbed me in the back."

Uziah backed around Mooch who was red faced and fuming and left by the back door. Mooch swung the office door open to face Georgia who was clearly putting on her clothes. She was fastening the back of her bra.

"You think that dumb ass Uziah can satisfy you and jump every time you say jump? He is not like me. He is straight from the sticks and has never been with a woman. He is interested in satisfying himself, not you. Barry and Bill tried to tell me. You promised them futures and educations paid for too. Fourteen and fifteen year olds are your choice. Isn't Uziah a little old?"

"Maybe my age preference is changing. Hannah informed me of all the old hags you have been sleeping with when you have known I expected you to be only with me. Go hit up Mrs. Begley and the other widows for your medical school bills. Our deal is off and Uziah is my new boy toy. Now, get out of my office?"

"You promised me my medical school bills paid. I have done everything you have asked since I was sixteen years old. You owe me!" He yelled.

"I am a promise breaker, so what? It is no worse than you telling Hannah that you plan to dump my ass after medical school? Hannah told me everything, not knowing that you were my boy toy."

"I broke it off with Hannah and chose you. Call her and ask her." Mooch stated desperate to get back in her good graces.

"My father was like you, worthless as they came. I listened to my mother cry and wait for him to come home from all of his flings with waitresses and call girls. I have chosen not to love a man but use them as my father used me and my mother. You are trash, Mooch, paid for trash. Now, I am throwing the garbage out. I don't love you. You mean nothing to me."

"I gave up Hannah for you, doesn't that mean something?" He yelled.

"No, I am saving her from you, Uziah, Pepper, Goldstein, Ohm, and the others. I am giving her a chance to go out on her own and be who she wants to be. You are all ropes around her neck. Hannah is probably the only person in this world that I do love and I have just saved her from you. Thanks for choosing me."

"Every time I made love the last three or so years to you, I pretended you were her. I have been a blind idiot. If I can get her to forgive me, I will never trust or sleep with anyone like you again. Someday, I will be a doctor. God willing, Hannah will be Mrs. Mooch Martin." He stated mad but also knowing that Hannah had told him she never wanted to see him again.

"Get out Mooch. Good luck in getting Hannah to listen to you. Forgiveness isn't one of her strong traits. She is a no nonsense woman."

Uziah asks Hannah to Leave

It was three-thirty in the afternoon on Thursday when Hannah was thru moving her treasures to the college campus student locker. There had been repeated knocks at the apartment door off and on all day. She had ignored them, sure in her mind that they were from Sergeant Pepper. She hadn't heard any more from Mooch and she was sad thinking how short that engagement was. She had lost two suitors in twenty-four hours and was starting to think that Uziah was right. Maybe she was hopeless when it came to men. She would have to cry about her loss of Mooch and Sergeant Pepper on Saturday when all was over. Right now, she didn't have the time to do that. She had to stay focused.

She was already signed up for the summer semester at the university. Renting a student locker had been easy. Her trips across campus with her things were uneventful. The only thing that she hadn't taken her share of, was the money beneath the loose board beneath their dining door table. They kept a rug over the board. She was reluctant to put her share of the money in a student locker. So, she would take it at the last minute. She knew that they had close to a hundred and fifty thousand dollars in their hiding place in one hundred dollar bills. They had run Zook's place five nights a week for the last almost three years and never touched a penny of the money except for Uziah's college tuition and books She bartered their rent from Sergeant Pepper in exchange for cleaning apartments that became empty and cleaning Sergeant Pepper's apartment twice a week. The guests of Zook's Place kept them fed with the feasts they brought to the dining club. Whatever came in, they ate it.

Uziah used his earnings as a dishwasher for his pocket money and Hannah took the money from her two houses to clean as her pocket money. Every penny coming thru Zook's Place, they had saved for their future educations. Uziah's college education and his tuition and books for the master program had been paid for in cash. Now, it was all coming to an end. Hannah was sad that the future that they had so carefully planned for was a fantasy. She would go to college, but Uziah would not be there for support as she had been there for him. In a way, she felt that she was getting the short end of the stick. However, she was thankful to not be on the farm and married to someone her father had chosen for her. She had no regrets about leaving home. She was well on her way to becoming an educated woman.

No matter what, she would keep her cool for now. She wanted to get thru her graduation tomorrow with no hitches if possible. She would leave after graduation. For now, she would stay inside her apartment and not answer her door for the next twenty-four hours. She did not want to have anymore confrontations with Sergeant Pepper or Mooch. She had not eaten, so she made herself a peanut butter sandwich to hold her over till dinner at seven. She was going to prepare Uziah and herself a shrimp feast to celebrate her new life that was on the horizon. However, only she would know that it was a celebration going away feast. She was leaving every one behind and that included Uziah.

Just after four thirty, the apartment door opened and a sarcastic, visibly mad Uziah entered and closed the door behind him. His clothes looked overly wrinkled for some reason. He looked like he had slept in them. Hannah didn't say anything. They were not married. If he wanted to roll around with a dog or a woman in the afternoon it was none of her business except for the fact that she had to wash his clothes. She could smell cigarette smoke on his clothing. None of their friends except Georgia smoked. However, Millie out at the restaurant did and Hannah knew that Uziah had a crush on her. He no longer talked about Endora, it was Millie this and Millie done that.

"Where were you at breakfast this morning?" He asked plopping down at the dining table. "A friend of mine saw you entertaining some halfwit down at the convenience store. What is that all about? I have told you that I don't want us associating with God's Will children."

"I had coffee and an interesting chat with a man who had a sister nicknamed Jelly Bean. This is my last two days of high school and I decided to celebrate and eat a doughnut and have a cup of coffee out for a change. I have worked hard to get us where we are and a morning out should not be a problem. I am not your wife, not even a pretend one now. I can come and go as I please. You are capable of fixing yourself a bowl of cereal." She retorted.

"You shame me, Hannah. You came home last night with your hair down. Sergeant Pepper has approached me several times today wanting to apologize to you. Have you become a whore, Hannah? Why else would all of these men follow you around like dogs? I am embarrassed and ashamed of you. I think I should send you home to your father and tell him that he should lay the strap to you."

"It is you that shame me. I am not the naïve cousin that accompanied you here and was willing to let you rule our world and me. I have cooked and cleaned up after you and your friends for three and one half years. None of my high school friends have been allowed at our table. I am now an adult and realize that you are a controller who would like me to be your slave and do whatever you deem appropriate. No more Uziah. It is over."

"I agree it is over. I want you to leave and go back home. I will give you two hundred dollars from the savings for a bus ticket and meals."

"Me go home? You have got to be kidding. You will take the end of a dish towel the same as Mooch if you want my help going thru medical school from here on out and you will share all of the chores, not just the ones you consider to be a man's. It is I that brings in the money in this apartment, not you. The Zook's Place money is at least two thirds, maybe more, mine. I am not a fool. I know that you have been taking a twenty here and a ten there and recently two one hundred dollar bills. You have used your two hundred. If anyone goes home on two hundred it will be you."

"Georgia says Zook's place is coming to an end." He shot back. "I want you out of here."

"Georgia does not run Zook's or provide the wealthy clients. It was Sergeant Pepper who arranged for two thirds of our dinner guests. The guests now call me, not Sergeant Pepper or Georgia. I control the reigns of Zook's Place and the money beneath the floor board. Keep your stealing hands out of it. I could stick any student Tom, Dick, or Harry actor in an Amish blue shirt and no zip pants and my guests would still come. You are not the attraction, Uziah."

"Georgia says Zook's is going under, and I believe her." He

shot back thinking of the afternoon in the floor with Georgia. He wanted more afternoons like that as well as her paying his tuition. He was tired of Hannah's hen pecking. He would take the money tomorrow when Hannah left for her high school graduation and move it to his student locker. It was his medical school money not hers.

"Whether or not Zook's goes under doesn't matter. I know how the private dining club is run and I can start up another. My old guests and future ones will provide for me comfortably as I go thru college. My only discomfort has been saving all of the money for you and your education. I have done without for you. I still wear the same two dresses I arrived here in. You need to get off your high horse and realize how easy you have had it. You have not had to work a forty hour week and go to school at night like many of our friends. You work strictly for pocket money and run your mouth at the table and outside on the balcony on Zook's night. I have no intentions of being your servant or slave anymore. I am the head of this house not you. Now back off and get out of my face. I graduate tomorrow and I have things to do and dinner to cook."

"You need to go home, Hannah! You are forgetting who you are and that a woman is not to head the man. You have become a Hen Pecking whore."

"Dream on, Uziah. I am not going anywhere. You are bigger physically than I and could possibly throw me out of this apartment. However, I will just rent one of Mrs. Begley's or one of the other apartments in the area and go on with my plans for college. I paid my tuition yesterday for the summer. Zook's Place is mine and the wealthy that come here will follow me. You can be a part of my world or not. It is up to you." She replied and then added sarcastically. "Perhaps you have in the back of your mind to become a man of the night like Mooch and take Georgia on for her money. You know that she pays Mooch, your best friend, for sex."

The Georgia remark did it. Uziah got up and stomped out taking a book he was reading with him. "I want you out of here after your graduation tomorrow night, Hannah. I have a money source for medical school. I don't need you." He yelled.

CHAPTER FIFTEEN

Ohm's Shocking Prediction

It was about twenty minutes after five. Once outside of his apartment, Uziah stormed down to the second floor landing and stood leaning on the wrought iron railing along the walkway. He was fuming at her inference that it was her that pulled in the money. He would show her. Georgia would put him thru medical school and he could have all the sex he wanted. He was sure that he had made her mad enough to leave. Georgia had made it clear to him. If he wanted her and her money, he had to send Hannah packing. He wanted more of her. Georgia was good in the lovemaking department. Now that he had Georgia, he definitely wanted more. She was worth breaking his vow of celibacy. He was hooked on sex with her. Plus, she was not Amish and he could start dressing like the wealthy and have a good looking socialite on his arm. Georgia represented who he wanted to be.

David Goldstein, seeing him thru his front window of the second floor, stepped outside to join him. Jelly Bean was on his apartment floor on her stomach with her hands under her chin watching television. He had removed and hid her shoes and socks so she wouldn't try to go outside. Quietly, he opened the door and stepped outside for a moment or so. The day had been a nightmare with his sister in tow. He was ready for a two minute breather. Plus, Mooch was in on the couch getting drunk.

"What is up Uziah, why are you standing out here?"

"Hannah and I have had words. I am standing here making plans to send her back to the Amish community. She has turned out to be a whore and I want to be free of her. She has forgotten her Amish ways and disrespects me as head of the house. I intend to send her home where her father can beat her."

"You what?" Inquired a surprised David. "That is dark ages thinking, Uziah. You should be thankful for Hannah. She has been the rock and foundation for all of us the last three or so years. You are a lucky man to have her. She is a gift from God that the rest of us wish we were privileged to have."

"She is a Hen Pecker that I wish to send home and get out of my hair. I just don't know how to accomplish the feat at the moment."

"Have you been sleeping with Georgia Macon? Mooch is inside getting drunk. He says you are Georgia's new boy toy. Is that the reason you want Hannah gone?"

"Yes, if you really want to know. Sex with Georgia is unbelievable. She told me that she has been in love with me for a couple of years and that she wants me to move in with her and that she will pay my way to medical school. I have accepted her offer and just now asked Hannah to leave." He replied ticked off that David was prying.

"I thought Mooch was lying to me. How could you do that to Mooch? You are stabbing your best friend in the back for no reason. Haven't you seen the morning paper? Georgia has made fools out of both of you. Hannah is the prize, not Georgia Macon."

"I have had it with Hannah. I have chosen Georgia and her money. Mooch deserves what he gets. Did you know he asked Hannah to marry him last night, used her, and then broke it off with her today? Don't compare me with him."

"Georgia Macon filed bankruptcy this morning. The courts will take everything she owns to pay off her debts. She has no money. She has been stringing Mooch along and now you have fallen for her lies. You are free cheap sex for her. She knew before she enticed you this afternoon that she had no money to send you or Mooch to medical school. She will be lucky to come out of the bankruptcy with the clothes on her back and maybe a couple thousand dollars. Since the interstate passed her restaurant by, she had been making less and less. She had been head over heels in debt the last three or four years. She hasn't been turning a profit. I showed Mooch the bankruptcy notice in the morning paper when he returned from the restaurant about an hour or so ago. You have been used for one last stand before Georgia closes the doors the first of next week. You are a fool."

"I don't believe you. You are Mooch's friend and you are trying to make me think ill of Georgia. She gave Hannah an expensive graduation present. She has to have money."

"Women will spend their last dollar on a present, a face lift, or a shopping trip at the mall. Georgia likes to impress Hannah because she knows what a fabulous income Hannah is pulling in. Come on inside and I will show you the morning paper and the bankruptcy notice. Mooch is on the sofa getting drunk. Just like you, he chose Georgia instead of Hannah."

"What do you mean he chose Georgia over Hannah? He just proposed to her last night."

"Georgia gave him an ultimatum. Either he dumped Hannah, or she wouldn't pay his way to medical school. It happened about thirty minutes before she apparently crawled all over you. She wanted Mooch to catch the two of you, you idiot. She just wants Hannah gone so she can continue to own Mooch. You were a tool to make Mooch come crawling and to get rid of Hannah."

"She has used me to get rid of Hannah?"

"I don't know what her intentions were, but it looks that way. You are two idiots. Mooch told Hannah that he had changed his mind and chose Georgia. Then he comes to the restaurant and finds you with Georgia and his final pay check on the time clock. She broke Mooch and Hannah up by threatening to not provide the funds she has promised him for medical school. She wants Mooch, not you. She wants Hannah gone."

"If you are telling me the truth, Hannah is never going to let me forget. I will be a hen pecked fool." Uziah stated. "Show me the paper."

Uziah followed David inside and listened to David further state, "Ohm Oto is a business major and has been helping Hannah keep her books. Last week, he told me that if the growth of Hannah's supper club continues over the next three years like it has, she will be pulling in a half million a year. Georgia in her best years at the Pancake Emporium might have cleared twenty-five or thirty thousand. Georgia is mortgaged to the hilt and the interstate has passed her restaurant by. Her business has fell off seventy five percent if not more. The Pancake Emporium is history as of next Monday morning."

"Mooch and I both dumped Hannah for a lying woman who doesn't have a pot to pee in." Uziah muttered in disbelief. He had just told Hannah he wanted her gone.

"Georgia doesn't have a pot to pee in as you have just said. Hannah will be pulling in a fabulous income, enough to put you and Mooch both thru medical school and have money left. You two have thrown away a woman with the Midas touch. The two of you are fools."

David pulled a crumpled newspaper sheet from Mooch's hands and handed it to Uziah. Mooch had a bottle of Vodka sitting next to him and had drank himself into a stupor. "I told Mooch about Hannah's projected income and about Georgia's bankruptcy notice about an hour ago. He is drinking to forget what a fool he has been. Hannah agreed to marry him last night. I would give my eye teeth for her to say yes to me. He dumped her this morning for the bankrupt pancake queen. The funny part is that he is actually in love with Hannah. There is no bigger fool than him."

Uziah turned to the bankruptcy listings and fingered down the row of listings till he came to Georgia and the Pancake Emporium. David was not lying to him. Uziah felt his face turn red and he had to swallow to stay calm.

"I have put my future at risk for sex and a woman who has an empty billfold."

"You and Mooch are fools. Now, it is my turn and I am not a fool. I plan to do everything possible to make Hannah fall in love with me. I know what a treasure she is. When I marry her, you and Mooch can eat your hearts out. She won't be paying for either of you to go to medical school, if I can help it."

Uziah left, but he didn't return to the upstairs apartment. He had to go to his student locker and retrieve the new clothing items including the dinner jacket. He would return the items to the mall and put the money back beneath the floorboard. Hannah had called him a thief and he was. He hoped that she didn't find out about his day of fool hardiness in the floor with Georgia. This was a light bulb moment for him. It was Hannah that he needed to get thru medical school and he was going to have to straighten up his act and crawl on all fours to make peace with her. It was almost six. He would hurry and return the dinner jacket and other items of clothing. He was a fool.

David Asks to Call on Hannah

At six, a knock came at the door of Hannah's apartment. She was busy cooking and reluctant to answer it. After the knocking continued, she went to the door and listened.

"Hannah, it is me David. Open up. I want to talk to you."

Relieved that it wasn't Pepper or Mooch, she cracked the door open to make sure he was alone. He was, so she opened the door.

"What do you need to talk to me about?" She asked.

"I have thought about what you said about Jelly Bean this morning and you are right. I am taking her back home Saturday morning. I have arranged for her to be placed in a group home till my parents are out of the hospital and then it is up to them to make a choice for her. I would never have had the nerve to make this decision if it hadn't been for you. Would there be any chance that I could talk you into going out to dinner with me Saturday night after I return?"

"I am moving, David. I will not be here Friday night after graduation. Uziah has asked me to leave and I will do so. It is time to move forward with my future. Zook's Place and I will be moving and I will hire a student actor to head my table. Uziah does not want me as part of his world anymore."

"So, you are leaving after your graduation?"

"Yes, I will go home to visit my parents for a few days, and then return here and start over. I am not that naïve seventeen year old girl that you picked up three and one half years ago. I am almost twenty two and capable of taking care of myself."

"Is there any chance that you would consider letting me date you. I have always been infatuated with you from the moment you crawled in my jeep on that snowy, blizzard night long ago. It was love at first sight for me, although I have not admitted it to anyone till now."

"When I am settled again, I will consider it. Right now, I am under the impression that all men are Jackasses and you fall a little bit in that category.

"I am one, I admit it. However, this jackass thinks you are the prettiest damn woman ever. Did you know that your dimples wink at me and drive me crazy?"

"Like I said, I will consider it. Right now, I am not thinking straight or making good decisions. One should never make commitments or decisions when they are angry or sad. I am both. Sergeant Pepper and Mooch have broken my heart this week. However, I will admit that on that snowy ride in your jeep, I thought that your nose was handsome and magnificent. I wondered what it would be like to work my Amish nose around it and kiss you."

"You little witch! I have looked at my nose for three and one half years wondering why it was so unattractive to you. Tell me again that you like it. I want to hear it again." He laughed teasing her.

"I will consider letting you call on me and I will consider telling you again that I like your nose. However, for now, I am mad at all men and you are one. It is not a good time for you to tease me too much."

"The teasing is over," he stated zipping his lip. "I am Jewish and know when to keep my mouth shut. I have watched my father who has been a good example. My mother rules him and you may rule me."

"There is one thing that I must tell you, David. I would never lie to you."

"What is it?"

"I have had feelings for Sergeant Pepper. I found out this week that he does not have the same feelings for me. I am still sad about it. Mooch and I got caught up in a moment last night and we should not have done so. He proposed and I accepted. However, today we called it off. It is Georgia he needs, not me. I was mad about it, but I have come to realize that we were there for each other last night but that doesn't mean the night means forever. I am laying everyone here from friend night down and moving on. It is sad, but all of you are Uziah's friends and not mine really. I never want to have to walk away again knowing I have no friends to turn to. It will be a lonely journey into my new life. However, when I get there, the ones that sit at my table will be my friends and I will have no need to walk away again."

"I love you Hannah and I understand. Could I kiss you just once so I will have it to remember?"

He didn't give her a chance to answer. He took her in his arms and kissed her like crazy. She pushed away when his hands slipped down onto her buttocks remembering what Sergeant Pepper had said. She should pull away when the man's hands came into play. At least she learned something from Sergeant Pepper, even if she was mad at him.

CHAPTER SIXTEEN

Gun Shots

At one minute after seven, Uziah returned home acting a little strange. Hannah didn't say anything as he glanced at the clock. He was breaking his own rule by being one minute past seven. Hannah could see that he wasn't happy with himself. Uziah was a rule follower and a rule maker.

"I am sorry that I am late," he stated and then pulled two one hundred dollar bills from his shirt pocket and placed them on the table. "You were right. I have been taking a ten and a twenty now and then. However, I have come to my senses. You may put this money back. I have been a fool."

"You may put it back after we eat. I have dinner fixed. Go wash up." She stated not wanting to comment on the money. She was just trying to make it thru the night and tomorrow without further words. She wanted to keep the peace for the evening if she could. A loud pop sounded in the distance. "Did you hear that Uziah? It sounded like a gun."

"I heard. It is probably a car back firing. They do that when they are out of time in the engine." He stated walking over to the bathroom and entering but leaving the door open to wash his hands.

"It sounded like it was coming from the area of Sergeant Pepper's apartment." She replied turning off the stove burners she had been using to cook dinner. She had a lovely shrimp and rice feast fixed to celebrate her going away.

"It is nothing to be concerned with, Hannah. Endora has been having trouble with her old car. If I were guessing, it is her vehicle that is making the sounds. I saw her getting into it when I was climbing the stairs." He stated sticking his head out of the bathroom door where he was drying his hands on a handmade towel that Hannah had cut from an old chenille bedspread that he had found in the dumpster.

Uziah then returned to the kitchen and took his usual place at the head of the table after helping Hannah put the plastic bowls of food on the door top. As they ate, he stared at Hannah all thru dinner, Hannah caught him staring at her, but she ignored him. She didn't want to get into another words war with him. She probably had her white cap on crooked or she had a bit of food on her face somewhere and was reluctant to tell her about it. When dinner was over, she cleared the table and did the dishes as usual. However, this time he took a dish towel and helped her. When they were done, she seated herself at the table and pretended to read the paper that he had brought home. Breaking the eerie silence between them, another pop sounded. Hannah got up and went to the window by Uziah's bed to look out.

"That sounded like a gunshot, Uziah."

"Ignore it and come back to the table to your reading. When you are done looking at the coupon ads, I have something I want to discuss with you."

Hannah returned to the kitchen sink and leaned on it, but didn't sit down. "I do not wish to discuss what we talked about earlier. I made my feelings known then," she replied.

"You were right in telling me what a jerk I have been. I have thought about it and have made a different decision. I do not want you to leave. I am sorry for my words." He stated rising and joining her in leaning against the sink.

"What decision have you made?" She asked wondering what he was up to. He wouldn't quit staring at her.

"I have been wrong about everything. My father thought you were right for me and that you could tame me like a horse. He was right. I want us to go to the justice of the peace and marry first thing in the morning. I was a fool chasing Endora and Georgia. Georgia filed bankruptcy today and recently Mooch informed me that Endora is a call girl and not a student at all. The reason she played ill on college graduation night is that she has never enrolled or attended classes. She has never been a student. She is a liar and a user of men. Today, Georgia promised me a free ride to medical school if I got rid of you. I am ashamed to have to admit to you that I have broken my celibacy vow with her. She also promised a medical school ticket to Mooch. David straightened both of us out and showed us in the morning paper a bankruptcy notice. Georgia filed for bankruptcy before she ever made me the offer. She used me and Mooch. Both of us have been fools. Looking at you tonight, I have suddenly realized how beautiful you really are. I think it is God's will for us to marry. You will wash and press your dress tonight. We will marry when the court house opens in the morning."

"We will what?" She asked standing up straight and the hairs on the back of her neck bristling.

"We will marry. I have lived with you all of these years and it is only right that I marry you. We are Amish and we belong together. I have been a fool not seeing it."

"In the first place, Uziah Zook, I don't love you. I turned you down as a suitor years ago. There is nothing between us other than being cousins who have worked together to obtain educations. Why would I want to marry you?"

"You have no choice. We will marry in the morning." He replied in the firm voice he always used when he was adamant on getting his way.

"I do have a choice and the answer is no. Why would I want to consider someone who has chased after Endora for years and apparently slept with Georgia today?" Hannah stated and then turned to walk away.

Uziah bit his lip and then spoke. "You will not defy me!"

"We are not married and I will defy you all I want." She stated walking away.

Then he followed her, grabbed her by the shoulders, and spun her around. "You are Amish and you will marry me. It doesn't matter who we may have kissed or wanted yesterday. It is the future that we must think of." He stated and roughly manhandled her into his arms and tried to kiss her. She turned her head and started pushing and shoving to get free from him.

Seeing that she was denying him, he pulled his right hand back and struck her hard across her face. She fell to the floor and he was immediately on top of her holding her down. She kicked and fought. He tried to kiss her again. Again she turned her head to try to avoid him. Then she screamed hoping someone would hear her from the apartment below. She heard a series of popping sounds from below. Frightened she screamed as loud as she could and continued to fight Uziah. It was evident to her that he was planning on raping her. He was pushing his suspenders down. She struggled and fought. Then there were popping sounds like those of a gun outside of the door and someone was banging on and kicking the door. Uziah let her go and went to the door reluctantly pulling his suspenders back up on his shoulders. Hannah took a deep breath trying to calm her emotions and then sat up halfway in a daze not knowing what to do.

Uziah opened the door to see Georgia standing there with a gun in hand. She pointed it at Uziah forcing him out of her way and entered seeing Hannah on the floor with a visible red handprint on her face.

"Lock the door behind us, Hannah." Georgia said and then she put a bullet thru the floor between Uziah's legs. Suddenly fearing for his life, he jumped back and broke out in perspiration. "Get outside ass hole before I put one thru your pecker John."

About that time, David Goldstein ran thru the open third floor apartment door but stopped seeing Georgia swinging a gun around.

"Both of you out on the balcony," Georgia yelled to David and Uziah. They did as they were told. Then Georgia exited the doorway with her gun pointed at them.

"Hannah, lock the door." She said one more time.

"Do as she says, Hannah." David stated. "She has killed Mooch, Endora, and Sergeant Pepper."

This may surprise you jokers; Hannah is my friend and she lives. However, Uziah has to my count of three to jump over this third floor railing. He deserves to be bruised up just like she is."

"Do it, Uziah." David said in a forced calm voice. "Pepper and Mooch are dead."

Then Georgia told them to back up flat against the third floor railing and they did so. David was eyeing the stairs. He was the closest to them and he would attempt to escape by making a dive for them and then running down them.

"Georgia. You and I do not have a beef with each other." David stated trying to keep himself from getting shot. "My mentally challenged sister is downstairs in my apartment. I have her for the weekend. She has the mind of a two year old. She needs me."

"Did you see Hannah's face?" Georgia asked. "This sucker was trying to rape her when I got up here. She was screaming for him to get off of her."

"Yes, I saw her face. Now let me go to tend to my sister. Her name is Jelly Bean and she has to be frightened. She watched you shoot Mooch. I want to thank you for not shooting her or Hannah. Jelly Bean could be your friend too. Please let me go to my sister. You and I have no quarrels between us." He had locked Jelly Bean in the bathroom before he made a run up the stairs following Georgia fearing that she was going to kill Hannah next."

Georgia then put another bullet between the two boys into the third floor wooden walkway. Screaming, Uziah went over the third floor railing and could be heard hitting the ground below with a thud.

"Down the stairs, ass hole. Hannah doesn't want to see any of you jackasses tonight. Now down the stairs before I change my mind. Kiss your sister for me. She is the only reason I am letting you live." Georgia stated pointing the gun toward the stairs.

David made a dart for the stairs and didn't look back. He had to get down to the ground and see if Uziah was alright. His sister would be fine locked in the bathroom. She might remove all of the toilet paper from the roll, having the mind of a two year old, but she was safe. He had to get help for everyone. He was surprised that there weren't police cars everywhere. He had called for help just before heading for the third floor to see if Hannah was okay. He was going to kill Uziah for trying to rape Hannah, if he were alive. He was mad.

Inside the apartment, Hannah realized she was trapped and that Uziah would return and finish what he had started. She did not know that he had taken a three floor leap to the ground. She glanced at the open window behind Uziah's bed. She had two to three minutes at the most till David and Uziah overpowered Georgia. She had to escape now. Running to her bedroom, she grabbed her pillow and shook it out from its pillow case. Taking the case, she ran to the dining table and pulled up the board where they kept their money hidden. Uziah had his college education and master degree program paid for. She told herself not to feel guilty leaving him two one hundred dollar bills. That was what he had intended to give her. She still had her college and master degree to pay for. She stuffed the pillowcase with the money and then put the board back on after pulling her white Amish cap off and putting it with the two hundred dollars and putting the board back on. She had been his slave for three and one half years. The money was hers. Running to the bathroom door, she set the lock. Then she pulled the door closed so Uziah would think she was in there for at least a few minutes. Then she heard pounding on her front door. He must have gotten free of Georgia. Running for the window, she crawled out pulling the window down behind her.

Sliding down across the roof of the second floor she made her way to the overhanging tree limb and began to climb down. Once she reached a lower height, equal to the first floor roof, she dropped her pillowcase to the ground. She had to drop from the last limb which was about eight feet off of the ground and she didn't have Mooch to catch her. She was a little frightened of the drop. However, she eased herself down and hung by her arms like a monkey. Uziah was tall with long legs. He would catch her if she didn't manage to get ahead of him and duck in somewhere. She was frightened and trembling. She couldn't give in to her fear and go to crying. She had to escape.

As she dropped to the ground, she closed her eyes. When her feet reached the ground, she felt a pair of hands grab her waist and steady her to help her gain her footing. Her heart exploded with fright. Uziah must have figured out what she was up to and ran around the building to stop her. Then she realized that the hands were much larger than Uziah's. She turned quickly to see who had her in their arms. It was her turban headed friend in white and he was smiling. "We both run away tonight. It must be the God saying that we should journey together. I will be your servant and take very good care of you."

"There is just one God," she said reverting to her Amish philosophy. "I do agree that he has apparently chosen for our paths to be one."

He let go of her once she had regained her footing. "I see beard man hit you. No man ever hit my Hannah Bird again. Hurry, we go. I am Ohm's servant no more. No one owns me, except you."

In spite of being frightened to the point that she had peed a little in her underwear, Hannah was pleased at what he had said and threw her arms around him and burst into tears.

"No cry gray dove. You are my Hannah Bird now and I will keep you safe." He said removing her arms from around him. "We must run before Ohm or Uziah come after us."

Chim picked up her pillow case and his grocery tote of bird drawings and slung them over his back. He pointed toward the university campus and then inner twined the fingers of his free hand in one hand of hers. Pulling her along, they ran until they were out of sight of the apartment complex. In the shadows of the night and the trees, they stopped to rest.

"Thank you for being beneath the tree when I needed you. Did you just happen to be standing there when I dropped?" She asked panting.

"I saw you exit the upstairs window and enter the tree carrying your tote. A peeping Tom is what the English would call me. Using my binoculars, I have watched you for three and one half years. A man's heart makes him do strange acts. The night before I met you at the all night convenient store, I prayed for a gray dove to come to me as a sign that one day I would not be an owned slave. You are the dove that the gods sent me. I have watched you in your third floor nest thru the windows to make sure you are asleep at night and safe. The bearded man would come to your bedroom and stand over you many nights when you did not know it. I feared for you. I wish my English was better and that I could say the big words that are in my heart. I saw you leaving on the roof after the man called Uziah hit you. I grabbed my tote of things and made my way to the tree knowing that you would need me to keep you safe. I am your servant now. The gods have given me and my heart to you. I will never leave you, hit you, or be mean to you. I am a good servant."

Hannah grinned. She had warned Sergeant Pepper about a peeping Tom, but she was the one that had one.

"I am going to Florida after I graduate tomorrow night. You are my friend and not my servant. We will share a new life together and God apparently has just made you head of my table."

"May I once kiss you, just once like crazy?" He asked. "I have never kissed a woman and just once I would like to experience that pleasure."

"I have been told that I am bad in the kissing department. If you want to practice your first kiss on me, I am willing." She replied.

Chim took Hannah in his arms and picked her up off the grass and pressed his lips to hers after closing his eyes. Hannah started counting to herself. She remembered what Sergeant Pepper had said about seven to ten seconds for a first kiss. Then she forgot to count. His kiss was what she had been dreaming about. He was turning her on and making her toenails curl up. Reluctantly, she pushed him away and stared at him in shock. Endora was right.

"Was my kiss bad?" He asked seeing the startled look on her face.

"You kiss like crazy." She replied not knowing what to say. On the day she had left the farm and ran away, she had wished for an Englishman who would kiss her like crazy. He wasn't English, but he was learning the English language. He had to be the one that only comes along once in a lifetime.

Chim grinned. "Does that mean yes you are willing to be kissed again or that I need to practice because my kiss is crazy like not good?"

"What it means is that I am tying you to my apron string forever. You are hot, as a friend once told me."

"Hot? I don't understand," he replied grinning at her.

"Well, you are making the woman in me sizzle and want you!

You are hot."

"I am pleased, Hannah Bird. I want you and I sizzle too." He replied. Then he took her in his arms a second time and pressed his lips to hers. This time, he pulled her body to his and secured her there with his big hands. Hannah did not resist. She was ready for a man to love her. Chim lay her down in the grass and they became one in the shadows of the night. He was more of a man than he had thought he was. His gods were kind to him and he was madly in love with the gray dove that they had sent. He would love her and only her for a lifetime.

Chim became the new head of Hannah's table and the love of her life. In Miami, Florida they opened up a new private dinner club called 'HANNAH BIRDS'.

~ ~ ~

Does Uziah die from his fall? Where is Osceola Black Lightning? Was she Hannah's guardian? Read book nine, 'Uziah's Dream', of the Black Lightning series.

Made in the USA
Middletown, DE
09 February 2021